SILENT

SILENT

ELLEN COLLINS

Moonshell
Press

ISBN: 979-8-218-50947-7

Manufactured in the United States of America

Cover Art painted by Ellen Collins.
Publishing Assistance, Interior and Cover Design:
Heimat Publishing, Crystal Heidel

Body of paperback typeset in Garamond Premier Pro
Title and Subtitle typeset in Serenity

PART ONE
2022

CHAPTER 1

IF IT WERE up to her, every day would be October. She loves the cidered light that filters through the pines, the lazy drift of pale butterflies over the last marigolds in the pots on her front porch, the sun on her shoulders that makes her feel lazy and contented. In the mornings she practices yoga facing the ocean, and in the afternoons she settles in a patch of sun where she can put her feet up on a hassock and read. Midday often finds her kneading a batch of bread or peeling apples for a tart. She has not lost her love of baking. The freezer is stocked with muffins and pies for Thanksgiving when Brent and Lindsay and their families will fill the small house with their voices and squabbles and appetites.

She still rarely goes to church, but she prays by herself. She prays for Owen, Brent's son. He's the same age Brent was when everything broke open. And she prays for Lindsay's twins, Rachel and Cecily, prays that they will be safe. It frightens her to think of them out in the world, so trusting, believing it is always a kind place.

The outspread wings of an osprey cast a fleeting shadow on the boards of the deck. Olivia looks up as the bird disappears over the roof, and she inhales the clean salt scent of the ocean. This is her favorite time of day in her favorite season. Early October mornings hold that hint of the cooling nights, but are already warming as the sun ladders up the sky. The summer crowds are gone, taking with them the bass notes of boom-boxes and the clomping of sandaled feet on the wooden walkways, the snarled traffic on the highway. Hers is the only house on the block that is inhabited off-season, and she savors the solitude and quiet.

It took a long time to get to this mindset, and there are still things that threaten to crack open the peace. A whiff of cigarette smoke. The mention of El Salvador on the news. And she has never been able to abide the taste of scotch. Things she thought she would forget rear up to grab her, and sometimes leave her shaken for days. When that happens, she sits for hours on her deck, waiting for the rhythm of the waves to soothe her, to slow her breathing. Telling herself that she is safe here on this stretch of sand where laughing gulls swoop overhead and clouds ride high in a blue, benign sky. That voice, though, that memory voice, is never completely silent. She has to coax it to recede.

Brent tells her she's crazy to live at the beach year-round. "You need people close by, Mom," he argues. "What will you do if you fall? Or if there's a storm and that straggly pine falls on the roof?" He keeps sending her brochures for senior living complexes. "They take care of everything," he says. "You know, you *are* seventy-four."

Every time, she answers that she knows exactly how old she is and she is perfectly capable of taking care of herself. She has friends. Maybe not in the immediate neighborhood, but closer to town. Close enough. "I don't want people breathing down my neck, dropping in day and night." She loves her solitude. People so often bring complications. And she's putting a book together, a cookbook with stories about the recipes. Her own and her grandmother's that her mother gave her all those years ago when she left Minnesota for D.C. The dining room table is covered with index cards, pages torn out of steno pads. Warm memories of gingerbread and chicken fricassee and stuffed acorn squash.

Now, though, she just breathes in the warm peace of a Wednesday morning. Later, she'll drive out to the farm market where pumpkins have replaced tomatoes and apples are piled in pyramids of red and yellow. Marcia and Charlie put a basket together for her every week with surprises and dare her to come up with ways to cook them. Last week it was rutabagas and Swiss chard. She always takes them a loaf of bread. A foil-wrapped loaf of banana oatmeal bread waits on the table in the foyer.

Sometimes it surprises her that she's not lonely. After a lifetime of being surrounded by people, to live these days mostly by herself. To be content with a short visit with a vegetable farmer or a conversation at the library check-out desk. A yoga class at least once a week. She gets her family fix when her kids visit with spouses and children and then leave after two days. As their cars disappear at the end of the street, the grandkids waving from the open windows, she relaxes, her house to herself again. Now and then she considers selling the beach house, for just the reasons Brent lists, and moving back full time to Chevy Chase. She still owns the house there, and would choose that over one of those retirement places. Or maybe one day Brent or Lindsay will want to live there. She holds on to it for them. But every time she imagines moving, she's filled with a deep, aching loneliness. How to live without the tides and the gulls, the flock of pelicans that skim the water every morning just after sunrise? Plus, D.C. still holds too much she'd rather forget.

The Sunday *Washington Post* is still unopened on the table beside her chair. She should at least *look* at the headlines before bundling it up for recycling. Why does she even buy it? More often than not, she ends up using the pages to wrap garbage, though she does enjoy the crossword puzzle in the magazine and the book review section. She'll scan the paper and then take a walk on the sand. Idly turning the pages of the Metro section, she slides over the stories, giving only marginal attention to local politics, the D.C. football team. But she sits up straight and almost drops the paper as she comes to the obituary page. Her eyes land on a small notice almost buried among the other tiny paragraphs. *Peter Kowolski, Former Priest.*

Pete is dead? Her fingertips tremble.

It's one of those small listings with no details. *Of Harrisburg, Pennsylvania. Formerly of Washington, D.C. September 27. Leaves behind a brother.* She never knew what happened to him, hasn't known if he was still alive, has tried not to think about him, but seeing the death notice makes feelings erupt she can't identify. Is it relief? Finality? Hope? There's no photo, and she struggles to remember his face. Thinks of what he might look like now. Fifty years later. He'd be around 80. Would have been.

He's gone.

Fifty years. Half a century. Fifty years that feel like a second.

It's news she wants to share with someone, but there is no one. Will has been gone for ten years (though would he have even cared?). Rebecca lives in a memory care facility. There's no one around to remember.

Except for her.

PART TWO
1971

CHAPTER 2

OLIVIA'S FATHER WAS at the grill turning bratwurst with a long-pronged fork, wearing that silly apron with the pig on the front. He had on a pale-yellow oxford cloth shirt, unlike the other men, brothers and uncles, who were wearing T-shirts. She smiled, remembering she gave it to him for his last birthday, and knowing this little touch of dressing up was his way of marking the evening as special. Her leaving would be hard on him. She was the youngest, would always be his little girl. He wouldn't say anything about how much he'd miss her. The shirt said it all.

She was standing next to the stone birdbath, the late June air thick with humidity and mosquitoes. This was her last night before leaving the Minnesota town where she had lived for twenty-two years for her new life in Washington, D.C. She pushed her damp auburn hair up from her neck and looked up to her bedroom window under the eave where pale green dotted Swiss curtains breathed in and out with the slight breeze. The room was almost empty now, the only furniture an old bookcase and a nightstand. She wondered where she would sleep, but it didn't really matter because she knew she'd be too excited to even try to close her eyes. Earlier she'd been up there, gathering the last few things to stow in her car, and the room felt lonely, outlines on the floor where the bed, the dresser, and her desk had been, patches on the walls where she had tacked posters. She had taken the posters down, thrown some away and given some to her younger cousin Emmy. John Denver. Crosby, Stills and Nash. Bob Dylan. A full-antlered moose. There was an old collage of photos that she had taped next to her bed when she was sixteen. Photos of friends mixed in with pictures she had cut from magazines, edges curling. It had "high school" written all over it, not the image she had in mind for her new sophisticated life in the Nation's Capital. She carefully slid the photos into a shoe box, debated whether to take it or leave it behind. After selecting just a few photos—she and Aubrey holding up a huge Douglas fir, her parents on their 30th anniversary, her brothers as teenagers goofing off in front of the camera—she pushed the box to the back of a closet shelf. Standing there in the nearly empty room, her bare feet on the well-worn floor boards, she heard the echoes of her twenty-two years.

But she was looking forward, and her bedroom furniture, along with an old daybed she was going to use for a couch and miscellaneous items donated by family members, had left on a moving truck that morning with her clothes, books, and dishes. She had no idea what the apartment looked like, because she had found it in a classified ad, but she told herself it would be fine. It would be her place, and she would make whatever it was into her new home. She hugged herself and grinned, seeing herself on the cusp of a bright beginning.

The move had originally been her best friend Aubrey's idea, back in the winter. She and Aubrey had grown up together, even gone to the same college, and Aubrey had landed an internship in D.C. with the Department of Agriculture. She planted the seed in Olivia's mind of coming along, finding a teaching job. Olivia was in her first year teaching in a small prep school. "It will be an adventure!" Aubrey said, and Olivia agreed, ready to leave small-town life for something more exciting and cosmopolitan. But then, after Olivia signed a contract to teach at Holy Redeemer Academy and found the apartment, Aubrey's job fell through in May (budget cuts) and she and Joe had gotten engaged. He convinced her to move with him to Chicago, where he had a residency in orthopedics. Part of Olivia was miffed at Aubrey, but how could she fault her for being in love? So now she was on her own, about to drive almost a thousand miles to her new life. She had tamped down any misgivings she had and now she felt like Mary Tyler Moore on that TV show, tossing her plaid tam into the air. "You might just make it after all," the words to the song said, and that's what she was going to do. There was no "might" in her mind.

Her parents objected at first. "All the way to D.C. by yourself?" Her mother said it was too far. Olivia didn't know anyone. She'd never lived in a big city. But Olivia laughed away her mother's warnings, assured her she'd be fine, and her mother had come around. "I just want you to be happy." Olivia would make new friends, and the school where she was going to teach sounded great. It was Catholic, so she'd feel at home, having been to Catholic schools her whole life and even teaching the year before at St. Anselm's. Small classes, all girls, lots of students from embassy families. She'd talked to the principal, Sister Helen, on the phone, and knew she'd feel right at home there just from the sound of her voice. The school itself had only two hundred students, and she'd be teaching freshman and sophomore English. Sister Helen told her that the lay faculty was mostly young people like Olivia. Instant friends.

Olivia didn't think of herself as particularly brave. She wasn't the first to volunteer for a new venture or to take chances, and she had chosen the safest routes, even going to a college only an hour away from her home. She had boarded there, but it was so easy to hop back for Sunday dinner or even mid-week to do laundry for free. It hadn't really been like going away, and Aubrey had been there as well as several other high school friends. And then she lived at home after college for a year to save money. She was restless, though, jealous of friends who had their own places, who had gone off to New York or Chicago or even as far as San Francisco. Her friend Mollie was on a fellowship in London, studying architecture. Barry, whom she had dated briefly, was teaching English in a small town in Nicaragua. That year after college, she almost felt as if she were back in high school, eating dinner with her parents at six every evening, helping with the dishes, putting her toothbrush in the family bathroom next to her father's menthol shaving cream. So when Aubrey hatched the plan to move east, Olivia jumped on board. And now that Aubrey wasn't going, Olivia was still determined to make it work, believing it was time, or even past time. It was going to be perfect.

The evening gathered around her like a shawl of memories. She felt the warm drape of it on her shoulders, fingered each tassel of the fringe. She looked around the yard and memorized it all. The rhododendron and lilac bushes by the front door, the oak tree with the tire swing. Her brothers Tom and Evan holding cold bottles of beer, Evan's wife sprawled uncomfortably in a lawn chair, eight months pregnant. Evan's son Spence tossing a baseball in the air and catching it in his mitt. Tom's twin boys were taking turns on the tire swing, arguing over who could make it arc the highest. Aunt Sarah was coming through the side yard with a strawberry cake. Olivia looked at the house with its gables and that wide screened porch, each room and nook as familiar as breathing. The sideboard in the dining room with the chipped china soup tureen, the turn of the stairway heading upstairs with that worn carpet spot, the black and white tiles on the bathroom floor. The basement cluttered with sports equipment, cans of paint, always smelling like damp earth and laundry detergent. But in her pulse now thrummed the excitement of being independent, having her own address in another city. This would always be the place of her roots, but she knew she had outgrown it.

The spicy aroma of sizzling pork filled the yard as her mother and Aunt Sarah carried out serving dishes and utensils from the kitchen: a bowl of sauerkraut, wild rice, potato salad, and the family signature salad made of canned fruit cocktail, Cool Whip, and mini-marshmallows. There was hardly ever a family meal without that salad. Olivia secretly hated it, but she loved the hands that prepared it. Hers was a big extended family, and someone was always dropping in or calling with a last-minute invitation for a pot-luck supper. They celebrated everything. First day of kindergarten. Getting a driver's license. A haircut. Nothing was too small to note with a cookout or dinner party. Tonight, they were celebrating her last night in Minnesota. She hoped no one would cry. She wanted them to be as happy for her as she was for herself, and tears might bring on her own. And then someone would think she was sad, was having second thoughts, and she'd have to explain all over again why she was leaving. No. She wanted to see this evening through clear eyes. She kept catching her mother looking at her, as if she were afraid she'd disappear. Olivia wondered what her mother saw—the little girl with freckles careening into the yard on her bike, the teenager pleading to be allowed to stay out until midnight? Or did she see the woman Olivia saw when she looked in the mirror, still with the freckles, but with a new determination in her eyes?

The only negative voice was Aunt Mamie, but then, she was negative about everything. As Olivia stood in the yard, with the late afternoon sun striping the grass, her mother's older sister came to stand next to her, a glass of iced tea in her hand. Mamie always had her nose in everyone else's business, and she had a way of turning even the happiest occasion into a problem. Olivia smelled the floral hair spray Mamie used to keep every gray curl in place, and she forced herself to smile.

"So, you're really leaving." Mamie leaned in close to Olivia, arching her eyebrows.

"First thing tomorrow!" Olivia was determined to keep things light. She wouldn't let Mamie's sourness taint the evening.

"Almost a thousand miles away." Mamie shook her glass so the ice clinked. "Suppose you get homesick?"

Olivia stiffened at the negative spin Mamie was putting on the move. She backed up a few inches to try to get away from the hair spray scent.

"I'll be fine. I'll miss you all, of course, but I have a good job and I'll make a ton of friends. D.C. is such a great opportunity." She sounded like a promotional brochure.

Mamie drained her glass and sniffed. "Just make sure you find yourself a good church." The tone of her voice made it sound more like a warning than advice. Like being part of a parish would be Olivia's salvation from whatever dangers the big city held. "Don't get so busy you forget you're a born and bred Catholic."

Church wasn't the highest priority on Olivia's list. First, she had to settle into the apartment, find a roommate, introduce herself to the school. Teacher meetings were starting the third week in August and classes the week before Labor Day, which she found strange. School in Minnesota never opened until September. She was leaving early because the lease started July 1. She'd have to find some temp work. There would be plenty of time to find a church, and she hoped she'd find one close to her apartment. She looked around for an excuse to escape Mamie.

Her mother was setting out placemats, pitchers of iced tea and lemonade. She, too, had "dressed up," shifting from her usual Bermudas and polo shirt for a dress patterned in small butterflies. She had spritzed herself with the Chanel No. 5 she saved for special occasions. Olivia went into the kitchen to grab plates. There was a basket of hand-hemmed napkins on the counter. None of them matched. They were made from the leftovers of quilts and dresses her mother had sewn, and Olivia picked up one covered in tiny orange stars, a remnant from the sundress she'd worn when she was thirteen. There were so many napkins—flowers and stripes and plaids. No one would miss this one.

She tucked it into the pocket of her denim shorts and took the rest outside to her family, seated around the long plank table, ready to eat. Her parents. Her two brothers and their families. Her aunts and cousins. They looked, for a moment, like a scene in a magazine. A Norman Rockwell painting.

CHAPTER 3

FOUR DAYS LATER, trying to fall asleep in her new bedroom, she thought she must be crazy. The excitement of arriving in D.C. had worn off, and when daylight faded, the half-empty rooms shrank to shadows. The rumble of cars on the street were the sounds of people going home to places they knew, places that knew them. After the moving men left, depositing her belongings in the middle of the living room floor, Olivia had looked around and saw how small the apartment was. Two bedrooms, a living/dining area, a kitchen that was little more than an alcove, and a bathroom. It wasn't what she had pictured, but now she couldn't remember the image she had held. She had known it was the top floor of a house, but she hadn't realized how tiring walking up the sixteen steps would be as she lugged things in from her car. Her back hurt. Her feet hurt. Her arms hurt. She put her dishes in the kitchen cabinets and saw how few she had. She didn't have enough hangers for her clothes. She hadn't thought to buy a shower curtain. Worst of all, she realized she had forgotten to bring the tool kit her father had assembled for her. She could see it on the floor of the closet in her room. Without it, she hadn't been able to put the bed frame together, and now she was spending the night on the mattress she had dragged over by her bedroom window.

It was his going-away gift to her. He put in it everything he thought she'd need. "I won't be there to fix things for you," he said, as he explained how to insert the bits in the small electric drill. Olivia had never used any of those tools, except maybe a hammer. He had patiently explained the difference between a regular and a Phillips screwdriver, while she pretended to pay attention. What she remembered most about that afternoon wasn't what he told her, but his hands, the nails cut straight across, that slightly crooked bend in his right index finger from an old break. And the way he picked up each tool with such reverence. She could imagine him in the hardware store, turning each tool over, debating this one over that one. Deciding to get her only the best. More than the tools themselves, she loved that he had done this for her and had put them in a shiny red toolbox. "So you won't lose it," he said. And of all things, she had forgotten to bring it with her. She was pretty sure he wouldn't go into her room, but what if he did and he saw it there? What if he assumed she didn't want it? Worse than not having the tools was the dread that he would think it meant nothing to her.

The dark sky she saw from the window disoriented her, because she had always opened her curtains to see the stars when she went to sleep, the tall oaks in the back yard. She imagined the stars now, sparkling behind clouds. Tree shadows played out on the wall, and lightning flashes warned of another storm. She looked around the room, the dresser and desk against one wall, cardboard cartons piled up in the rest of the space. Their shadowy silhouettes crowded toward her. Each box was labeled with a thick red marker—linens, sweaters, records. She had been too tired to unpack much beyond the kitchen things. Earlier, she had run through rain to a deli where she bought a tuna sandwich. Now the air was heavy with moisture and the dull shake of thunder. She thought she heard scratching in the walls. Back in Minnesota, they had kept a tennis racket in the upstairs hallway because bats snuck in through the chimney. What sort of creatures might inhabit the walls of a brick house on the East Coast? What had possessed her to rent an apartment sight unseen? Of course, she had done so thinking Aubrey would be with her. With her friend along, they might have laughed at the odd noises or not heard them at all. But alone—every sound was magnified. Was it mice? Big, hairy spiders?

Even if she had been able to put her bed together, she would still feel disconcerted. Nothing was where it belonged. Was that really the best place for the desk? Shouldn't the dresser be next to the closet? She was a thousand miles from home, and there was no one to talk to, no familiar sounds. She didn't have a phone yet, and even if she did, there was no one here she could call if she needed help. For the first time in her life, she was totally alone. She wrapped the sheet tighter around herself, rolling into a ball. The sheet held the scent of lavender her mother had tucked into the folds. Never had she felt so small.

Her father had wanted to ride east with her and then fly back home. But she had insisted she do it on her own. Having him drive with her would be like having a parent go with her the first day in a new school, and she was way past that. If she was going to be independent, she was going to do it all the way, and that meant driving by herself. There had been something very appealing about crossing all those state lines, seeing skylines of cities she'd never visited, knowing with every mile that clicked on the dashboard gauge that she was getting closer to her new life. Now, as the rain started again and spit against the window, she wondered if that had been the right decision. She saw the disappointment on his face when she said no, sensed a sadness in him as he went over with her the route AAA had mapped out. He really wanted to do this for her, and she rejected his offer. Would it have been such a big deal to say yes if it would make him happy? He would have made sure she remembered the tool box, and he would have known how to find the wall studs to hang that heavy mirror, which screw driver to use to fix the wobbly kitchen cabinet door.

She watched headlights arc over the ceiling as cars passed on the street below. Listening to the hiss of rain and the growl of thunder, she willed herself not to cry. She made a mental list of all the reasons this had been a good idea. Opportunities. Life away from a small town. New people. Independence. She tried to imagine the living room after she unpacked everything, the green shag rug unrolled on the floor, her books in the bookcase, lighted lamps, her favorite music on the stereo. It would be fine.

But a second later, as lightning cracked the sky, she found herself fighting tears.

CHAPTER 4

TWO WEEKS LATER, she thought it was the best decision she'd ever made, and she wondered why she'd ever doubted it. She loved everything about D.C.—her apartment (even though it was small), the brick sidewalks in Georgetown, the little shops where she could buy candles or muffins. She loved waking up in the morning and looking out to the backyard where the green leaves of a small tree shimmered in the sun. She loved knowing museums and art galleries were only a few miles away. The traffic that snarled the downtown streets day and night made her nervous, and parking was nearly impossible, so she consulted a bus schedule and learned to find her way downtown to the National Gallery and the Smithsonian Museum and out Connecticut Avenue to the zoo. There were no entrance fees, which was a plus on her limited budget, and the bus fare was only forty cents. One hot afternoon she spent hours in the art gallery, meandering through the wide, cool rooms and looking at paintings by Vermeer, Fragonard, and Copley. She bought a handful of postcards and, flooded with momentary nostalgia, a print of Monet's *Woman with a Parasol*. The blue sky, high clouds, and the windblown field of wildflowers reminded her of the countryside around her town. Not that she wanted to be there. She just felt comforted by memories of picnics and hayrides, and she loved the colors. She tacked it up on the bedroom wall over her desk.

Having spent twenty-two years in a small town where excitement was two-for-one night at the bowling alley, she felt drenched by culture. Her world had suddenly expanded, and even though she didn't know them, she knew she was living in the midst of congressmen and ambassadors. Why, that guy running to hail a cab on Wisconsin Avenue could be a lawyer who worked "on the hill"—what locals called Congress. She must truly be on her way to being a local if she was learning the lingo. And that woman wearing heels and clutching a briefcase could be heading for a meeting at the White House. Olivia breathed in deeply, heady with excitement. She still wished Aubrey were there to share it with her, but she'd write and tell her everything.

Her mother had secretly mailed her the toolbox, and she had finally assembled her bed. There was a grocery store, a Peoples Drug Store, and a book and record store within three blocks of her apartment. True, she didn't have a roommate, and she'd have to do that temp work for a while before she got her first paycheck, but she'd work it all out. Every morning she had to pinch herself to see if it was real, to prove that she had driven almost a thousand miles and now had a home in the Nation's Capital. She smiled as she wrote her return address on the postcard she was sending to Aubrey. She smiled when she memorized her new phone number. She smiled when she opened the kitchen cabinets and saw her glasses and plates on the clean sheets of shelf paper, the soup pot and the muffin tins. She smiled when she unscrewed the top of the nutmeg container and the room filled with the scent of snickerdoodles. This was where she was supposed to be.

The only time she felt lonely was in the evening. The field trips around the city kept her busy during the day, and would until she registered with the temp agency, but after dinner she had little to do but leaf through the textbooks she had picked up at her school. She didn't have a TV, wondered how long it would take her to save up to buy a small one. She did have her stereo, so as she read, she listened to her favorite records. Still, those hours were long, and she wished she had someone to talk to. The second bedroom echoed with emptiness. She didn't like going to movies alone, nor did she want to go to a restaurant by herself. Would she have to wait until school started to meet new people? That day felt so far away. Some evenings she tried out one of her grandmother's recipes, but they were designed for a crowd, and she didn't want to eat Swedish meatballs for a week.

The house settled into itself as darkness fell, and the window air-conditioning unit in the living room window rattled as it tried unsuccessfully to cool the space. Most of the time she turned it off and opened the windows. Instead of toads and crickets, she heard city sounds. Sirens. Cars honking. Conversations of people on the sidewalk. She looked around at the sparse furnishings—the day bed with its maroon corduroy slipcover, the armchair and the matching hassock from Aunt Sarah's spare room, the coffee table that was an old steamer trunk that doubled as a storage place for extra blankets, the small table Aunt Mamie had given her that was both a workspace and a place to eat. She decided to think of her bedroom as "cozy" rather than "cramped," even though the bed, desk, and dresser took up every inch of space. Still, sometimes even the small rooms dwarfed her, magnified her solitude. She remembered sitting on the wrap-around porch of her Minnesota home, or driving with friends to a tavern and gathering outside at a rickety table drinking beer. As she sat on the lumpy daybed in her living room, she sensed the city pulsing around her, and she felt isolated. But then she'd go to bed and sleep and when she woke up in the morning, with the sun on that tree in the yard, she'd be eager for a new adventure. Daylight infused her with energy, and she'd look around the apartment and the way she had arranged her meager furniture to make it look like there was more, at her to-do list on the fridge where she was steadily checking things off, and she'd know she had done the right thing.

CHAPTER 5

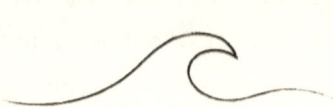

IT WAS MRS. Trimble, Olivia's landlady, who introduced her to Rebecca. Mrs. Trimble worked the night shift at Suburban Hospital and knew that Olivia needed someone for the second bedroom. She ran into Olivia one hot afternoon when the mail had just been delivered. The mailman left it all on a small hall table, and Mrs. Trimble was sorting through it. Olivia's mother had sent her a thick envelope last week of local newspaper clippings she thought Olivia would enjoy, but there was nothing today.

"Settling in OK, Olivia?" Mrs. Trimble had pretty much left Olivia alone in the three weeks she had been there. "You know, if you need anything, or if there are any problems, I have a great fix-it guy." Olivia appreciated that, and also appreciated that the landlady didn't barge in every five minutes. She didn't need another mother. At the same time, she was worried about the whole roommate search, because she didn't know where to start.

"Everything's fine, Mrs. Trimble," Olivia replied, disappointed at her lack of mail. Aubrey had promised to write every week, but so far there had not even been a postcard. Even though she knew Aubrey was busy with her wedding plans and a new job, it hurt her that Aubrey hadn't taken the time to send a card or a short letter. Surely Aubrey would know that she would be lonely. They'd been able to read each other's minds since they were kids. In the time Olivia had been in D.C., she hadn't met anyone beyond store clerks, Mrs. Trimble, and Sister Helen, the principal at Holy Redeemer Academy, and she ached to hear a familiar voice or just see Aubrey's handwriting on an envelope.

"Listen, I know you said you planned to have a roommate to share the rent—" Mrs. Trimble paused, absent-mindedly riffling through a pile of circulars.

Olivia definitely needed a roommate to help with the rent. She had saved money by living with her parents the past year, but she had bought the Chevy (used) and now she was discovering that everything from food to gas cost more than it had in Minnesota. And her job at Holy Redeemer Academy would put her on a strict budget. Catholic schools were notorious for low salaries. Utilities were included in the apartment rent, but she had to pay for a phone and car insurance, and she needed more furniture and some area rugs. She hadn't calculated how much she'd have to spend on gas to get back and forth from work, since the school wasn't on a bus line, and even the little things she had to buy piled up—a shower curtain, a teakettle, a new lampshade to replace the one that had been bent in the move. She was starting to wonder if she could afford groceries past October. The entire plan had been predicated on Aubrey being with her. Yesterday she had registered with a temp agency. She knew she should have done that right away, but she'd been busy settling in to the apartment and getting to know the city.

"No. I need to do that soon." She took a sip from the can of Coke she was holding. She didn't want Mrs. Trimble to know how tight her money was.

"Well, I know a couple of nurses at the hospital who are looking for places. One in particular, Rebecca Wertzman, works in the emergency department." She went on to describe Rebecca, how she was just about Olivia's age, had been renting a room in a private home for the past year, was eager for a place of her own.

Olivia wondered what it would be like sharing an apartment with a stranger, but then, everyone here was a stranger. And a nurse sounded good. Reliable. Mrs. Trimble promised to have Rebecca call her and headed into her downstairs apartment. Olivia figured it was worth a try, and if this Rebecca didn't work out, Mrs. Trimble said she knew others. Olivia perked up a little at this, some of her bank account worries receding.

And so, Olivia met Rebecca. She was short, with dark curly hair and her nails painted an outrageous shade of purple. She promised to be neat, confessed to being a lousy cook, and said she knew where all the best thrift stores were to buy used furniture. She moved in two days after they met, complete with her sewing machine (she made most of her own clothes), a brand-new electric skillet (gift from her mother), and dozens of Reader's Digest Condensed Books. "I never have time to read the whole books," Rebecca said, laughing as she set them up on the bookcase in her room she made of milk crates and the top of an ironing board. Olivia couldn't imagine not reading a whole book. She, in fact, devoured books. One of the first things she had done in D.C. was to get a library card, and there was a stack of books next to her bed. She would peruse a unit in the literature texts she had to teach and then settle in bed with one of her library books. Steinbeck, Eudora Welty, Vonnegut. She looked at some of the titles on the spines of the condensed books and wondered what parts had been left out.

But reading aside, Olivia liked Rebecca from the start. Nothing seemed to faze her, and she was one of those people who wake up talking as if yesterday's conversation had never ended. Although she rarely cooked, she was more than happy to do the grocery shopping as long as Olivia gave her a detailed list, though she was apt to substitute at will or come home with some odd item just because it had been on sale. Maraschino cherries. Sardines. Drinking straws. Olivia would find working with terrible injuries, heart attacks, and even death depressing, but Rebecca chattered about the successes, the guy who almost lost his arm but didn't, the joy she felt rocking a baby who had a high fever. The day something went wrong with the hot water heater, Rebecca joked about how they could pretend they were at camp showering with rain water. She knew how to bargain at the thrift stores, something Olivia never would have dared to do, and that accounted for the drop leaf table Rebecca had wrangled for less than the asking price. When she wasn't in her white nurse's uniform, she wore flamboyant clothes, like the long skirt with a purposely uneven hem she had sewn by combining a collection of paisley scarves. "You just have to learn to see possibilities in things," she told Olivia, whose wardrobe mainly consisted of Villager blouses and tailored skirts.

There might be days on end when they didn't see each other. Olivia took a couple of temp jobs every week, and Rebecca was often asleep when Olivia left in the morning. Or she came home after Olivia had gone to bed. They left each other notes on the kitchen counter. *Want to see a movie Wednesday? We're out of milk. Can I borrow your red blouse?* But when Rebecca was around, she was true to her word. She didn't leave her bath towel draped over the side of the tub, always washed her dishes, and she did the clean-up when Olivia used the electric skillet to make pancakes.

Olivia was happy on the days she came home from some random job (receptionist at a real estate office, ticket-taker at a movie theater, cashier at a fast-food place) and Rebecca was there, sanding a piece of furniture or laying out a tissue paper pattern for a new dress. There would be wood shavings or scraps of fabric everywhere, and Rebecca happily humming as she worked. Rebecca added sparkle to the apartment. Olivia remembered her first couple of weeks alone, when the rooms didn't feel like home yet, especially on empty mailbox days. With Rebecca around, the apartment came to life.

CHAPTER 6

IT WAS ONE of those August days when the humidity had lifted, leaving behind a lazy warmth that invited you to go outside and soak up the end of summer. Olivia and Rebecca were eager to get out of the apartment. Rebecca had lived in the city for two years, and she knew where to go to find things to do that were free.

"There's a rec center just off Wisconsin Avenue," Rebecca said at breakfast. "There are minor minor minor league games there every Saturday afternoon." She explained that the teams were so minor they didn't even have uniforms. "It's really just guys who like to play baseball. A lot of med students, lawyers. You never know who you'll meet." It sounded good to Olivia, who was tired of thrift store shopping and writing lesson plans for her fall classes. Being outside also appealed to her, since she had just spent four days working in the back room of a shoe store doing inventory.

The park was in walking distance, and they managed to snag seats on one of the three-tiered wooden bleachers on the side of the field. Rebecca went over to the snack stand and brought them back big red paper cups of Coke. The guys were milling around on the field, tossing balls back and forth, taking some practice hits. Rebecca had been right—they all looked like they were in their late twenties and thirties, and they had made an attempt at uniforms by wearing either white or blue T-shirts. Olivia took a sip of her Coke and settled in, slipping off her sandals.

She loved baseball. She loved the thwack of the bat, the arc of a ball sailing toward the outfield, the dust from a slide home. She loved taking off her shoes and wiggling her toes in the grass, the heat of the sun on her shoulders. She loved the concentrated stance of the batters, their fervent focus on the pitcher. She loved the wind-up of the pitcher's arm, and the way the outfielders ran backward to catch a ball. She loved that no one plowed into anyone else, like in football, and that the scoring was so easy to understand. She had played a little softball in high school, not varsity or anything. Just a community league. The best part, she thought, was running the bases. She had always loved running.

There was no scoreboard, just a card table with two wooden easels. As the game progressed through the innings, it seemed that no one really cared about the score. It was all about the playing. It was all about being outside on a warm cloudless day. A few guys in the blue shirts even cheered when someone on the opposing team made it home. It was a perfect afternoon. The sun was high and the chirr of birds a soft lazy refrain. Olivia crunched a last sliver of ice from her half-full cup.

It was the bottom of the ninth, and the score was 4 – 3, with the white team ahead. One of the white team players was at bat, swaying slightly side to side to set his stance. He already had two strikes. The breeze had died down, and Olivia brushed a damp lock of hair off her face. She heard the smack as the bat hit the ball, saw the white sphere arc up into the air. Instead of streaking for the outfield, though, the ball veered to the right. A foul, she thought. Then, before she could even register what was happening, the ball landed right in her cup. Warm coke splashed all over her, and she dropped the cup on the ground. Rebecca shrieked and then started to laugh. Olivia tried to mop up the Coke from her shirt with a paper napkin, realized the shirt was clinging to her and the outline of her bra.

Ten minutes later, when the game was over, the batter walked in front of them, looking like he was heading to the snack bar. Olivia called to him, held up the ball, and said, "Do you want your ball back?"

He looked over and grinned as if he was putting two and two together. "Is that the one I hit?"

"It landed in my cup."

"I'm so sorry. I thought it had rolled under the bleachers."

He was tall, maybe almost six feet. His dark brown hair was cut short on the sides and a little longer on top. He had the shadow of stubble smudging his face, more like someone who hadn't shaved in a day or two than someone who was seriously considering growing a beard. His eyes glinted green in the sun, and his smile made them crinkle at the corners. A pencil-thin scar crossed the bridge of his nose. He looked seriously apologetic as he pointed to her empty cup. "The least I can do is buy you another Coke," he said.

"Oh no," she said. "I'm about to leave anyway. It's fine." The heat was making her thirsty, but she wanted to get home and out of the embarrassingly clingy shirt. She heard Rebecca beside her, snorting a laugh.

"I insist," he said, pointing to the snack stand. "I'll be right back." She watched him trot away, noted his firm calves above droopy socks, his broad shoulders. Rebecca nudged her, raising her eyebrows, as if to say, "I told you there were some great guys here."

In less than two minutes he was back with a brimming cup. He chuckled as he handed it to her. "What are the chances of that happening? Like a hole in one, only the wrong sport." He sat down next to her, stretched out his long legs. He smelled like sweat and late-summer grass. She wondered what he did for a living. She took a furtive glance sideways and saw he was smiling. Turning to her, he held out his hand. "By the way, I'm Pete." He had freckles on the back of his hands, and very long fingers, though the nails were nibbled down to the quick.

"Olivia, and this is Rebecca." He seemed in no hurry to leave, and she would have liked to stay and talk with him, but she and Rebecca were meeting two of Rebecca's nurse friends for an early dinner, and now she'd have to change her clothes. She and Rebecca stood to leave, and Olivia turned her head once as they crossed the field toward the street. He seemed to still be looking at her, and she wondered if he'd be playing again the next week.

CHAPTER 7

"HE'S A WHAT?" Rebecca looked up from spreading jam on her croissant.

"A priest. I saw him when I went to Mass this morning. My mother's been nagging me every time I talk to her. 'Have you found a church?' So I went to the 8:00 service and there he was." He hadn't said the Mass, but he approached her at the coffee hour in the church hall. She almost spilled the spoonful of sugar she was about to stir into her decaf. The guy she'd met the afternoon before wearing shorts and a T-shirt, the guy whose baseball had splashed into her Coke, stood in front of her in black slacks and a black shirt with a Roman collar. She felt a warm flush climb up her cheeks as she remembered her shirt plastered to her chest. She was at a loss for words and also surprised that he remembered her name. Was this the best introduction to her new parish?

"Shit. He's so good looking. He didn't act anything like a priest. Not that I'd know." Rebecca was Jewish.

Olivia had a flash of his green eyes. No, he hadn't acted like a priest the day before. Playing baseball. Wearing those athletic shorts. Every priest she had ever known was so formal and always so much older. Even when her parents had invited the pastor, Father McConnell, to dinner, he arrived in his black suit, and no one ever called him Phil. But Pete hadn't even told her he was a priest. Did he not want her to know? Was he careful to keep the different parts of his life separate?

Olivia nodded and pulled a tea bag out of the box. "He just seemed so normal at the game. Like he was going to go home and feed his dog and head out to a bar with friends. And then when he came up this morning and said hi, well, I . . ." She remembered nothing of what she said to him, just a feeling of astonishment. He seemed completely at ease, reaching into his pocket for a cigarette, wearing the same easy grin she noticed the afternoon before. He asked her where she was from, why she had chosen St. Andrew's. He told her there was a very active young adult group (Aunt Mamie would be happy) and if she was a singer, there were two choirs she could join. Olivia hadn't given any thought to joining any groups; she had enough on her hands with preparing for school, the boring temp jobs, and fixing up the apartment.

"Are priests allowed to wear regular clothes? I thought they always wore black and had shirts with those weird collars." Rebecca took a bite of her croissant.

"Well, yeah. I mean, a lot of them do, though I've never known priests that well." She had always seen them as up on a pedestal, existing on a level above everyone else. Priests didn't hang out with lay people, play cards, mow lawns, or go to the movies. The priests in her home parish had either worn black or been draped in vestments during liturgical services. They certainly didn't wear shorts and play baseball. "The church is more liberal now. I don't know about priests, but a lot of nuns wear regular skirts and blouses instead of those long black dresses. A few of them wear short veils, but some of them don't even do that. You can always tell a nun, though."

"How?"

"They wear clunky shoes and don't pluck their eyebrows. And they carry purses like our grandmothers." The two of them laughed, and Olivia selected a mug from the cabinet. The kettle shrieked on the stove.

"He barely looked old enough to be a priest." Rebecca ran her finger through the jam that had dripped on her plate. "But how would I know?"

Olivia thought for a second, captured again by the memory of those green eyes. "He has to be at least in his late twenties, but probably early thirties. Priests study for a long time. College. Seminary. And he told me he'd been at St. Andrew's for two years. So yeah, probably early thirties. At least thirty-two."

Rebecca took her plate to the sink. "Huh. Seems like a waste for such a good-looking guy to be out of the dating picture." She turned around to face Olivia. "And it's not just that he's good looking. He was so thoughtful. He went and got you that new Coke, and he really sounded sorry about what happened with the baseball. Some guys wouldn't have taken the time." She glanced up at the wall clock. "Yikes! I'm gonna be late! I have to work 'til eight, so I won't be here for dinner. Save me something."

Olivia felt the silence settle around her after Rebecca left. Sundays always stretched out long, and she was restless. The room felt too small, and she wanted to be outside in the golden late summer afternoon. Maybe she could go for a walk, but what she really wanted was someone to go on a walk with. Often it seemed like the world was made up of couples. A mom and dad pushing a stroller. College kids with their arms draped around each other, laughing at a secret joke. Even older people came in twos. When she had gone out to buy croissants, the ones she and Rebecca had just polished off, she had seen an elderly couple sitting on a bench outside the bakery. They weren't talking, but there was a well-creased newspaper between them open to a crossword puzzle completed in ink. They had looked so content, as if they didn't even need words. She wanted some of that.

In her room, she looked at the overflowing laundry basket. She really should go to the laundromat. But she didn't want to spend two hours watching her clothes tumble around in the machines. The *cheer cheer* song of a cardinal wafted in from the backyard. That decided her. She could do her laundry later. What she wanted was to sit and laze in the sun. The apartment felt suffocating, and the silence too thick. Cooler days would be here before she knew it, and then she would be stuck inside. She picked up a paperback and took a soda from the fridge. She'd go back and sit in the park. There wouldn't be a baseball game, but she could just enjoy relaxing in the warm air. And maybe someone would come along. You never knew who you'd meet on a bright Sunday afternoon.

CHAPTER 8

IT WAS ONLY two weeks into the school year, and Olivia was feeling overwhelmed. The initial euphoria of being in a new place had worn off, to be replaced by the reality of having to get up at six, grab something to eat, and be at school by eight. Then teaching five classes a day with only thirty minutes for lunch, and more often than not, a staff or department meeting after classes. Taking home piles of papers to grade every evening. As a new teacher, she was on the evaluation loop, and she had to turn in weekly lesson plans every Friday afternoon. While the other teachers were zipping out of the parking lot at three-thirty, she was stuck at her desk writing plans to turn in to Sister Helen. She had never realized how hard it would be. Maybe she was just too conscientious. Was she the only one up until eleven every night getting ready for tomorrow? Plus, she was discovering how expensive everything was, and her modest savings were rapidly dwindling, in spite of Rebecca sharing the rent. There was no time for more temp jobs.

The staff had been welcoming and supportive of her as the youngest teacher. They showed her where to find the bulletin board supplies, helped her gather textbooks and pens and glue sticks. Advised her to bring her own lunch unless she wanted the leftovers from the nuns' dinner. As

Sister Helen had said, many of the teachers were also in their twenties, though most were married. There was one math teacher, Sylvia, who was in her fifties and took a motherly interest in Olivia, often sitting with her at lunch and even bringing her little treats like a brownie or a tangerine. The exception to the friendliness was Sister Anna, who was the English department head, and who locked herself in her classroom during her free period, making her inaccessible if Olivia had a question. She never said anything, but Olivia got the distinct impression that Sister Anna didn't approve of her. The occasional raised eyebrow, the tiny frown. Olivia found this disturbing, because she was so intent on making a good impression, so determined to succeed. She thought Sister Anna might just think she was too young, that she didn't know enough about teaching. Why, then, wouldn't she want to help her? Eventually, Olivia was too busy to think about it. She shrugged and ignored the closed door.

Late one Tuesday afternoon, Rebecca breezed into the living room where Olivia was sitting on the couch surrounded by piles of papers. Off duty from her job at the hospital, Rebecca was home only long enough to change clothes for her second job at Footnotes, a local bookstore. She invited Olivia to come with her, because there was going to be a book signing.

"Come on, Olivia," she said, tossing her purse on the floor. "It'll be fun. And there are always great snacks." Neither of them had been grocery shopping since the week before.

Olivia chewed on the end of her pen and pointed to the pile of papers. She shook her head. "Wish I could. But as you can see, I'm held captive by these vocabulary tests."

"I'll help you grade them when we get back. You spend every evening holed up here."

Olivia was tempted. It was true that she hadn't been anywhere but school and church and the grocery store since school had started. She looked down at her outfit—a pair of old khaki shorts and a faded gray T-shirt. She could change into a dress, maybe that jade green A-line that made her feel like dancing. Put on the new gold earrings her brother Evan had sent her as an early birthday gift. She could just feel herself hurrying down the brick sidewalk with Rebecca, free from the stuffy apartment. Then reason took over, and she felt the vision deflate, and she sank back into the couch, deflating with it.

Rebecca came out of her room a few minutes later, wearing a turquoise tank top and one of the calf-length skirts she had made out of silk scarves. She had pulled her curly black hair into a clip, and was wearing magenta lipstick. On anyone else, it would be too much, but on Rebecca it was perfect. It made Olivia feel like the ugly stepsister. Only instead of staying home to scrub floors, she was stuck grading papers for teenagers who didn't care about correct spelling. I'm missing out on everything, she thought, still seeing herself in that green dress. Tears, whether of anger or disappointment, threatened to fall. She took a deep breath and willed them away. What good would it do to feel sorry for herself?

Rebecca tried to tempt her by suggesting that there might be some eligible and fascinating guys at the book signing. That was another thing. Where were all the cool guys Aubrey had assured her swarmed around D.C.? She had not had a date since she got here. Well, there was that one guy she had met when she and Rebecca had gone to happy hour one Friday afternoon in August at a waterfront bar. She had accepted an invitation to go out to dinner, but he was such a pompous ass that she had been tempted to leave before her meal arrived. She might have, but she hadn't had enough cash with her for a cab. And a Catholic girls' school was no place to meet men. Father Pete had mentioned a couple of choirs, and a young adult group, but she didn't want her social life to revolve around the church. She wanted something broader, more cosmopolitan. Something like a book signing where there would be teaching assistants, professors, or just unmarried men who liked to read. She could see herself standing next to the table of half-price books and reaching for last year's Robert Ludlum at the same time that another hand grabbed it, and the two of them laughing and discovering they both devoured espionage stories.

"Are you sure?" Rebecca raised her eyebrows. Olivia thought she looked like freedom. As a nurse, she never had to bring work home with her. She clocked out of the emergency room and floated seamlessly into her other life, the life where she got to dress up and go to bookstores and concerts. Hadn't she seen Neil Young at the Cellar Door just a week ago when Olivia had to spend hours on lesson plans? She stabbed her pen into the quiz in her lap, then took a deep breath and willed herself to calm down. She forced a smile and gave a little wave as Rebecca grabbed her keys and headed out, leaving behind her a wisp of jasmine scent. Olivia's image of the book store faded.

Olivia missed Aubrey. She missed her family. She even kind of missed Trevor, her old boring boyfriend, and that told her how desperate she must be. On nights like this, she wanted to talk to one of them, to hear a familiar voice, but long distance was expensive. And she was afraid her voice would give her away, and she wanted them to believe that she was fine, that she had made the right decision. She had done what any twenty-two-year-old would do. She was starting her life, the life she was entitled to. No, she didn't want them to think she had failed or that she was anything but happy. In the occasional letter she wrote home, or on the phone, she even made up some stuff about her social life. They weren't really lies, she told herself. They were what everyone wanted to believe. Olivia off on her own and loving it. They were what Olivia wanted to believe would be true one day, and maybe believing this might make it happen.

Thinking about her home town made her think about Trevor. He had wanted to marry her. It was part of his life-plan, which he had worked out when he was in high school. Go to college. Major in business. Take over the family hardware store when his father retired. Marry Olivia when he had saved enough money. Have three children. Join the Knights of Columbus, that Catholic men's group that did charitable work in the community. Make a good life for them all in the drab Minnesota town. She had said no because she didn't want to be part of anyone's plan. She wanted to live out her own plan. Shuffling Trevor out of her mind, she picked up another quiz.

Her mind wandered. Maybe she should get up and fix a snack. Or a glass of chardonnay. Maybe she should toss the tests aside and go to the bookstore after all. Surprise Rebecca. The living room suddenly felt small. As she sat there, undecided, she got that weird feeling in her throat that had been coming off and on. It had first happened two weeks ago, driving through the rush hour traffic to school. It started to feel like her throat was closing up. She could barely breathe, had to gulp in air, and her heart was racing. She had wrenched her car into the parking lot of a Peoples Drug Store and put her hand on her chest, felt the hard fluttering. I'm too young to have a heart attack, she thought, as sweat started to bead on her forehead and drip down her ribs. She kept drawing in air, and gradually the pounding calmed, her throat felt open and normal, and she drove on to school. It had happened again while she was teaching her freshman class to diagram a sentence. She had stood at the board, felt that fluttering choking, not that bad this time, but she had the same trouble breathing. It felt like a hand was at her throat, closing off her airway. She didn't want the students to see her distress, and she had to grip the chalk and will her heart to slow, take quick shallow breaths. "Do the next one on your own," she said, and she walked over to stand by the open window, hoping fresh air would help. In a few minutes, the feeling subsided, and she returned to the board, hoping the students didn't see her shaky fingers. What was happening? She had always enjoyed good health, took her vitamins faithfully, ran a mile without losing her breath. Was she losing her grip?

It happened several more times, and it washed over her with no warning. In the pasta aisle at Safeway, once in church, yesterday standing inside the downstairs door getting the mail. She had no idea what caused it, and she had thought of asking Rebecca, since she was a nurse. But it wasn't like anything she had ever heard of, and maybe her roommate would think she was crazy. Maybe she was crazy. Maybe she was having some sort of breakdown. How could she explain this weird symptom that came and went? The worst part was that it rushed in with no warning. She would be brushing her hair and suddenly be fighting for breath. There was no way to prepare for it, to ward it off. And once it hit, she was afraid she wouldn't get over it. It was suffocating. Fresh air seemed to help, but not always.

The words on the quiz in her lap blurred. It wasn't tears. She wasn't crying. She was in a place where even tears didn't help. A blank place. She felt herself start to flush with sweat, sensed the deepening of that throat thing. No, she said to herself. You won't go there. She tried to think of peaceful things—snow on the banks of a lake, the clear call of a loon, a sky jeweled with stars. She sat like that, the school papers momentarily forgotten, until gradually she returned to herself, to the room, to the rattle of the air-conditioner in the window.

Then she went back to work.

CHAPTER 9

SHE RAN INTO Father Pete a few more times after the baseball game. At church, of course, when he stood at the back at the end of Mass greeting people, but also once at the record store, and once in Peoples where she was buying shampoo and he was choosing something from the candy bar display. Neither time away from church was he wearing his clerical clothes, so he looked like any guy in a T-shirt and khakis. In the drugstore, they chatted for a few minutes, and he added a roll of lime Lifesavers to his Snickers as he headed for the cashier. And then he invited her to join a committee at church when he saw her at coffee hour after Mass the next Sunday. "It's people your age, and they do good work." Their current project was collecting school supplies for children in El Salvador. She had often worked on service projects back home, and she thought it would be a chance to meet some people. The teachers at Holy Redeemer were friendly, but they didn't have time to socialize during the school day, and they all left after dismissal in the afternoon. She needed to broaden her circle. Pete had assured her it wouldn't take up a big chunk of her time.

Even though she had balked at joining a choir or a young adult group, Olivia accepted his invitation, seeing it as community outreach, and they were gathered now in a first-grade classroom. St. Andrew's had an elementary school. They were sitting on tiny chairs around low tables. There were four people besides Father Pete and her. Ben, a guy in his thirties, his hugely pregnant wife Susanna, a grad student named Nelda, and Bryana, an ESL teacher. Father Pete explained that there was another couple, Marianne and Greg, who were usually there but had a conflict that evening. The room smelled like rain and crayons. Through the open window she could hear the splash of rain from the gutters. Father Pete introduced her to the others and sat on the edge of a table. Olivia had been concerned, despite Father Pete's insistence, that being on the committee might be too much work, would take up the time she didn't have, but it seemed simple enough. He had been so nice to think of her, and it would be rude to turn him down. Tonight, they were going to sort the supplies collected over the summer. Parishioners had donated boxes of crayons, yellow #2 pencils, looseleaf paper, composition books, sets of colored markers. It would only take about an hour, and she'd still have time to reread the chapter in *A Separate Peace* for her sophomore English class the next day.

Olivia smiled at the others and said yes, she was new to the parish. Nelda said she hadn't seen her at church, and Olivia said she usually went to the early service, and the others confessed to sleeping in and attending the late afternoon Mass. Yes, she was a teacher. Yes, she loved D.C. But her smile started to feel pasted on. Did she love D.C.? She glanced up and saw Father Pete looking at her, and for a flash she saw him in his baseball clothes. And standing at the candy display trying to decide between a Milky Way and a Snickers. Back in Minnesota, all the priests in her parish had been at least as old as her parents, if not older. Father Pete seemed like one of them as he sorted through packs of looseleaf paper and composition books. He was wearing a black shirt and black slacks, but he didn't have his Roman collar on.

The tasks tonight were mindless, her fingers wrapping rubber bands around bunches of pencils, counting plastic rulers and protractors. The clean, new pages of the notebooks reminded her of so many first days of school, sitting in a freshly ironed uniform jumper, her feet wiggling in stiff new saddle shoes. Then she brought herself back to this classroom, with large construction paper letters taped above the chalkboard. She laughed at a joke Ben told as he taped up the box she had just filled.

The women were mostly silent, with Ben and Father Pete keeping the conversation going, talking about baseball and which teams would make it to the World Series. Olivia joined in a few times, feeling a burst of energy from the shared camaraderie. It was fun to be with a group, giggling at stupid jokes, sobering as she listened to Father Pete giving them the hard facts about what life was like for the children in El Salvador. When she heard about the poverty, she packed the boxes with more care, wished she had some pretty ribbon to wrap around the pencils instead of the dingy rubber bands.

Father Pete pointed to the clock on the wall, said time was up, he didn't want to keep them past eight-thirty. Ben stacked the cartons on a dolly and he wheeled it out of the room, followed by Susanna who was rubbing her low back. Bryana and Nelda pushed in the chairs and waved good-bye. Olivia was about to leave herself, looking around to see if they had forgotten anything, taking her car keys out of her purse.

"Thanks, Olivia." His voice was warm and low.

She realized Father Pete was standing behind her, and she turned, a little startled. "Oh, it was fun," she said, thinking how lame that sounded. Surely, she could have thought of a better word than fun, but her mind was only half on his words, the other half thinking about the chapter questions she had to copy on the ditto machine in the morning.

"How's it going?" He sat again on one of the children's tables, crossing his ankles. "The new school. Getting around in a new city." He reached in his pocket for a pack of cigarettes, shook it absent-mindedly, and put it back.

"Fine, Father. Everything is fine. I love my school, and I have a terrific roommate." She paused. "I forgot—you met her that day at the baseball game." She smiled inside, remembering how Rebecca had remarked what a waste it was for such a good-looking guy to be out of range for dating. But there was no time for chatting. She still had to pack her lunch for the next day and put gas in her car on the way home. "I have to go, but thanks for inviting me," she said as she picked up her umbrella and headed out.

CHAPTER 10

AT THE NEXT meeting, early the next week, Ben explained that Susanna wasn't coming. "Swollen ankles," he said. "She's close to her due date."

Father Pete looked concerned. "Ben, let me know if there's anything I can do to help." He gave a little laugh. "I'm available for a midnight run to the hospital if you need it. Parking can be a problem."

Olivia thought that was above and beyond the role of a parish priest, though maybe Father Pete saw it as part of his ministry. And Ben smiled and said maybe he'd take him up on it. "I'll probably be a wreck." Really, Olivia thought, Father Pete seemed so generous.

That Wednesday, she found it hard to keep her mind on packing pencils and composition books. Interim report cards were due (she'd never heard of that), her car was making a funny noise, and she had had two incidents of that hard-to-breathe thing in the past three days. Again, they were when she was doing something ordinary, like trying to decide between McIntosh and Red Delicious apples in Safeway. And then Sister Helen (usually so pleasant) had frowned at one of her lesson plans ("stick to the curriculum, Olivia") where she had included an idea to have the kids write essays based on popular song lyrics. Olivia thought that if they used lines from Joni Mitchell or Bob Dylan songs it might spark more creativity. Rebecca had brought a date home the night before, and the two of them sat in the living room until after midnight listening to records. Olivia had to put her pillow over her ears to try to get to sleep. She had almost skipped the meeting, but she hated to go back on a promise.

She was also distracted because the other couple, Marianne and Greg, were there. When Olivia and Nelda went down the hall to the supply closet to get more cardboard cartons, Nelda explained that Greg was a former priest, and Marianne had been a nun. Olivia knew that priests and nuns sometimes left religious life, but she had never known any. Nelda said that they had come from a parish in Maryland, where he had been assistant pastor and she had taught fourth grade in the school. It took a while for Olivia to digest this. How did a priest go about leaving his vocation? Did the Pope have to approve? Greg was older than Pete. He looked early forties. Marianne looked to be in her early thirties. Olivia wondered how difficult it had been for them to leave their former lives, or maybe love trumped everything. As Greg spoke, he brushed the back of Marianne's neck. They looked so natural together.

As they were wrapping up, and the others filed out to their cars, Father Pete motioned for her to stay. "Is everything ok?"

"Sure." Why was he asking? Had he noticed the circles under her eyes? She pushed in the chair where Ben had been sitting.

"You just seem distracted tonight." He rolled a piece of chalk around in his hand. "Not your usual bubbly self."

Olivia hardly thought of herself as bubbly, but she had been distracted. Maybe Father Pete had noticed all the times she looked at the clock.

"You know," he continued, "it's not unusual to feel a little lost in a new place."

"I don't feel lost," she said. "I'm fine." She was. Usually. And she didn't feel lost. Just tired.

He went on, as if she hadn't spoken. "A new city, a new school. D.C.

traffic." He chuckled as he said that. "When I moved here from Raleigh, I couldn't figure out the traffic circles. I ended up driving around one three times trying to find Massachusetts Avenue."

"Oh, that hasn't been a problem. I'm pretty good with directions." But she was exhausted, and if she wanted to wear that lavender blouse tomorrow, she'd have to get home and iron it. He didn't seem in any rush to leave, though. He put the chalk on the blackboard ledge and perched on top of the teacher's desk, pushing aside folders and a stuffed kangaroo.

"I'm sure you are. After all, you got all the way here from Minnesota. I just meant—oh—sometimes being in a new place can feel overwhelming. So, if you wanted to talk about anything . . ."

Olivia didn't know what to say. He went on to tell her more things, besides the traffic circles. about his first impressions of the city when he had come here two years ago. How it had been hard to get a prescription filled, the bureaucracy around the Department of Motor Vehicles, the weird parking rules during the winter. He seemed, then, not so much a priest as—just a guy.

Maybe because it was getting late and she was tired. Maybe because he was being so nice. Maybe because she felt like she didn't have to live up to an image around him. Suddenly she felt tears prickle behind her eyes. She blinked to try to hold them back, but one, then another, rolled down her cheek. "I'm sorry," she said as she swiped her hand across her cheek.

"Nothing to be sorry about," he said. "It happens to all of us."

And then he explained that he did some counseling in the parish, that maybe she'd like to come in and have a chat. "Sometimes all a person needs is someone to listen," he said gently. He took a leather appointment book out of his pocket. "How's next Tuesday at five-thirty?" He picked up a pencil from a cup on the teacher's desk.

CHAPTER 11

OLIVIA KEPT GLANCING at her watch to check the time. She liked
to be on time, but she hated to be early. She didn't know anything about
counseling sessions, what to expect. All she knew was that she was not
going to cry. She would be calm and show the priest that really, she was
in control. She had just been overtired last week. Wasn't counseling for
people who had serious problems? But Father Pete had been kind to
offer, and he seemed so earnest. The times she had been around him, he
was always easy to talk to. They would just have a brief chat, and that
would be it.

The rectory was a three-story row house across the parking lot from
the church, a few steps away from the back door of the school. Father Pete
said the door would be open and to just come in. She checked her watch
for the third time and pushed the heavy door. She blinked to adjust to
the dim light of the hallway, but she could see a couple of chairs and a
small table with the statue of a saint. Saint Andrew, she assumed, said to
be Jesus' first disciple. Straight ahead down a short hall there was a door
to a room she figured was the kitchen, because she could hear a radio
and the clank of pans. It reminded her a bit of her grandmother's house,
with a center hall, living room on one side, dining room on the other,

stairs straight ahead. She ran her fingers through her hair and straightened the waistband of her skirt. She wondered if she should sit on one of the chairs to wait or if she should just stand, but there was no need because the door to her left opened and there was Father Pete, grinning and beckoning her in.

He was holding a legal pad covered with scribbles. "Working on Sunday's homily," he said as he closed the door. "It takes me all week because I'm a slow writer," he explained, putting the pad on his desk. Olivia looked around the room. If it were a regular family home, it would be the living room, or "parlor" as it was called decades ago. The door had most likely been added to turn it into an office. There was a couch with a coffee table in front of it, magazines fanned out on the table. At the far end of the room, near the window that faced the street, there were two straight-backed chairs on either side of a small table set up with a checkers game. The window was cracked open, and she could hear traffic sounds from outside and the voices of people passing by on the sidewalk. Father Pete's desk, the largest piece of furniture in the room, faced the door, and there were two club chairs in front of that. He held out his hand, inviting her to sit in one of those. He sat behind his desk, leaning back and smiling. They exchanged pleasantries about the weather, noting that the last week of September still felt like summer. She felt comfortable and began to relax, and she was able to smile back at him.

Father Pete already knew a bit about her, from their chats at coffee hour and the mission meetings. But he asked her more, about her family, about life in Minnesota, about what had prompted her to make a move halfway across the country. He encouraged her to tell him about her job, about the other teachers. He was a teacher, too, he said.

This surprised her, because she thought parish priests just worked in the parish. He explained that while he lived in the parish, and helped out by saying Mass, his principal job was a teacher. He taught history at a boys' prep school. That they had something in common would make talking to him easier. While they chatted, he pushed a clunky glass ashtray around his desk with one hand. She noticed a thin hint of smoke in the room, despite the open window. She wondered if he was touching the ashtray because he wanted to light up, and she hoped not, because she couldn't stand the smell of cigarettes.

As the hour wore on, she grew more and more at ease talking to him. There was something about the way he listened, looking at her intently with slightly parted lips, nodding thoughtfully as she spoke. When she faltered, ran out of words, he would be right there with another question, drawing her out. Finally, she sank back into the chair, feeling her shoulders melt, and she told him about the breathing episodes. "I know it's silly," she said, "but I thought maybe I was having some kind of breakdown." There, she had said it. She hadn't thought she would have the courage.

"Panic attack," he said, putting his elbows on his desk. "You have the classic symptoms." He assured her that it was perfectly normal for someone who had been through so many changes in a short time. "Moving. New apartment. New job. All major life hurdles. I totally get why this would happen."

She felt a wave of relief. Yes, it did make sense. All the changes. Thinking about that, she lost track of the fact that he was still speaking. He seemed to be looking at her for a response and she had to apologize. "I'm sorry. My mind drifted for a second."

"I was just asking . . . is there anything else? You seemed so upset at the meeting last week."

Olivia shook her head. "No . . . I don't think so." In truth, she often felt as if she were completely over her head with all the schoolwork, and she felt that the work cheated her out of any kind of social life. But he was a teacher, so he'd know about that. And as a priest, he wouldn't understand about the social life. She doubted there was much to his life beyond teaching, saying Mass, and these counseling sessions.

He looked at her for a long minute, as if he were waiting for her to say something. "Boyfriend trouble, perhaps?"

She laughed. "Who has time for a boyfriend? I'm way too busy with school for that."

"Everyone needs to play. No good prospects on the staff?"

The only man on staff was about sixty years old and had been teaching chemistry since the invention of the Bunsen burner. She shook her head.

"Well, I'm sure you'll meet someone soon." He chuckled as he told her about couples meeting at unlikely places like the grocery store or the carwash. "I married a couple who first saw each other when they were buying asparagus at Safeway." He rolled a Lifesaver around in his mouth and she could hear it click against his teeth.

She snuck a glance at her watch and saw that it was almost six-thirty. Time to go.

He looked at his watch, too, and stood. "This has been great, Olivia. You seem a lot more relaxed than when you came in." He explained again how natural it was that she was feeling "out of sorts," and warned her that the panic attacks probably weren't over, but at least she understood what they were all about. He picked up his appointment book and turned the page. "Would you like to come back again? Say next week at the same time?"

Olivia didn't know how to say no even though she didn't think there was anything else to talk about. But it had been a relief to talk about what he called the panic attacks, and Father Pete understood the pressures of teaching. She didn't know how to say no. Maybe one more time would be good. She nodded, put the strap of her bag over her shoulder, and thanked him. She realized she was smiling.

CHAPTER 12

AND FATHER PETE was right. The panic attacks came less and less frequently, and when they did, she knew how to breathe through them. He showed her how in her second counseling session. He stood up from his desk chair and sat in the club chair next to hers.

"It's all about the breathing," he told her. "When you're tense, you don't take in enough air. You just breathe into the top of your chest. You want to bring the air down farther, so you feel your ribs expand."

Olivia was impressed that he knew so much. She had never thought about there being different ways to breathe. She tried it, but her inhales still felt shallow, and she was a bit self-conscious with him watching her. Breathing seemed like such a personal thing, and usually you just did it without even being aware of it.

He was looking at her intently. "Here, let me show you." He reached over and put his hand on her back. "Now, breathe until you feel it all the way down here to my hand." She tried it a few times, until he assured her she had it. "Feel the difference?"

She did, and she was also acutely aware of how close he was to her. She kept her eyes straight ahead, counting the pencils in the jar on his desk. Six, and three ballpoint pens. He removed his hand, and she went back to her regular breathing, relieved when he returned to his chair and there was space between them. It was just a little weird, having him, a priest, put his hand on her like that.

He crossed his legs and smiled. "You're doing great. Just do this any time you start to get that panic feeling. Do you feel better?"

She nodded, more relaxed already. He took out his little appointment book, raised his eyebrows as he wrote down her name. She forgot she was going to tell him she wouldn't be back.

For the next few weeks, they talked mostly about school. He wanted to know what had drawn her to teaching. Truthfully, she wasn't sure. It just made sense that an English major would choose that profession. There weren't many editing opportunities in a small Midwest town, and what else would she do with her degree? Yes, she enjoyed it, but it was so much *work*, and she had to bring so much home with her. So they talked about that, and she asked him about playing baseball, and sometimes there was the latest *Time* magazine on the coffee table, which led to a conversation about the upcoming election. He was decidedly a democrat.

Then she missed a session because she had to stay late at school for an English department meeting. He called her at home that evening, to make sure she was okay. At first, she was surprised to hear his voice on her phone, but then she realized she had filled out a little information sheet the first time she went to see him. Thoughtful, she mused. She had left a message at the rectory, so he didn't have to call.

"Don't leave me in the lurch next week," he joked, right before he hung up. Knowing he wanted her to be there made her want to be there. He was really interested in what she had to say.

The next time she saw him, sitting in his rectory office, he asked her if she'd help him that weekend with a flyer he was designing to raise money for the mission project. "I know you're busy, but—"

"Oh, no, I could do that." She did have two sets of book reports waiting to be graded, and Rebecca had proposed a barge ride on the canal on Sunday. But how could she say no to the parish priest? And how long could it take? He wasn't charging her anything for the weekly sessions, and this could be a way to pay him back.

"Let's meet at the school Saturday afternoon. In that same classroom where we have the meetings."

"Oh." She had thought they'd meet in his office. But of course, he'd have a key to the school building.

He must have seen her confusion. "The copy machine is there. And lots of art materials." Well, then, that made sense. And now she had something to do on Saturday besides grading papers and shopping for groceries. Even if it was only meeting a priest for a service project. Rebecca was working Saturday, and they could still go on the barge ride the next day. An art project would be a good distraction because otherwise she'd just be rattling around alone in the apartment trying to avoid grading those book reports.

There was a big smile on his face. "You're so creative, Olivia. I know we'll work up something great." She wasn't sure about her creativity, but it was good to be needed.

CHAPTER 13

HE CALLED HER at home a couple of times. Could she check with the other mission committee people to see if they could change the date of their next meeting? Could she start collecting cardboard cartons for the committee? Once, he had the title of a book he thought she'd like (they'd had a short book discussion the time she saw *The Winds of War* on his coffee table and told him she had read Wouk's *Marjorie Morningstar* in high school). She started trying to be the one to answer the phone because she didn't want Rebecca to know it was Pete. It was silly, she knew, but how would she explain? She'd never told her about the counseling. When she started going to see Pete (he was Father Pete then, something that changed after a couple of weeks), she hadn't known Rebecca that well, wasn't sure what she'd think. And now, how would she explain that the priest was calling her on the phone? Rebecca would tease her, and Olivia knew there was nothing to tease her about, but she didn't want to deal with it. There was just no reason for Rebecca to know.

Often Olivia and Pete just happened to be in the same place at the same time. Late one afternoon he saw her walking and it was raining, so he gave her a lift. He took her and the other mission project people for coffee, for pizza, after their meetings. It felt good being close to him, especially when he made such an effort to include her in the conversation. And after he gave her the name of a garage to take her car to for a tune-up, she mentioned that she had taken it in that day and he insisted on driving her to pick it up. And yes, there was that time they went for a beer. It was supposed to be her and Nelda and Bryana, to talk about starting a clothing drive for El Salvador, but the other two had canceled at the last minute. When she walked into the bar, he waved her over and said, "The other two stood me up." She started to turn around to leave, making a comment about doing it another time, but he said, "As long as we're here . . . " and she sat at the table. At first it felt a little awkward, drinking a beer with him, but he soon put her at ease. An older man, a parishioner, stopped and greeted Pete, and she saw him shoot a questioning glance at her, but Pete casually introduced her, saying, "She's my right-hand helper with the mission project." He pointed to the clipboard on the table. "We're gearing up for a new phase." The man smiled and left, and Olivia dipped her fingers into a bowl of peanuts.

That evening he told her he'd be playing what was likely to be the last game of the season that Saturday and did she want to come? "I need a cheerleader," he said. "And I promise not to lob a ball into your cup."

"I'll bring one with a lid," she quipped back.

She invited Rebecca to come along, not mentioning that Pete had asked her. Rebecca said she hoped that "hot priest guy" was playing, and Olivia shrugged. But she turned away and realized she was smiling.

The afternoons were growing chilly, so she grabbed a sweater. It was a quintessential autumn day. The trees still held their leaves, now tipped with gold and veined with russet, but the air had lost its humidity. Wispy clouds floated in the cerulean sky, dissolving almost as soon as they formed, and people seemed to walk with renewed energy. At the field, a group of enterprising kids had set up a stand selling cider and popcorn balls.

At the top of the seventh inning, Pete jogged over toward them. Rebecca saw him coming and said, "Look who's coming! What did you say his name was?"

"Pete. Father Pete." She noticed the broad smile on his face.

He sat down next to her, wiping sweat from the back of his neck. "Great to see you!"

"Good game," Olivia said, taking off her sunglasses. "You almost had a home run!"

"It must be my fan club here," he said, looking at the two women.

They chatted for a few minutes, and it seemed natural to be sitting next to each other on the bleachers. Around them there were families, some small groups who were probably friends of the players, a woman pushing an umbrella stroller back and forth as if trying to lull her baby to sleep. Pete squinted into the sun and looked toward the dugout. "Oops, I'm up next." He turned back as he started to jog around the edge of the field. "See you Tuesday, Olivia."

Rebecca's eyes widened. "What's Tuesday?"

"Oh. Um, counseling."

"You go to counseling?" She sounded shocked. "Father Pete is your counselor?" Her eyes grew wide as she spoke.

"Well, yeah, I was—having these panic attacks. Silly really. And I started crying one night at a mission project meeting, and he offered to help me."

"And did he—help you?"

Olivia nodded. "I don't have the panic attacks any more. It was just moving here and the new job and all, and I guess I was overwhelmed."

"I had no idea. I mean, you looked fine to me. Why didn't you say something?"

Olivia shrugged. She hadn't told anyone but Pete about those panic attacks. She hadn't even written Aubrey about it. She had so wanted everyone to believe she was doing fine, didn't want Rebecca to think she was some kind of nut case.

Rebecca held out a bag of pretzels to Olivia, who took one.

"Oh, I don't think I'll go much longer. It seems kind of silly, now that I'm over the panic stuff." She took a bite of the pretzel. "Let's watch the game." She felt the beginning of a blush on her cheeks, but didn't know why. She really should think about stopping the counseling sessions.

CHAPTER 14

SHE DIDN'T, THOUGH. Every Tuesday she walked into the rectory, and suddenly it was November. She looked around the room. The clock on the wall read six-thirty. Time to leave. Olivia noticed that the second hand jerked with every move, as if startled at the passage of time. Reaching down to pick up her purse from the floor, she wondered if she should make an appointment for next week. She had been thinking more and more that she didn't need the counseling. She wasn't having the panic attacks. But not to come back would be to lose this really enjoyable hour.

In the weeks she had been coming here, the room had become so familiar that she felt at home as soon as she settled into her usual spot, which was now the couch instead of the club chair. She couldn't remember when or why she had changed her seat, but it didn't matter. She knew the rough texture of the upholstery, the worn spot on the carpet near the door, the faint aroma of cooking from the kitchen down the hall. Pete either sat behind his desk or in one of the leather chairs. He tended to choose the desk because he seemed to like to fiddle with things, clicking a ballpoint pen, unfolding a paper clip, all the while keeping his eyes on her as he listened to her talk or offered his comments.

She had learned a lot about him, too. Their casual conversations prompted her to ask him about *his* growing up, *his* teaching. She knew that he had worked summers in college at a camp for special ed kids, that he was allergic to cashews, that he spent at least four hours a week preparing his Sunday homily. He was thirty-three, and his birthday was in February.

Today he had been telling her about his brother. "Larry's kind of a renegade," he said. "He dropped out of college and works in a record store and takes weird jobs like walking dogs." He shook his head and laughed. "So what? If it makes him happy . . ." She told him about her large extended family, her brother Evan who collected old comic books and her cousin Lucy who raised ferrets.

It wasn't all light-hearted, though. There was something about Pete that made her open up in ways she never had before. She told him about how, under her bravado of moving east, she doubted herself and her ability to become that independent, successful self. How she was afraid of disappointing her family, and more of disappointing herself. This, he told her, was what was behind the panic attacks. No matter what she told him, he had an answer or words of advice. What he told her built her up, made her lift her spine straighter when she left the rectory. He talked about himself, too, about how in his family it had been expected that he, as the oldest boy, would enter the priesthood. "It was just the way things were. It was like that for half the families in our neighborhood in Scranton. My mother had been praying for my vocation since I was a little boy." Whether it was that tradition, or something inside of him, it had been a seamless, simple decision. When he spoke that way, she had a glimpse of a part most people probably weren't allowed to see. She found herself counting the days until she would have the next session. Six days, three, one.

Today she had brought brownies. She had started to do that sometimes, offering him a plate of sugar cookies or snickerdoodles. Nibbling a chocolate-chip-laden brownie, he told her she should consider baking as a profession. "Remember," he said, "you've not been completely happy in the classroom." True. She had told him that teaching wasn't nearly as glamorous or exciting as she had thought it would be, that it was much more demanding than her first year back in the small school in Minnesota. But she didn't know the first thing about becoming a professional baker, or, as he suggested, a part-time caterer. And really, she had a tiny repertoire of recipes. Still, she couldn't help but think about it as she made muffins on the weekend or pulled a pan of oatmeal cookies out of the oven. Baking and cooking made her happy. But there was more than three-quarters of the school year to get through. She'd think about that later.

Then he changed the subject and asked her opinion about the Sunday homily he was working on.

"I never would have thought of that," she said, when he explained a tricky passage in John's gospel. She had never studied the Bible that much, even though she had attended Catholic schools. Religious instruction had centered more on the sacraments, church history, stories of the saints.

He smiled, saying, "I hope you'll be there on Sunday in case someone in the congregation walks out."

"Hardly." She beamed at him. "Everyone loves you and your homilies."

And it was true. At the end of Mass, parishioners lined up at the back of the church hoping to get a word with him. More than once, she had heard someone say, "That Father Kowolski—he really knows what he's talking about."

Since both of them worked in a classroom, they often swapped teacher stories and traded crazy homework excuses. "I can do you one better than that," he said when Olivia told him about the freshman who used the dead grandmother excuse three times in two weeks.

Now, as she dug around her purse for her car keys, he went over to the window and closed the blinds. "The glare from those streetlights," he explained as he crossed the room. Daylight savings time had ended the weekend before, and now evening came an hour earlier. Two slats on the top were missing. Instead of returning to his chair, however, he sat next to her on the couch. Not too close, but still. It startled her. Didn't he know it was time for her to leave? Her session was officially over, but she would stay if there was something he wanted to talk about. Maybe he had a student he needed help with, or maybe there was a snag with the mission project. Whatever it was, she sensed, by his presence on the couch, a slight change between them. She straightened, a little nervous but curious.

He didn't say anything, though, and the silence felt awkward, so she started to rise. "Don't go," he said, putting his hand on her arm. His voice was husky as if he had a cold or had not spoken in a long time. She could smell the spice of his aftershave, something like citrus and licorice. What was he doing? Was it instinct or just the surprise of someone coming unexpectedly close that made her inch away to the farther cushion? She couldn't explain this sudden uneasiness, but then when the moment stretched out too long for her not to look at him, she lifted her eyes and relaxed. It was just Pete, after all. How many evenings had she sat here with him, talking about her problems and swapping school stories? How many times had she received the Host from his hand at Mass? Don't be so skittish, she told herself.

He must have sensed her ambivalence, because he pointed to his collar. "Is it this?" he asked. He reached up and snatched it off, tossed it on the floor. "There. I look just like a regular guy." She remembered meeting him at the baseball game, thinking that he *was* just a regular guy. But now, even without the collar, in his black shirt and pants, he still looked like a priest. He put his hand back on her arm, higher now, and stroked it gently, up and down. She felt heat through the fabric of her blouse. "Don't look so scared. It's just me. It's just the two of us relaxing after a long day. And I am just a regular guy, under this uniform I have to wear."

Then he pulled back, something like confusion on his face. "Listen, I'm sorry. I didn't mean to make you uncomfortable."

Olivia nodded, not sure what to say. Pete was a priest. And his hand on her arm didn't equate with that role. One moment they were talking about homework excuses and his Sunday homily, and the next he was sitting so close to her she could see glints of gold in his green eyes. She didn't know how to process that. Nor did she know how to process her reaction. Did she like the touch on her arm?

He picked up the collar from the floor and stood. "I don't want anything to stand in the way of our friendship." There, he said it, friendship. Because they were becoming friends. "And if it disturbed you in any way that I touched you like that, I apologize. It's just that all day I have to be the priest. I have to look the part of the priest. And sometimes, I—well, it shouldn't have happened." He looked at her as she pulled on her jacket. "We're still friends, right?"

She nodded. Of course, they were. She didn't know what had made him touch her, but their friendship was too important to let anything come between them. They could go right back to where they were. He in his chair. She in hers. Talk of sermons and homework. Panic attacks and mission projects.

Still, that night it took her a long time to fall asleep.

CHAPTER 15

THE NEXT WEEK, there was a hug. He stood next to the door as she prepared to leave. They had been laughing again about kids' homework excuses. They were still chuckling as she began to zip up her jacket. And then he reached out and gave her a hug.

"Oh, Olivia, you're too funny!"

And then he pulled his arms back, opened the door for her, and said he'd see her next week.

It was so fast, she didn't have time to be shocked. But as she walked through the dark streets to her car, she thought about it. It wasn't a serious hug, not arms around and holding on. It had just been a quick gesture, like you might share with your cousin when you leave the café after having lunch. Or like you might give one of your students who scored the winning point in a basketball game. The kind of hug where you barely feel the other person's hands on your back, where you hardly feel their bones under your hands.

It was the kind of hug a friend gives a friend.

And then there were other hugs, and none of them were lingering, but when she looked back, she would remember that it was always when they were alone. At the door to his office when it was still closed. In the classroom when the other mission project people had left and he asked her to hang back and help him take supplies to the storeroom. Always quick. Always with a thank-you for something unrelated to the hug. And then breaking apart to talk about a completely different topic. She never hugged him back, not because she didn't want to, but because the hugs were so quick and over so soon. And she never initiated one. They always seemed to come out of the blue, catching her unprepared.

But later in November, everything changed. After the time when he sat on the couch with her, she moved back to one of the club chairs in front of his desk. She was still confused about the way he had touched her, had stroked her arm like that. They hadn't talked about it again. It had made her uncomfortable, and he had apologized, and she didn't know how to bring it up. Maybe she should have stopped going to see him, but she really did enjoy their times together, their chatting and sharing. She shouldn't have to give that up because of a misunderstanding. She still hadn't made that many friends, and when she sat around the apartment by herself, she felt lonely. He was a friend. That was all.

One evening, a week before Thanksgiving, she was in her usual chair, and Pete was in his swivel chair behind his desk. He wasn't wearing clerical clothes. He was in a blue oxford cloth shirt with the sleeves rolled back at the wrists and a pair of jeans. For once, he didn't ask her how her week had been. He didn't ask her anything. In the silence, and under his gaze, both of which made her a little nervous, she started to notice little things around the room to distract herself. His raincoat tossed over a hassock. The cover of the TIME magazine on his desk with Nixon giving the peace sign. The philodendron whose leaves looked dusty. Maybe she should ask him something. If he had plans for Thanksgiving. If he was still planning to buy a new car.

Suddenly, he sat up, put the pen down. "Hey," he said, "I could really use a glass of wine. Be right back." He went across the hall to the dining room, and she heard the clink of glasses. He came back with a half-filled bottle of Merlot and two glasses. "A chilly evening like this calls for an early Thanksgiving treat." She relaxed a little at the return of his usual voice. He poured the wine into the glasses, set one on her side of the desk, and went back to his chair, holding the other glass in his hand. He lifted it in a toast, and took a long swallow. He had never offered her wine before. It had always just been talk. Or the brownies and cookies she'd brought. She picked up her glass, trying to think of something light and humorous to say. Drinking wine in his office made her jittery, though she couldn't say why.

He sank back again into the silence that felt odd, heavy. She sipped the wine, and it tasted sweet and faintly metallic at the same time. She pointed to the magazine and was about to make a comment about the election, when he put his glass down and leaned forward.

"Olivia." His voice was soft, barely above a whisper.

She looked at him. The air felt different in the room, as if charged with a low level of electricity. She put her wineglass on the desk, waiting to hear what he'd say. Not the usual bantering, the casual chatting. Just her name. He sounded serious. She hoped it wasn't bad news. Maybe he was being transferred to another parish. Maybe he had too much work at school and in the parish to keep having counseling sessions. Maybe he was going to tell her that since she didn't need the actual counseling, he had to cut off their meetings. She felt suddenly chilled and looked around at the familiar room, thinking how hard it would be not to sit here anymore.

"You know, Olivia, I was attracted to you the first time I saw you." Suddenly her senses were on alert. She hadn't expected this. The first time? Back at the baseball game, when the ball splashed soda all over her? When she sat sweaty in the sun, in bare feet, her T-shirt soaking wet? She had thought he was just being friendly. And then when he invited her to join the mission project committee, when he had given her a lift in the rain—wasn't he just being pastoral? She hadn't sensed any attraction, just an outreach, a welcome to her new parish. Certainly that was all he had in mind. And certainly she wasn't attracted to him, at least not in the way he seemed to be implying. He was funny, yes, and friendly, and he had given her helpful advice about her panic attacks. She felt completely at ease with him. Despite Rebecca's insistence on calling him "the hot priest," to her he had just been Father Pete. She hadn't thought about any "hot" factor. She couldn't be attracted to a priest, not like that.

"Do you have any idea how hard it's been for me to sit here and talk with you and not touch you?" He picked up his wine glass, and she saw his hand was shaking. She had never seen him be anything but calm and in control. The phone rang on his desk and he ignored it. She realized she had not taken a breath since he first spoke, and her thoughts swirled. She felt hot and cold at the same time. Slowly, she let her breath out. How long had he felt this way?

"But you can't," she said when she found her voice. "You're a priest." Surely a priest couldn't, shouldn't, have feelings for a woman. Friends, yes. And hadn't he declared them to be friends? She was comfortable with that, knowing they were friends. His friendship had been a bright light for her in the past couple of months. She loved talking with him, sharing stories, bantering back and forth. She loved when he consulted her about his sermons, when he praised her brownies, and she loved all the things he had done to make her feel at home in the parish. How long had he felt this way? All the way back to the summer?

And then she thought about the hugs. Had he wanted them to be more? Had he hoped she'd hug him back? Again, she searched her mind for things he'd said, looks he'd given. She came up empty. Likewise, she couldn't recall anything she'd done to lead him on. Did he think she had been doing that? The thought was mortifying. She never would have come on to a priest.

He drained his glass, reached for the bottle but drew back his hand. "Ah, Olivia, how could anyone not be attracted to you? You're witty and smart and talented and beautiful."

She had never thought of herself that way. No one had ever told her that. She was just—herself. It made something pop around her heart. To be noticed that way. Oh, she remembered the occasional whistle when she walked across the college cafeteria with her tray, but she assumed the whistle was for whoever she was with. And was it the guy casting parts for the drama club production of Romeo and Juliet who said she should try out because "no Romeo could resist you"? She knew he was kidding. The drama club was full of exaggeration. Trevor had never spoken to her like that, and yet he had wanted to marry her. But now here was Pete saying she was beautiful. Had she really heard him say that?

He leaned forward, his hands stretching out over the desk blotter. "And right now, all I want to do is kiss you."

She repeated the only words she could think of. "You can't. You're a priest."

"There's nothing wrong with a kiss. It's what people do who feel close to each other. And you do, don't you? Feel close to me?"

Olivia didn't know what to say. She turned the wine glass stem around in her fingers. Outside, an ambulance rushed by, its siren pulsating in the darkness.

He looked confused, frowned slightly. "Or have I read the signals wrong? Because if I have, I'm sorry, I just thought—"

Close to him, yes, but not in the way he meant. She wished he hadn't said that, because it made her want to be somewhere else. She wanted to be friends with him, she wanted to laugh with him and share teacher stories and work with him on the mission project. She looked forward to Tuesday afternoon every week. But there had been that touch back in October, and maybe she shouldn't have let herself put it out of her mind. Did he think she kept coming back because of that? The room shrank, and she had to remind herself to breathe.

She felt a blush start at the roots of her hair and work itself to her cheeks. What was he talking about? Signals? That would be flirting, and that would be unthinkable. She had just been enjoying a simple friendship. Had she been wrong to see it that way? "Oh, no, you didn't. I mean, I do feel close to you." And then, like a veil had been lifted, she spooled back to the past months. When she was lonely, it was Pete she thought of. When she had good news, it was Pete she wanted to share it with. When her father fell and broke his leg and she thought she should take a week off and go home to help, it was Pete she asked for advice.

"So, then, what's the problem?" He poured more wine into his glass, lifted the bottle toward her. She shook her head, too muddled to think about drinking. "Don't you know you can trust me?"

"Of course, I do." He was smart and funny, and she felt so comfortable with him. And he was a priest. Who wouldn't trust a priest? He had devoted his life to God, to serving the church, and she was a parishioner. All the more reason why she couldn't even consider kissing him. "But it's different."

He ran his finger around the rim of his glass. "Not really. Not really at all. It's just an expression of strong feeling between two people."

"But a kiss means—"

"It means just what I said. It's not a big deal. You're a desirable woman, and I'm a man. It's simple."

She couldn't think of what to say, because to her it wasn't simple. To her it was a big deal. Right now he was dressed like an ordinary man, holding an ordinary glass of merlot. But tomorrow morning he would wear satin vestments and change wine and water into the body and blood of Christ. He had taken vows. He had promised to give his life to the church. Kiss him? She couldn't. Besides, she knew where a kiss would lead. It was never "just" a kiss. What red-blooded man would settle for a single touch of the lips? She saw something in the narrowing of his eyes that reminded her of that look her college dates would get, when they would start with soft kisses that quickly became urgent and deep. How could Pete be looking at her like that? She put her wine glass down on his desk, her mouth gone dry, and after a few awkward moments, stammered a good-bye.

CHAPTER 16

THEY DIDN'T MEET the next week. Pete left Monday afternoon to visit his parents in Pennsylvania. Olivia was relieved about the break, because she needed time to think about the shift he saw in their relationship. He told her on the phone, when he called the day after she had hurried away, that he respected her reluctance, that he wouldn't force her to do anything she wasn't comfortable with. He said he didn't want to jeopardize their friendship. She didn't say anything to Rebecca, though she thought about it. She needed someone to help her sort it all out, but to tell about it felt almost gossip-y. The closeness she felt with Pete was something she didn't want to risk losing, and talking about him behind his back seemed—disloyal. And how much would Rebecca understand, being Jewish? She and Pete would go back to the way it had been before any talk of kissing, and they'd be fine.

On Thanksgiving, she roasted a chicken and made her grandmother's stuffing with apples and chestnuts. Rebecca set the table with a centerpiece of dried grasses she found on a walk in Rock Creek Park. Rebecca had to work on Friday, but the rest of the time the two of them lazed around the apartment eating chicken sandwiches, listening to records, and doing crossword puzzles. There was even a very light snow on Saturday afternoon. It made Olivia nostalgic about her family back in Minnesota, where there was probably a foot of snow by now. She missed their big crowded family dinners, the battle for the wishbone, the dining room table extended with card tables at each end. Still, this was her home now, and the dusting of snow on the grass would have to do. She talked with them late Thursday afternoon, the hubbub of cousins and nephews in the background, and when she hung up the phone, she felt the distance echo between her and her family.

On Tuesday, Pete was true to his word. She almost didn't keep the appointment, because his talk of kissing had unnerved her, but she thought they should talk about it, and maybe then she would say she wouldn't be back. It seemed only fitting to do that, to actually put words to the ending. He asked her to proofread a sermon he was working on, and they drank coffee, and they talked about the holiday. Every time she started to say something about it, he brought up something else, and the moment would be lost. It was as if the talk of kissing had never happened. Maybe it was the wine that had loosened his tongue, and he now saw what a mistake any physical affection would be. They fell into their usual easy talk, and he seemed to have forgotten all about kissing. He said he was thinking about getting a dog from the shelter. They discussed the merits of the various sizes and breeds (though the shelter probably wouldn't have anything with a pedigree), and he asked her if she'd like to go with him to check it out, help him decide. She had always wanted a dog (her mother was allergic), and they made a tentative date to go to the shelter on Saturday. The hour was over before she knew it, and he didn't even give her one of those quick hugs. Olivia left feeling comfortable in the way things were between them. Happy to imagine what kind of dog he'd pick. Happy with herself for squelching any physical stuff between them. Happy that they were back where they belonged.

That Saturday the weather was miserable, sleet and rain that glazed the streets, and the dog-search was put on hold. Olivia was disappointed, because not only had she looked forward to seeing all the dogs, but she had loved the idea of spending an afternoon with Pete. The uneasiness she had felt at the mention of kissing had dissolved, and he had obviously given up on that, and she had filled her head with images of the two of them walking up and down in front of the cages, debating the pros and cons of each one. Maybe after he chose the perfect pet, they'd go shopping for a leash and dog toys, one of those crates, a feeding dish. On the way back from the shelter, she'd get to hold the dog in her lap while Pete drove. Two friends out having fun. Instead, she was sitting at the dining room table looking out at the slick street and feeling lonely. Rebecca was working. Olivia didn't have anything she wanted to read, and the only shows on tv (they had finally bought a small portable) were sports and reruns of game shows. By two in the afternoon, she thought the day would never end.

And then he called. The weather was supposed to clear the next day, and the animal shelter would be closed, but did she want to go with him to pick out a Christmas tree for the rectory? He explained that the pastor, Father Walker, usually did it. "He has these vivid childhood memories of going out to get the family tree." And even though church rules prohibited putting the tree up until after the fourth week of Advent, the pastor wanted to get it while there was a good selection and set it in a bucket of water by the back door. Olivia had never heard of this rule. Her parents always put their tree up by the second week in December. But maybe it was different for priests.

He told her he'd pick her up, said to make sure to wear warm socks, and her mood brightened instantly. After all, she knew a lot about Christmas trees, from all those seasons working at Aubrey's family's tree farm. "I'll swing by at two." Her lethargy lifted, and she started a pot of lentil soup and rummaged around to find ingredients for peanut butter cookies. She hummed as she creamed the butter and stirred in the brown sugar.

Pete knew of a tree place out near Leesburg. Olivia didn't understand why they had to go so far—there was a perfectly fine tree lot right up on Wisconsin Avenue. "It'll be more fun if we're out in the country,"

Pete said. "We can pretend we chopped it down ourselves." He went on to describe childhood Christmases in Pennsylvania, when he and his brother and his dad actually did chop down their tree.

The sun had melted the thin rime of ice on the streets, and although it was cold, it felt festive to Olivia to be going out to find the perfect tree, even if it was for the rectory and not her apartment. She'd be in Minnesota for the holiday, and by the time she arrived a huge tree would be crowding the living room, covered with lights and ornaments. She stood inside the front door until she saw his Fairlane pull up to the curb, noted that he was right on time, and they were off. In her lap was the tin of cookies she had packed for them.

It took a little over an hour to get to Leesburg, but to Olivia it felt like ten minutes. She barely noticed the scenery as they left the city and drove past empty fields, the occasional strip mall, and boarded-up roadside stands. They traded stories about Christmas trees and holiday traditions, and he convinced her to open the tin so they could munch on cookies. "M-m-m," he sighed. "Just what I needed."

The tree lot where they stopped was next to a small hardware store. Most of the trees stood in rows, but some were propped against the outside wall of the store. There were also a couple of tables piled with wreaths, some simple ornaments, and a collection of pre-tied bows and bunches of holly and bittersweet. It was a miniature version of Aubrey's family Christmas tree farm, and her thoughts spooled back to those frosty afternoons with Aubrey laughing and taking crazy photos of themselves with their faces peeking out of wreaths. Children darted around in the chilly afternoon, and dads held trees up while their wives stepped back to assess them. "Too bare on the side." "Way too tall for our living room." "Perfect!"

After wandering around for about thirty minutes, Pete found what he deemed the ideal tree, and he strapped it to the top of his car with the rope he'd brought. They wrapped their hands around Styrofoam cups of hot cider from a refreshment table, and she found a little felt reindeer for

Rebecca, because even though she didn't celebrate Christmas, she loved holiday decorations.

By the time they finished their cider and he paid for the tree, it was almost four o'clock and the shadows were lengthening. It was growing colder, and Olivia wrapped her scarf around her neck, pulled her coat collar up.

"Cold?" he asked, and he put his arm around her shoulder. She didn't think twice about it, though later she would wonder why. It felt natural, what you would do when you were out in the cold with another person. There were pine needles on his jacket, and she inhaled the fresh forest scent. "Listen," he said, "if you don't have anything else to do, why don't we stop on the way back and have an early supper? I noticed an inn down the road, and I'll bet they have a fireplace. I don't know about you, but my feet are freezing." He stamped them on the parking lot, as if to emphasize this.

A cozy dining room. A fireplace. Olivia could picture it in her mind. She had lost feeling in her toes twenty minutes ago. She had nothing at home for dinner except the leftover soup. Rebecca had a date with an intern from the hospital. It had been such a perfect afternoon, and she didn't want it to end.

CHAPTER 17

WHEN SHE WENT for her "counseling" session on Tuesday, the memory of Sunday's outing was still with her. Although Pete had explained why the tree couldn't be put up in the house yet, she imagined it decorated and twinkling with strings of multicolored lights. When she closed her eyes, she felt herself spin back to the afternoon in Leesburg. The cold crisp air, the mulled cider, the fresh woodsy scents, and most of all, sharing it with Pete. They found the inn he mentioned, and they sat next to a huge fieldstone fireplace sending out warmth from crackling logs. Candles flickered from wall sconces, and they ate beef stew and hot biscuits, shared a bottle of red wine. She forgot, for that hour, that he was a priest. It just felt so natural, sharing a meal with him, seeing him across the table as he pulled out a credit card to pay the bill. Another surprise—priests had credit cards? Today she'd remind him about going to the animal shelter. Maybe one afternoon after school?

But he seemed distracted, even fidgety. While they talked about the coming vacation (he was going back to Pennsylvania Christmas morning after saying Mass, she was leaving for Minnesota on the 20th) he kept fiddling with things on his desk. Straightening a pile of index cards, picking up pens and putting them in a glass jar, turning a cigarette lighter over and over in his hand, moving a file folder from one side of the blotter to the other. They were drinking white wine, and she had brought cheddar cheese straws, and it should have been festive, but it felt flat. She broached the dog topic, but he shook his head, saying it probably wasn't a good time, with him away at the end of the month.

Was he regretting their afternoon together? He had been so animated on Sunday, had seemed to enjoy being with her, picking out the tree. And it had been his idea to go for dinner. Had she said something wrong?

"About Sunday," he said. Here it comes, she thought. He thinks it wasn't a good idea for them to be out together. He regrets the dinner. He's fine being her counselor and her friend, but people might talk if they saw them out having a meal, buying a dog. Doing the things that couples do. Even if it was perfectly innocent. Which it was. Because they weren't a couple at all, they were just two people buying a tree and picking up the loose branches from the ground for her to use in decorating her apartment. True, he had put his arm around her, but it was because she was shivering as the sun started to set. There had been no talk of kissing.

She forced herself to smile. "I had a good time." She pointed to the office door. "And I can't wait to see the tree when it's up out there!" She wanted to steer the topic back to the light-hearted Sunday afternoon.

He didn't speak right away, and she couldn't read anything in the deep green of his eyes as he looked straight at her. She found herself babbling about tree ornaments. Who would decorate the tree? The housekeeper? Did the three priests make a party of it, did they string popcorn and cranberries? Was the pastor happy with what he had chosen? She doubted the pastor knew she had been part of the outing, and wondered for a second if he would have thought it odd that she went along.

And then he did it again. One word. Her name. "Olivia." Almost too faint to hear. No other words followed. No questions, no compliments, no requests.

The air in the room shimmered. There was something behind the word, the way he said it.

"I tried, Olivia." His voice came back to him, then. He slid his elbows on the desk and leaned forward, his hair falling over his eyes. "I tried to keep my distance, like you asked me to. You have no idea how hard it's been."

Now, when she heard him speak, she knew. He hadn't given up on wanting to kiss her. To taking their relationship to a new level. And he was thinking about it right at that moment. Her face grew warm. Should she leave? She glanced back at the door and then at him. And what happened in the next few moments would be something she'd never forget. How he stood up and crossed around his desk, how he had one dark green shirt sleeve rolled up to his elbow, and the other had fallen down around his wrist. How his black crepe-soled shoes made no sound on the floor. How she seemed to stop breathing. How she stopped thinking.

And then, as if she herself were in a film and not herself at all, she watched her body stand to meet him, watched her body turn toward him instead of toward the door. The door, the front hall, the street, her car, her apartment. All that disappeared and she was acutely aware of him, the nearness of him, the way his breath caught in his throat when he spoke her name again.

It was no longer about thought, about reasoning. It was all about his arms circling her back, all about his lips that were grazing hers, gently, and she, who a moment before might have thought to run away, answered with her mouth, reached around to splay her hands on his back. There was just the one kiss, light, tasting of wine, and then they simply stood with their arms around each other. She felt his heart beating through the fabric of his shirt. He was solid and sure, and she felt warm and enclosed.

"See?" he said, pulling back a little. "I told you it would be fine. The floor didn't open up and swallow you." He chuckled, that low rumbling sound she loved. "We're still the same people we were five minutes ago. You're perfectly safe."

She nodded. She felt better than safe. How could anyone not feel safe with Pete?

"And now," he said lowering his arms, "you'd better go." He pointed to the closed door and tilted his head out toward the hall. There was a distant sound of pot lids and a ringing phone. "I don't want our nosy housekeeper to come knocking on my door saying it's time for dinner."

At the door, she paused. When she looked back at him, he was standing in front of his desk holding his glass of wine. He was smiling.

CHAPTER 18

THAT NIGHT SHE sat on her bed, brushing her hair. Rebecca wanted to make popcorn balls, but Olivia needed to be alone. Something huge had happened, and her mind was reeling with it. It was just one kiss, and it would stay there. It wouldn't happen again. Yes, it had felt good. Yes, she trusted him. But he was a priest, and priests didn't kiss women. And women didn't kiss priests back. Nothing terrible would result from that one kiss, but it wouldn't be repeated. She told herself she had just been carried away by the moment. She would stop seeing him altogether, even quit the mission project. There weren't any more meetings planned until January, and she'd say she was too busy. It was partly true. Sister Helen had asked her to help plan the annual Valentine's Dance.

Nevertheless, as she pulled the brush through her hair, she kept seeing him sitting at his desk, his eyebrows knitted together, his nervous hands playing absent-mindedly with things on the blotter. The way his hair fell over his right eye. She heard the whoosh of heat from the vents, the clang of pans from the kitchen, the dull sound of traffic out on the street. She kept asking herself why she had let it happen, why she had stood and let him kiss her, why she had kissed him back. Why she hadn't pulled away. She had been so adamant about not kissing him. What had changed in her? She should be ashamed of herself. Her hands were shaking. She didn't think she could ever look at him again. It would be hard, giving up the friendship, the Tuesday afternoon conversations, the jokes they shared. But it was the right thing to do. It was only one kiss, and she could put it out of her mind. She had to.

Two nights later, he phoned. Rebecca was in the shower, and Olivia was gathering papers to take to school the next day. Hearing his voice smashed all her resolutions. Later she would ask herself again and again why she hadn't hung up the phone.

"Are you okay?" he said.

"Of course. I'm fine. I—"

"I just had to call. I can't get Tuesday out of my mind. And I want to see you again."

She laughed, her mouth spontaneously spreading into a smile. There was magic in his voice. "Sure. Next Tuesday, as usual." Was she really saying this? Hadn't she decided to stop the "counseling"?

There was a pause. She could hear the intake of breath as he took a drag from a cigarette.

"No. Sooner. Like tonight."

"Tonight?" She couldn't just go out at eight-thirty at night. What would she tell Rebecca? A bubble of laughter escaped. "I can't. It's too late, and I have to get ready for tomorrow." She had to wash her hair, make her lunch. Was there leftover vegetable soup? Her words sounded flimsy to her, but she wasn't ready to see him again. He had kissed her, and she had kissed him back. She knew she liked it, and she didn't know what that meant. If they were to meet, what would happen? Probably not just casual conversation. She was afraid of that, and that was why she had decided to break off with him. Even the counseling. She had to put distance between the two of them. So what if she was lonely? She'd try to go out with Rebecca more, to those book signings. She'd even ask Rebecca to fix her up with one of her intern friends. Rebecca had been talking a lot about some guy named Drew.

Still, a wave of regret rippled through her when she told him no. His voice made her tremble, loosened something in her. A good trembling, like when something you've been waiting for is about to happen. Or has just happened. She loved those Tuesday afternoons drinking coffee or wine in his office, laughing about their students, talking about their pasts. She loved helping him with his sermons, doing little tasks for the service project. That was so much to give up. She felt her resolve crumbling. It wasn't as if he were someone dangerous. He was just Pete. And the two of them had so much in common. They would just keep the relationship at a safe level.

"Tomorrow, then." Did he have office hours on Friday evenings? "But not here. Let's meet somewhere."

A restaurant? A bar? Wouldn't people look at them suspiciously, a priest and a woman? Where would they go where no one might recognize him? As if to answer her questions, he described where they could meet, a dead-end off of Macomb Street. "You can leave your car there and drive with me." She forgot about saying no. She saw herself opening his car door, could feel the rough edge of that torn place on the passenger seat, could smell the minty air-freshener tree that dangled from the rear-view mirror. She had been in his car that time he took her to the service garage and when they bought the tree. Why did she remember these details? Through the phone, he sounded like he was right next to her. It would just be an outing, though. No more kissing. She'd make that clear. And better to tell him in person than to do it over the phone.

"But where—"

"Don't worry." He sounded excited, like he had a great plan. "I'll take care of everything."

"Okay, but what will I tell Rebecca?" She knew her roommate would have at least a dozen questions. Olivia had more than a dozen questions, but forgot that one of them was why was she even considering this.

He chuckled. "You'll think of something."

"Can we do this? I mean, is it like—"

She didn't want to use the word "date," because of course it wouldn't be. But what would it be? Before she could finish the question, he spoke. "We've been working hard all week. We both deserve a little fun."

CHAPTER 19

ON FRIDAY, THEY met the way he said they would, and he was in such a happy mood. As he drove, his fingers played out a beat on the steering wheel in time to the song on the radio, and when she asked where they were going, he just smiled and said, "You'll see." She had changed after school into jeans and a thick black sweater and borrowed a purple wool poncho from Rebecca. He was wearing a maroon ski jacket and chinos. She'd told Rebecca that she had a date with "Michael," the brother of a teacher at her school, and that she had to pick him up because his car was in the shop. They were going to a movie. She had checked out the listings at the Avalon.

She hated to lie, but she couldn't tell Rebecca she was meeting Pete on a side street and they were going to a surprise destination. It was one thing to run into him at a baseball game or at church, but how would she explain this? Rebecca had been so curious about the counseling that time at the baseball field that Olivia told her she wasn't going any more. She made up trips to the library or a drink after work with a teacher friend or a mission project meeting. Half the time Rebecca was working, anyway. Pete was her secret. Not that there was anything to hide about meeting with him in the rectory, but Rebecca wouldn't get it. She could just hear her. "Geez, Olivia, go out on a real date. Why do you want to hang around the rectory with a priest?" So Olivia made up the little stories. When she told Pete, he laughed. And when she was sitting in his office, he'd make it into a joke. "So where are you now? Hechinger's? Can I interest you in a new socket wrench?" And she'd go home and tell Rebecca that the hardware store was out of vacuum cleaner bags or whatever she said she was looking for.

This would be even harder to explain, because Olivia barely knew how to explain it to herself. Before the kiss, it really had been about companionship, about the gratitude she felt, about how that gratitude had bloomed into friendship. Tuesday afternoons were an oasis in her week, a time of shared talk and comfortable camaraderie. With Pete, she never felt like she had to be anyone but herself, and she could tell him anything. They talked, too, about deeper things. Their Catholic upbringings, his reasons for becoming a priest. And when she saw him at Mass, raising the chalice at the consecration or laughing with parishioners at the church door, she warmed at the knowledge that he was her friend. Priests had always been on another plane, but this one was right here with her. They were equals. That, too, she didn't think Rebecca would get. "You can't be 'just friends' with a man. A priest or not a priest. A man always wants something more." She could hear Rebecca saying something like that, but she didn't want to hear it. Not Pete. He wasn't that complicated. He had been honest about the kiss, and she knew he wouldn't force her to do anything she didn't want to do. She would tell him it couldn't happen again.

Still, she had a long debate with herself about Friday. She should say no. She should only see him in his office, if at all. But then the idea of going out after a long week, of having uncomplicated fun with another person, won the argument. They were probably just going to drive around, maybe check out the holiday displays down around the Mall. Lily, one of the teachers at school, had told her that the light displays were fabulous and famous.

The night was chilly, and she wrapped the poncho around herself. He noticed and turned up the heater as he drove onto the ramp to Key Bridge.

"Where are we going?" she asked again. The hotels in Rosslyn, just over the bridge, sparkled with lights.

"I was going to wait until we got there," he said as he flicked on his turn signal, "but I'll tell you now. We're going to the airport."

"The airport?"

He just chuckled, looked sideways at her.

"Really, Pete. Why are we going to the airport?"

"Not the airport itself. Someplace near the airport. I have a surprise for you. Something I guarantee you've never done before."

He wouldn't say any more about it, and as he drove along the parkway they talked about Christmas and the gifts they had for their parents. She had found a beautiful illustrated book on fly fishing for her dad, and he'd bought his father a sweater vest. "Same thing every year, but he says he loves them." She liked that about him, how he made even gift-giving simple.

They didn't go all the way to the airport, but he pulled over into a small park. There were no other cars there, and she could see the towers on the landing strips and the blinking lights of planes on the runways on the other side of the road.

"Every newcomer to D.C. should experience this at least once," he said, as he cut the motor. Silence fell around them like a curtain, except for the tick of the cooling engine.

They were right under the landing pattern of the planes, he explained. They flew so close overhead you'd think they could touch you. "It's truly amazing," he said, squinting at his watch. "I checked out the arrival times, and we have a few minutes. So, while we wait—" He pulled out a pint bottle of whiskey from under his seat. "Something to warm us up," he said as he unscrewed the cap. He extended the bottle to her. "Sorry, I forgot glasses."

Olivia wasn't a big drinker, and he knew that. She certainly wasn't going to drink straight from the bottle. She shook her head. "You go ahead."

And he did, tipping his head back and taking a big swallow. "Ah," he said. "Warms the cockles of me heart, as my grandfather used to say." He spoke in a fake brogue.

"But you're Polish, and that's Irish whiskey."

He laughed then. "Everyone's Irish when they drink this. Sure you don't want some?"

She shook her head. It was getting cold in the car, and for a moment she wished she were back in her warm apartment, playing cards with Rebecca, drinking wine in her pj's. This wasn't her idea of a Friday night out, sitting in a chilly car. She pulled the poncho closer around her neck.

Suddenly, he put the bottle back under the seat, and reached across to open her door. "Come on," he said, "a plane's coming." He sounded as excited as a kid.

They stood in the dark parking lot. She craned her neck to see the sky sequined with stars that looked close enough to touch. And then one star was moving, rushing toward them, and she realized it was not a star but an airplane. She could hear it then, the roar and whine of the engines, and as it hurtled closer through the night she thought surely it would crash into them, miss the airport entirely. She reached out and clutched Pete's arm and buried her face in his sleeve. It smelled of pine and smoke. And just as suddenly, the noise receded, the air stilled, and she dared to peek out as the lights of the plane grew smaller and the wheels touched down on the runway across the road.

"Amazing, right?" he asked, putting his other arm around her. She was shaking, whether from fright or cold she didn't know. "I told you." Amazing, yes, and terrifying. She really had thought the plane was going to land on top of his car. "If you look, you can actually see the rivets on the underbelly of the plane. And if you're standing to the side, you can wave at the passengers."

He sounded like he thought it was fun. She couldn't imagine wanting to do it again, though maybe in daylight it wouldn't be so scary. At least then the pilot would have a clearer view of the ground.

He kept his arm around her, and she felt his fingers combing through the ends of her hair. She shivered.

"Did you like it?" His mouth was close to her ear.

She nodded, just because she didn't want to disappoint him, but thought "like" was hardly the right word.

He guided her back to the car and opened the door for her. When he slid back in, he reached down for the bottle. This time, when he held it out to her, she took it. She needed something to stop her pounding heart. Dimly, she wondered if the pounding was from the plane so close overhead or his fingers in her hair. She drank a little and he was right. It did warm her instantly.

They stayed like that, talking casually about nothing very important, passing the bottle between them. The warmth spread from her middle all the way to her fingers and toes. She thought maybe she should try whiskey more often. And then his arm was around her and he leaned in close and he was kissing her, and she turned to him and knew she was kissing him back. This was nothing like the kiss in his office. A slow curl of desire opened within her. The air rumbled a few more times as planes continued to pass overhead to the landing strip, but they seemed to be very far away, seemed to have nothing to do with her at all.

CHAPTER 20

THEY MET TWO more times before she left for Minnesota. Not at the rectory. He told her he had canceled all of his counseling appointments until the new year, and there was a lot of traffic in and out of the house as the parish geared up for the holiday. Instead, she parked her car in that same spot and climbed into his Fairlane. They kissed right away, her shyness gone. It surprised her that it would feel so natural. He seemed to take for granted that they would kiss before they even spoke. She was so caught up in it that all her resolutions melted.

Olivia didn't understand it. She was kissing a priest. She knew it was wrong, but she was doing it anyway. Maybe it was because in his car, away from the rectory and the church, he didn't seem like a priest. He was just Pete who, aside from Rebecca, was her only real friend here. She felt as if she were being carried by a tide, and she didn't stop to think about its direction. Both times, he brought a flask of scotch (he had switched from the Irish whiskey), and he remembered two small glasses. She was unsure about the taste, but she liked the tingle it gave her. The first time he drove them to a side street near an elementary school where there was no traffic. He kept the heater on but turned off the headlights. "No one will see us here," he assured her, as he gently caressed her face. They didn't stay there long. He seemed to know when enough was enough for her. He said, even though the heater was on, "I don't want you to get too cold," and he pulled away from her and started to talk about something unrelated to the fact that they had just exchanged kisses that started out soft and slowly deepened in intensity. He knew how to take it slowly. She liked that he was so careful with her.

The second time, he took her to a deserted park. He had brought along a small telescope that he propped on the hood of his car. She had no idea he was an amateur astronomer, and she loved this, this learning new things about him. He focused the instrument and showed her how to look through the lens. "See up to the right?" His mouth was right next to her ear. "That's Castor and Pollux." She knew the mythology stories from teaching English, but she had never seen the constellations. To her they just looked like abstract clumps of stars spread out in the dark sky, but she nodded anyway, wanting to let him feel like a good teacher. He promised to get her a guide to the stars, so she'd know what to look for the next time they used the telescope.

The next time. She loved hearing that. "The next time" implied that it was to be one of many. She vowed to learn as much as she could about the night sky.

And then he folded up the scope and put it in the back seat, and they sat in the car and he poured them each a few fingers of whiskey. That helped the dampness of the December night to recede, and when he brought his face close to hers she met it eagerly.

In between kissing, they sipped the scotch and he asked her about her trip to Minnesota. She'd be gone ten days, returning on the 30th. When she started to tell him about the complicated system her family had for opening gifts, he put his thumb on her lips. "Sh-h," he said. "You're not there yet. You're here with me." And then he shifted in his seat so he could be closer to her. "We don't have much time left until you have to leave." It was Sunday the 17th, and she had the staff Christmas party the next night, and on Tuesday the holiday concert at school. This would be the last time they'd see each other until January. Part of her wished she were staying in D.C., so they could have more time together. They really had to talk about this, whatever it was that was happening between them, and he wasn't leaving until Christmas Day. But she hadn't seen her family since the summer, and her mother was calling now at least once a day. What did Olivia want for dinner her first night home? Aunt Sarah was planning a caroling party. Don't forget to bring your boots.

She tried to talk to him that night about what they were doing. The fact of his priesthood kept nagging at her. He told her there was nothing for her to worry about, that he knew what he was doing, that they weren't hurting anyone. And, he continued, "Don't you like it?" Of course, she did, but she kept hearing that voice that told her she shouldn't like it. And then he asked her, "You trust me, don't you?" And when she said yes, he told her to let him worry about what they could and couldn't do. "And if you really want us to stop, we can." She felt better then, and in a moment he was telling her a joke and they were laughing. All that was good between them helped her worries to fade.

As she started her car on the dark street where she had parked, she was missing him already. Ten days. Two weeks. It seemed like an impossibly long time. He waited until she drove away, and she looked through her rear-view mirror to the yellow spots of his headlights. He didn't follow right away, giving her a few minutes' head start. "I'll watch until you turn the corner," he told her. She giggled—it sounded like a script for an espionage movie.

The scotch made her a little fuzzy, so she drove slowly, keeping her eyes on the road. He probably should have brought a thermos of coffee instead. Or cocoa. Maybe she'd do that next time, when they met in January. She rolled down the window halfway, and the night air was like cool silk on her face.

Rebecca was in the living room watching TV when she got home, and Olivia didn't want her to smell the alcohol. "Gotta pee!" she called out as she shrugged off her coat and disappeared into the bathroom. Her hair was tangled, her cheeks red. She splashed water on her face, brushed her teeth, yawned loudly as she glanced into the living room where Rebecca sat with a bowl of Fritos. "I'm exhausted," she said, hanging her coat in the closet. "I'm going to bed."

"But how was your date?" Rebecca asked from the couch. "Who was it? That Michael guy again?"

"Oh, nothing special," Olivia replied, yawning again. "I'll fill you in tomorrow. I have to be at school early."

But she stayed awake for hours, watching the moonlight fall through her window, replaying every moment of the evening. The stars, the telescope, the nearness of Pete as he adjusted the lens. Gone was the Minnesota girl who had never colored outside the lines. The two words, "Pete" and "priest," were losing their connecting edge.

CHAPTER 21

THERE WERE BUNK beds in her old room. "Tom's boys come to spend the night every couple of weeks, and it seemed so much easier to have beds for them instead of dragging out the sleeping bags," her mother explained as she fluffed a pillow on the lower bunk. But even with new beds, even with a Matchbox car parking lot on top of the new desk and a crate of Legos on the bookshelf, the room still felt like her. Olivia could close her eyes and know she was there. There was something in the scent a room held. This one was ballpoint pen ink, wool sweaters, lily-of-the-valley cologne. She could look out the window and there were the maple trees she loved, and she knew that under the piles of snow her father's small garden plot waited for spring. She could almost smell the lilacs and the peppery marigolds, see the straight rows of radishes and peas and squash he planted every year, feel the crumbly earth between her fingers when she helped him turn over the soil.

Her mother left her to get settled, and Olivia opened the door to the closet that still had that faded pink floral wallpaper from her early childhood. The rest of the room had been painted and repainted over the years, and was now a very pale blue. As she hung up her clothes, she thought of the prom dresses, plaid uniform skirts, and oxford cloth blouses that had crowded the small space, and the jeans and snow pants and sweaters stacked on the shelves. Now the shelves were nearly empty, but there were new padded hangers, and a sachet ball hung from the rod. She smiled at this touch, at her mother wanting to make the room special.

After she unpacked, she hefted the empty suitcase to the top bunk, and sat for a moment on the bottom mattress, and there before her, between the edges of the new rag rugs, were the scuff marks on the floor from the year she had tried tap dancing. She could see herself sprawled on her bed reading a book or doing homework, or crouched by the door with the hall phone cord stretched out as far as it would go, so she and Aubrey could have their private, girl-talk conversations. She was so far from that girl now, so far from the tap shoes that had long been thrown away. When she left last summer, she had anticipated changes—living in a big city, renting her own apartment, being on her own away from family and lifelong friends. She had seen herself dating men who hadn't grown up in her small town, who were as independent as she would be. She had imagined dinners at restaurants where she'd sample international cuisine, conversations about literature, concerts at the famed Kennedy Center. None of that had happened. Instead, she was in a forbidden relationship she couldn't even explain to herself. What had begun as an innocent counseling session had deepened into something else. A friendship, yes, and that was okay. She would have kept it at that. She tried to figure out if she had done anything to make him think differently, to have him see her as a desirable woman, but she came up with nothing. His words circled in her mind. Him telling her she was beautiful. Him saying how hard it had been not to touch her. When was it that she began to believe him? When had she forgotten how to say no? When was it that she had become her new self, this woman who was falling in love? And what was she to make of that woman? Was it really her?

As she wandered around the house, feeling the thrum of that new self, the rooms worked their magic on her. Looking at the family photos displayed on top of the piano, reading the titles of beloved books with their faded covers, discovering the hall closet was still stuffed with coats and outgrown boots, she knew she would always have roots here. She would call other places home, but this would be where she had started, and because of that, she would never let it go. A thick tree stood in the living room, with the multi-colored lights her father loved, and the ornaments carefully placed on the branches. Many of the ornaments had been in her family for years. Thin glass globes, tiny wooden train cars, gold-plated stars. One day some of them would be hers. She ran her fingers over the branches and inhaled the scent of pine and sap, and all of a sudden she was back at that tree lot in Leesburg with Pete, their breath white smoke in the chill air as they laughed about that one tree with the really crooked trunk. Two weeks in Minnesota seemed like a long time.

Her mother wouldn't let her help with dinner that first night, but fussed around the kitchen while Olivia sat at the table playing with the salt and pepper shakers. Cows. She remembered buying them at a county fair when she was eleven and giving them to her mother for her birthday. Her father showed off the new ice-maker in the fridge. "No more of those pesky trays that someone always forgot to fill." He looked pointedly at Olivia's mother, who smiled and shook her head as she chopped carrots. Olivia loved the gentle bantering of her parents. They had always been that way, going back and forth with teasing barbs that no one believed were anything less than expressions of love.

Her father brought Olivia a glass of ginger ale with a slice of lemon, the way she liked it. She wondered if her parents could detect a change in her, if it showed in the way she smiled, the way she spoke. Or did she appear to be the same person who had left last summer? It had only been a few months, but she felt like someone else. And what would they say if they did know? She couldn't imagine her mother, who had never even called a priest by his first name, accepting that her daughter was romantically involved with a member of the clergy. And her father wore his traditional values like a badge. He wouldn't understand it at all. She watched him check the thermometer at the window over the sink. He still had a slight limp from the broken leg. "Bet you're not used to this cold. We'll make sure you have extra blankets on your bed." Olivia had felt the bone-chilling cold as soon as she walked out of the airport, but she didn't mind it. It brought back so many wonderful memories. She had breathed it in deeply, and it was like inhaling frozen lakes and skating parties and snow so white it was blue.

She was sure her parents believed her to be the same person who had left in the summer. The Olivia who liked chives in her scrambled eggs, who read three library books at the same time, who always made her bed. The Olivia who followed the rules, who had been so embarrassed that one time she got a speeding ticket. What she was doing was much worse than driving over the speed limit, worse than not making her bed. Her parents would never understand that. They would be ashamed of her. How would she ever make them understand? If they knew, would they even welcome her back to the home where she had spent most of her life? It was a choice she had never considered. Pete or her family. She shook her head to chase the thoughts away and allowed herself to return to the aroma of roasting pork with thyme and rosemary that filled the kitchen. Her father poured himself a beer and looked thoughtful as he dipped his hand into a bowl of salted shelled walnuts. "So, Olivia, tell us all about life in the Nation's Capital. Phone calls and your infrequent letters"—he frowned at her over the rims of his bifocals—"haven't filled in enough of the blanks."

It was a question that would be repeated over and over in the next few days as she visited familiar shops and drove down remembered streets. Morrie, the guy who ran the Esso station where she filled up her car, inquired about the price of gasoline. Andrea in the post office asked her if she'd be moving back any time soon. Old Mr. Phillips, the pharmacist, said he'd heard all they had back east were chain drugstores. "Bet you don't get anything like the personalized service I give," he said, tucking some lipstick samples into the prescription she was picking up for her mother. Everyone was hungry for details, and she felt like a celebrity. You'd think no one ever went anywhere beyond the town limits. And then she realized that few did. Her brother Tom, who had gone to Ohio Wesleyan for college, had returned after graduation to work at an insurance company. Her old boyfriend Trevor was proud to be next in line to run the family hardware store. "All that traffic," her mother sniffed, speaking of big cities. "I couldn't stand it." Businesses stayed in the families for years, and houses were handed down to younger generations. They became "the Wesley house," or "the Connick house."

As she drove through the town or walked through the business section thronged with last-minute shoppers, everything looked the same to her. It was like one of those towns people build around toy train tracks where nothing ever changes, and the church is always next to the café and the same five trees sit in the middle of the park. It just wouldn't feel like her home town if she returned to find parking meters in front of the library or to discover that the book store (owned by the Wembley family for years) had been bought out by a big chain. She asked herself why, if she was so adamant about leaving because nothing ever changed, did she still honor that constancy. Why she wanted to make sure Ida would still be the cashier at the Piggly-Wiggly and Koffner's Bakery would still have their two-for-one doughnut special on Saturday morning.

She had left because she wanted more excitement, more opportunities. She had even wanted a certain amount of anonymity, where the postmark of every letter she received wouldn't be scrutinized by Andrea, where the pharmacist wouldn't know about her UTI. Living in this town had been like living in a fishbowl, but at the same time she couldn't help but wonder how well these people really knew her. They knew her as they wanted her to be. They knew her as Frank and Alice's daughter. They knew her as the reliable babysitter, the winner of the 4H essay contest senior year in high school, the girl who organized the church charity car wash. Whereas Pete, she mused, when she thought of him for the hundredth time since she had arrived, knew her as she really was. He listened to her talk about her doubts, about her panic moments. He knew her not as who she had always been but as who she was right now. In spite of her shaky moments facing life in the big city, he accepted and applauded the new Olivia she was trying to be.

Every day, whether she was visiting friends or popping into shops, thoughts of Pete hovered around her like a physical presence. When Aunt Sarah asked her if she had a new boyfriend, she shook her head, but she couldn't help but smile inside. If anyone had inquired two months ago, her denial would have been real, but now she was bursting with the realness of Pete. She wished she could tell them that she had met a wonderful man, and when she described him, they would say they couldn't wait to meet him. When she retreated from the busyness of the days before Christmas, she ran a movie in her head of their times together, played a soundtrack of his voice. But, of course, he had to be a secret. She couldn't tell anyone she was becoming romantically involved with a priest. She couldn't even explain it to herself.

On the rare quiet afternoon when she had a few hours to herself, or at night when she lay in the bunk bed listening to the wind, she gave herself over to memories. The Christmas tree shopping, the star-gazing, the night they watched the planes land. The intimacy of passing a flask back and forth in the car. The first kiss in his office. The deeper kisses in his car. The flip of her stomach when she heard him say her name over the phone.

She wished she could hear his voice now. She wished they could walk down a snowy street together, peering into shop windows, drinking coffee at that new café near the library. She wanted to hear him sing in his off-key way at the caroling party. She missed the nearness of him, and little things like the calluses on his thumbs. But there wouldn't be any phone calls. She had explained that the two extensions in the house were right in the middle of everything, and she was too old to pull the phone into her room. Plus, long distance was expensive, and her parents might question the charges. "Who'd you call in D.C.?"

So she stored up things to tell him when they were together again. He'd grin when she described herself as a celebrity in her little town. She found her old camera in the downstairs closet, and she took pictures of the snow, of the frozen lake sparkling in the sun. He'd tell her how much he had missed her, how he had thought of her every time he passed that Christmas tree in the front hall. She still thought of it as "their" tree, even though it belonged to the church.

Apart from being separated from Pete, though, the vacation was wonderful. She loved having her family around, seeing how much her nephews had grown (Wyatt had learned to ride a two-wheeler). She loved eating her mother's cooking and seeing the way her father could concentrate for hours tying fishing lures. She loved reading the town newspaper with its descriptions of the minutiae of daily life. *Mrs. Henrietta Wycroft Entertained the Seven Pines Bridge Club in Her Home on Wednesday Afternoon. Annual Fish Fry on the Ice Planned for January 14.* She loved the snow, and one morning she helped Wyatt and Tommy make a snowman in their front yard. She loved sleeping for ten hours every night in her old room, waking to the aroma of coffee and cinnamon rolls. She loved it all, but it was the way you love a scene in a Christmas card. It makes you reminisce, but you know you have another, wider life.

There were times when his name was on the tip of her tongue, when she almost said, "Pete and I—" or "Pete always says—" and stopped herself just in time. It was so hard not being able to talk about him. Two days before Christmas she was sitting at the kitchen table drinking cocoa, watching the mini marshmallows melt into a sugary glaze on top of the chocolate. Her parents were out doing last-minute errands, and the house was quiet except for the tick of the heater deep in the pipes. Aunt Sarah and the rest of the family were due to arrive in an hour for the caroling party, and Olivia was savoring the quiet and the rich aroma of vegetable soup simmering on the stove. The knock on the kitchen door startled her, and when she opened it, she shrieked with joy. "Aubrey! I didn't know you were coming home!" There was her best friend, her blond curls poking out from layers of scarves, her cheeks red from the cold.

"I wasn't going to, because Joe didn't think he could get off work, but I convinced him that this is my last Christmas as a single woman, and my mother has this huge list of things for me to do. Plus, I knew you'd be here." They embraced and jumped around like kids, and there was just so much to talk about. Life in Chicago. Life in D.C. Aubrey's wedding coming up next month (Olivia had saved money for the plane ticket). They giggled and clasped hands, each one talking faster than the other.

Soon, however, the frantic conversation wound down, and they were just two best friends sitting in a well-lit kitchen, even comfortable with silence. Olivia topped off their mugs with hot cocoa and looked across at Aubrey, who was the same yet different. Yes, the same glass-blue eyes and blond hair, the same way of leaning forward when she spoke. But changed, too, something more serious about those eyes, her voice a shade deeper. Was it that she was about to be married? Was it that she and Joe were sharing an apartment in Chicago, something neither of their families would have condoned? Aubrey's parents thought she lived alone, and she had sworn Olivia to secrecy. Did living with a man give you an edge, something that Olivia could detect but not define? And would she, Olivia, ever have the confidence that seemed to radiate from her friend?

"But what you haven't told me," Aubrey said, pulling a marshmallow from the bag on the table, "is whether you're seeing anyone. Remember how we talked about all those eligible bachelors swarming around D.C.?"

Olivia started to give her usual flip answer. No one yet. Playing the field. So busy with school. But then that nagging feeling scratched at the back of her mind. She wanted to tell Aubrey about Pete. She needed to sort it all out, and since Aubrey hadn't met Pete, she could be completely neutral. Not like Rebecca, who still sometimes referred to Pete as "that hot priest." To Aubrey, Pete would be faceless and anonymous. And the need to tell someone had been uncurling in her the whole time she'd been here. In between her Kodachrome memories of him, there had been a question. Should she be with him? Could she keep seeing him?

She squared herself in her chair, pushed her mug away. "Actually, there might be—"

Aubrey's face erupted in a wide grin. "Tell all!"

Olivia didn't know where to start, so she began by swearing her friend to secrecy. "It's a little unusual," she said, and then she started with the externals. He was a teacher. He was at her church. He was into astronomy. As she spun out the facts, she knew she was skipping the important part. But weren't the parts she was telling also important? These were what drew her to Pete. It wasn't the fact of his priesthood. That was, well, a complication. Was she taking a long time getting to the point because she was afraid Aubrey wouldn't understand?

She was just about to get to that when the front door banged open and there was Aunt Sarah, her three kids trailing behind, carrying wrapped packages. And Mamie was behind them, and then her parents and her brothers and their families came in the back door on a blast of cold air, and the moment was lost. There were hugs for Aubrey, everyone wanting to see that engagement ring again, and Aunt Sarah exclaiming, "Can you believe the wedding's only four weeks away?"

Then there were so many family events, and Aubrey was busy with her relatives and her mother's endless wedding to-do list. She and Joe left the day after Christmas. Olivia wished she could have told her the whole story, but then thought maybe it was better to keep it to herself.

CHAPTER 22

THE DAYS FLEW past, and suddenly it was December 30, and she was in a cab on her way back from the airport to her apartment. As much as she enjoyed being back in Minnesota, seeing her family, walking through piles of snow, it would be good to be back. Back home, she almost said to herself, and she wondered if that little apartment was beginning to be home. If it was becoming *here*, and everyplace else, including the Minnesota house on Fremont Street, was turning into *there*.

Walking up the front steps from the street, checking the front hall table for any mail Rebecca might not have picked up, and then dragging her suitcase up the stairs to the apartment, she did feel a sense of homecoming. The apartment was the place where she could unwind and be herself.

She spent the ten days in Minnesota with people always looking at her, as if expecting to find her altered in some way, or as if they wanted to reassure themselves she was still the same. She wasn't sure which, but it was sometimes unnerving to be under such scrutiny. Her mother was always asking her if she wanted anything, when she was perfectly capable of getting her own snack, when she knew where everything was in the kitchen. Now that she was back, she could take off her shoes and make a cup of tea without her mother leaping up and saying, "Let me get that for you."

As much as she loved her parents, and her entire family, the prospect of settling back into her apartment, where there were no prescribed meal times, where no one dropped in to see if she wanted to go shopping/take a walk around the lake/check out the new coffee shop, beckoned to her as a vacation from the vacation. She still had four days until school started again. In her bag was *The Day of the Jackal* her brother Evan had given her, and she couldn't wait to open it.

She heard the phone ringing as she put her key in the lock, and she felt a thrill go through her. Maybe it was Pete. He knew when she was getting back. This could be his way of surprising her, of welcoming her. Maybe he was calling to see if she wanted to get together that evening. She was tired, but seeing him would perk her up. Any thoughts she might have had, any misgivings she might have shared with Aubrey, any doubts about the "rightness" of the relationship, had disappeared as her plane dipped down to the runway at National Airport and she remembered that night she and Pete had watched the jet land, soaring right over their heads.

Rebecca was putting the receiver back when Olivia got the door open. "Roomie! You're back!" Olivia loved how her roommate was always happy to see her. "I would have picked you up at the airport, but you didn't give me your flight info."

"No problem," Olivia assured her, setting down her suitcase and rifling through the mail on the table by the door. "There was a line of cabs waiting outside. And navigating the airport traffic is such a pain." She sniffed the air. Onions.

"I made onion soup!" Rebecca said. "A welcome home gift!" Later Olivia would find the red and white Campbell's can at the bottom of the garbage can, but she wouldn't let on. Rebecca had many talents, but cooking wasn't one of them.

"Mm-mmm," she said. "Perfect for a winter night. All I had on the flight was a little bags of nuts." And miniature bottles of scotch. She had taken one because it reminded her of Pete. Drinking it, thankfully over ice and not straight the way he drank it, made the journey seem shorter, made her think that maybe this very evening, or tomorrow at the latest, they'd be sharing a drink together. He said as much to her before she left. That as soon as they were both back in town they'd get together and celebrate the holiday season. "We'll ring in the new year!" She smiled when she reflected that she, who had always stuck with wine, was developing a taste for whiskey. It was so much more sophisticated.

"Who was—I mean, I thought I heard the phone ring just now." Olivia wiggled her feet out of her shoes.

Rebecca shrugged. "Wrong number, I guess. There wasn't anyone there. Second time it happened today. I hate it when people don't even have the courtesy to tell you they were calling someone else. Come on, I have a nice bottle of red. Let's have some wine and I'll serve the soup." She reached into the top drawer for the corkscrew and took a loaf of garlic bread out of the oven.

It had to have been Pete. Who else would call and hang up? He wouldn't want Rebecca to know it was him. Olivia felt her lips curve into a smile. She accepted a glass of wine from Rebecca, and the two of them sat at the table, where Rebecca had set out bowls and bread plates, had even lit a candle.

But the phone didn't ring again that night. And Olivia couldn't call him because Rebecca was there. The two of them drank half the bottle of wine, ate the soup and the bread from the French bakery on Wisconsin Avenue, and they played gin rummy until Olivia couldn't keep her eyes open.

Tomorrow was Sunday. She'd see him at Mass, and maybe he would send her some sort of signal. If they were alone at the donut table after the service, he might suggest they meet later. She fell asleep feeling happy about that. Only twelve more hours.

CHAPTER 23

THEY GAVE UP the "counseling" sessions, because she was afraid someone in the rectory would notice how often she was there, and because she was uncomfortable making out with him on the couch when the housekeeper was right down the hall and the pastor might be passing by outside the door, even though the door had that pebbled glass that made it hard to see through. The rectory was his priest turf. She couldn't forget that he was a priest when she was with him there. She still went to the mission committee meetings, but they were tapering off until the spring. So the only time they were together was when they met secretly one or two evenings a week. They always met in the dark. Olivia would park her car on different streets and get into Pete's Fairlane, and he would drive them someplace where no one would see them. The back of a shopping center parking lot, the edge of a deserted park, once down by the waterfront near a warehouse. He would bring out his flask of scotch. Then they would make out, and it didn't take long before it went beyond just kissing. More than once she came home with beard burn, prayed it would fade by morning. How would she explain it when Rebecca thought she was at the library or out to dinner with the blind date that Angela from school had arranged?

And how could she go in to teach high school girls who would giggle behind their textbooks?

So many times she came home to the apartment and retreated to her room, pleading fatigue to Rebecca but too keyed up to sleep, and in the darkness her "good girl" Catholic admonitions kicked in. When she was with him, she was carried along on a tide of passion, with the nearness of him, the magnetism that drew her to him. But back home, where photos of her family sat on the dresser, where textbooks and student papers were piled on the desk, a pesky voice nagged at her. She shouldn't be doing this. Pete was a priest. She could imagine the shock on her parents' faces, her brothers appalled at what their "little sister" was doing. Aunt Maisie would literally have a heart attack. And good Sister Dorothea, her high school principal, would press her lips together and shake her head. "We always thought better of you, dear." But then she would hear Pete telling her that they weren't hurting anyone, and she knew that was true, and her hesitation would melt away. She had no idea what his experience was, what he had done in college before he entered the seminary, but she doubted that he, with his eyes on the priesthood, would have lived a very wild and reckless life. He told her that what they were doing was a natural expression of their feelings for each other, and he reassured her when she voiced her doubts. "You know I'd never hurt you." He was so earnest, and he praised and complimented her so much, told her how love was a gift from God. Told her he prayed for her every day. And so she let the cautions and reprimands of her provincial parochial background fall away. She told herself that this was the '70s, she wasn't in high school anymore, and how could something that made her feel so good be as bad as others might think? Or was she rationalizing all of it to absolve herself? There were too many questions, and too many nights she tossed and turned, and in the pale morning light her bed was a tangle of sheets.

He made her laugh. He asked her for help with his sermons or when there was an unexpected task related to the mission project. "You can always count on me," he told her, "and I love how I can count on you."

Inside his car, sheltered by the dark, it was thrilling to do something so far removed from that color-inside-the-lines-person who had always followed the rules, something exhilarating about being daring for the first time in her life. While she worried that something might go wrong, that they might be discovered, she pushed back the voice of caution that told her to stop. Pete knew what he was doing. She could trust him. After all, he was a priest, an educated man. Hadn't he studied ethics in the seminary?

It was winter, and it was cold, and even though he usually kept the heater on in the car, it didn't work all that well, and the seal around the passenger side window was worn down. It was uncomfortable twisting around in the front seat with the steering wheel and the gearshift, fumbling awkwardly with winter coats. And she was always nervous, afraid that even though they were in dark places where probably no one could see them, where probably no one would come along, there was always a chance that there would be a patrol car or a night watchman. If a guard or a police officer came along, would they have to show identification? Was it against the law to park behind a closed supermarket? She didn't know how long they could keep this up. Mostly, she wanted to be with him in a place that was lit, where she could actually see his face and the shine of his eyes.

She flew to Chicago one weekend for Aubrey's wedding, where she wore the dark green bridesmaid dress and danced with one of the groomsmen who asked her for her phone number. On another weekend, Pete had to chaperone a retreat for his students. A surprise storm blew in and the city closed down for three days. At those times they had to be content with clandestine phone conversations when Rebecca was at work.

So, in late January, when he suggested they go away overnight, she said yes.

He checked the schedule and found a weekend when he was saying the noon Sunday Mass. It just happened that it was the same weekend Rebecca was going to New York to visit some old friends and see a Broadway musical. Olivia would have the apartment to herself, but they couldn't risk Mrs. Trimble knowing he was there, and the apartment was too close to the church anyway. "I'll get a room," he said. "You just pack something sexy."

Sexy? He never used words like that. It seemed flippant, almost too casual. What they were going to do wasn't casual. It marked a huge step in their relationship. Nevertheless, it made her realize that she couldn't spend the night with him wearing one of the old T-shirts or flannel nightgowns she usually slept in. So, one afternoon after school she went to Sears and bought a lacy midnight blue nightie with spaghetti straps. It made her blush just paying for it. She thought the saleswoman, who looked a lot like her Aunt Sarah, eyed her a moment too long as she took the money. Did she guess that Olivia was about to have a romantic encounter? It was 30 degrees out. No one who was just going to snuggle under a quilt would buy something like this. She was afraid she was blushing as she pulled the two twenties out of her wallet.

The first time. It was something she had thought about since high school. Most of what she knew she had learned from college friends and Aubrey, who had lost her virginity to a guy she had dated for two years, told her she would know when the time was right. But she hadn't given Olivia many details. She had just used words like "unforgettable," and "amazing." What she hadn't gotten from friends, she gleaned from books. "The earth moved," Hemingway wrote, but Olivia didn't think that actually happened. She was more worried about pain. But Aubrey had told her that the whole pain thing was an exaggeration. She pushed that thought away.

She had no idea what it would be like to be in a motel room with a man, to be in the same bed. To be naked. One night after a shower, she stood wrapped in a towel in front of the full-length mirror on the back of her closet door and let the towel drop at her feet. She didn't think she had a very remarkable body. What would Pete see? Would he be disappointed? And there was the issue of birth control. She wasn't on the pill. She'd never even been to a gynecologist.

That was something they hadn't talked about. Birth control was against church law. How was he going to justify using it? She wouldn't take a chance on getting pregnant, and she knew he didn't want that, so he'd probably get condoms. Should she remind him? But how would he feel about breaking a church law to be with her? She almost laughed. It wasn't the only church law he was breaking. The more important question was if she would know what to do when they were actually in bed together. She decided instinct would take over. It wasn't something you rehearsed. And Pete would no doubt be as nervous as she was. It was probably his first time, too. Even though he was 32, he had been in seminary for all those years, and had been a priest for three.

She thought the day would never come. By Thursday she was so keyed up she walked around her block six times after school, and she started counting the hours. There were moments, too, when she considered calling it off. It just seemed so unreal, that she, Olivia, who had only had a handful of serious boyfriends, was going to spend the night with a man. With Pete. With a priest. She could hear Sister Dorothea telling them senior year in high school to "save themselves for marriage," and she could hear one of the girls in the back row commenting, "Easy for her to say—she's a nun." They had all laughed then, but the words had lodged in Olivia's mind. For the most part, she believed in what Sister Dorothea had said. She wanted it to mean commitment. She might be out of sync with the times, but she couldn't see herself having casual sex with any man she dated.

But Pete wasn't just any man. She loved him. And she could tell he loved her, too. He had said it, several times. There was commitment there. She knew it. Why else would he, a priest, be taking this step with her? It was what allowed her to say yes.

As the day approached, she knew she could still back out. It wasn't something she *had* to do. It was her choice as to where and when she would have sex. If she was bothered by misgivings, even on Friday afternoon, she could change her mind. He would understand if she said she wasn't ready. He had always treated her with respect. Thursday night, she looked at herself in her bathroom mirror. "I'm doing this because I want to," she told her image as she wiped away the steam.

CHAPTER 24

WHAT SHE WOULD remember most afterward was the mixture of scents. The sharp spice of Pete's aftershave, the industrial soap residue on the sheets, and the faint sweat of their bodies. She could not draw a picture of the room, remember if there were framed prints on the walls or the color of the drapes. Pete had flipped on the lights when they went in, but had quickly turned on a bedside lamp and switched off the ceiling light. "Atmosphere," he said. She had a vague notion of a small table, a TV, a striped bedspread.

Details of the room that she couldn't bring to mind were inconsequential, overshadowed by the reality of what had happened in that room. She and Pete had made love. They had fused their relationship even deeper as everything around and within them fell away. That she was a teacher. That he was a teacher. That she drove a Chevy and loved to cook. That he wanted a dog and liked astronomy. And most, that he was a priest. What was real was that it was the two of them and they loved each other and he wanted to break the rules to be with her.

She waited in the car when he went into the small office to pay. He was wearing a leather jacket, jeans, and a wool cap. She told him he looked like a motorcyclist. There were only a handful of cars in the parking lot, and most of the rooms were dark. The motel was over the bridge in Virginia, near Falls Church, a place she'd never been. A lighted sign out by the road flashed Vacancy in big orange letters and also had the words "free TV." She didn't think they'd be watching much television. He was back in five minutes, holding a key on a black plastic tag. He tossed it to her with a smile and drove down the row of parking spaces, stopping in front of #8. She looked at the number on the door and knew she was taking the biggest step of her life. It still wasn't too late to back out, but it no longer seemed like an option. This was the moment, and it was the right moment.

All day she had wondered how it would work. Would they sit around and talk for a while? Have a drink? Would she go and change into her negligée in the bathroom? Maybe they'd drop off their stuff and go out for something to eat. Or would they just fall immediately into bed? She hoped not. She wanted the evening to build up to that, to enjoy the luxury of spending time together somewhere other than a car or a rectory office or a school classroom. Somewhere where it would be just the two of them, where they didn't have to keep their voices down or worry about someone seeing them. All those hours together. A whole night seemed like an eternity. In truth, she wanted to take it slowly because she was nervous.

He seemed to get her apprehension, so he made an effort to help her relax. He took the ice bucket out to the machine outside the motel office, plumped the pillows against the headboard so they could sit comfortably, opened the nightstand drawer and made a joke about the Gideon bible. He asked her if she wanted the radio or TV on. As they sat side by side on the bed, sipping scotch, he let his foot curl over her shin, his fingers played softly with her hair. It felt so comfortable being next to him this way that she sank gratefully against him, inhaling him, feeling his heart beat under his shirt. They were cocooned away from the world. He poured more scotch into her glass, and that warm feeling spread through her chest.

And then they kissed, and it was so much better than being scrunched up in the car. She felt herself loose and languid, and also filled with an eagerness she'd never known before. She wanted it to go on forever. He said her name once or twice, but it came out muffled, and she couldn't find her own voice.

When she awoke in the middle of the night, she thought she was dreaming. She tried to connect the edges of the dream, but they wouldn't knit together, and then she heard Pete snoring softly, and she remembered. Was it real? Was she really lying in bed next to him? She hugged herself, knowing she wasn't the same person she'd been yesterday. Amazed and exhilarated at what had happened. She looked across the bed and saw the mound of Pete's shoulders under the spread. What would he say when he woke up? Would he be as happy as she was? Orange light from the outside sign outlined the drapes at the window. The sheets felt clammy, but the room was overheated. She wanted to crank down the heat, but she didn't know how, and she didn't want to turn on a light. And even though Pete was asleep, she was embarrassed to walk across the room. She had never put on the midnight blue negligée.

Sitting there in bed, she was aware of her nakedness, of the feel of the sheets against her skin. They weren't soft like her own sheets, and the pillow was lumpy. But it didn't matter. All she could think of was that the two of them had been together. Were together now in these hours before dawn. She had to pee, but that would involve getting out of bed with nothing on. The clock on the bedside table read three-thirty, way too early to get up, but she was too keyed up to go back to sleep. Her skin felt alive, and she kept replaying the evening before in her mind, wanting to hold and savor every second.

She found her underwear on the floor, along with the turtleneck she'd been wearing. She pulled them on and slipped out of bed, tiptoeing across the room to the tiny bathroom, where she closed the door carefully so the latch wouldn't make any sound. When she was done, she walked softly across the room to the window, glancing over to make sure Pete was still asleep, and pulled back the edge of the heavy curtain, letting in a sliver of moonlight. The parking lot was dark and still, dotted with small rain puddles. There were no cars on the road in front of the motel, and no sounds. It felt like time had stopped.

She let the curtain drop, and the room was completely dark again. She crept back to bed, still partially dressed, and waited for morning.

CHAPTER 25

OLIVIA WAS GLAD she had the apartment to herself after her night with Pete. She wanted to hold it all close to her and savor the memory, reliving every moment. When she got home, she took a long shower and then sat on her bed in a faded flannel nightgown, her skin still alive from his touch. She decided not to go to church because she didn't know how she'd feel seeing him in his vestments, preaching, distributing communion. She didn't know which was the real Pete—the one on the altar or the one in the motel room.

Images shuffled through her mind—his leather jacket hanging on the chair by the window, an open pack of Winstons, his wallet and loose change on the dresser, his red toothbrush on the rim of the sink. She saw the way he brushed back the hair that fell over his forehead, and his feet, bare, tangled in the sheets. There was something so intimate about a person's bare feet, especially when you had only seen them before in shoes and socks. It had been hard not to stare. Not just at his feet, but at his whole body. The way he slept with his mouth half open, the curly thatch on his chest. At the reality of him there with her.

It would be impossible to go back to the way she had been, to the person she was Saturday morning. It wasn't anything anyone could see.

To her students, she would still be the same woman in the denim skirt collecting weekend homework. To the overweight attendant at the Gulf station she would still be the woman behind the wheel of the blue Chevy who bought gas every Saturday morning. She didn't even think Rebecca would detect the change, and Rebecca noticed everything. The change was too deep to see, but she felt it in every pore of her body. And she couldn't stop smiling.

It felt odd to be spending a Sunday morning alone in the apartment. Rebecca rarely worked on Sunday morning, and they usually had breakfast together. Pancakes or omelets. But she was in New York. It was too quiet. And odd, too, not to be going to church. As she sat on her bed drinking tea, she knew Pete was two miles away standing at the back of the church holding the song sheet, waiting for the guitars to start strumming the opening song. Was he distracted? Did he see her in the back of every woman's head in the pews? Would he be able to keep his mind on his sermon, or would he keep spooling back to their night together?

Most likely, he would call her as soon as he got back to the rectory. He'd want to make sure she was okay, wonder why she hadn't been at church. He'd want to connect with her. Their parting had been hurried. He was anxious to get back to go over the notes for his sermon. He apologized that there wasn't time for breakfast, and she shook her head at the Styrofoam cup of tepid coffee he brought back from the motel office. They spoke little in the car, and she sensed his preoccupation with the Mass. He had seemed almost dismissive, even cold, but she told herself he was probably tired.

After she finished her tea, she checked the refrigerator and saw nothing there beyond some yogurt, a stalk of celery, and a bag of apples. She'd go to Safeway, buy meat for a pot roast, potatoes, carrots, sliced turkey for her lunches. Lettuce. It would be cozy sitting in the living room grading papers with the aroma of onions and garlic and simmering beef, waiting for the phone to ring. How great it would be if he could come to dinner, if the two of them could sit at the table, a regular couple. She had fantasized about that before, but now, now she wanted it even more. Now they had taken a further step, and it would feel so right to do all those normal things couples do. Sharing meals. Going out to the movies. Choosing a bottle of burgundy at the liquor store.

She smiled at the idea of all of that, and then felt a sinking inside when she realized that of course it couldn't happen. Pete couldn't drop over for dinner. They couldn't go to the movie theater at Dupont Circle or browse the shelves for a red wine. Not now. Not now while he was still a priest.

But who was to say what the future held? One step at a time, she reminded herself. Think about this afternoon. Think about putting on a record while you cook. Think about that moment when the phone rings and you hear his voice.

That would have to be enough—for now.

CHAPTER 26

TWO WEEKS LATER, at a faculty meeting, Sister Helen announced the final plans for the annual staff retreat. This was a big deal for the teachers (and for the students—they got a day off from school). "Good news," she said. "Two parents have generously offered their houses, right next door to each other, in Rehoboth Beach." The teachers would leave early Friday morning for the Delaware shore and return Sunday afternoon. From what Olivia had heard, everyone loved this retreat.

"It's not like a religious retreat," Angela the P.E. teacher explained to her when they took a short coffee break. "It's supposed to be a planning time for the second half of the year, but most of the time we just relax and eat a lot of great food."

Olivia couldn't picture going to the beach when it was still winter, though she did look forward to seeing the ocean. Of course, there had been waves on Lake Superior, but she thought the ocean waves would be much more dramatic. And while she liked most of the teachers, she wasn't sure she wanted to share a room with one of them, and it would mean giving up a whole weekend. But there didn't seem to be a choice, and everyone else was excited.

She stopped paying attention, surreptitiously grading papers on her lap, and jolted when she heard Sister Helen say her name. She looked up to see the principal looking at her, eyebrows raised in a question.

"Pardon me? I didn't hear—" Olivia clicked her pen shut and tried to look attentive.

"I was just saying that you probably know Father Kowolski. Don't you go to St. Andrew's?"

Olivia went hot and cold at the same time. Surely Sister Helen didn't know anything. If she did, she wouldn't have worded her question that way. Olivia tried to cast around for whatever the nun had been talking about before the question. The retreat. She remembered that much. But what did Pete have to do with that? Had Sister Helen gone on to a completely new topic and she had missed it?

"Oh, yes. Sure. I do. I go to St. Andrew's." Careful, she told herself. Don't sound like the panic you feel.

Apparently, Pete was going to be the chaplain for the retreat. Her first reaction was over the moon excitement. They'd be together all weekend! But wait, they would be together along with about ten nuns and a dozen lay teachers. She'd have to call him "Father." They wouldn't dare act as if they were anything more than the most casual of acquaintances. No covert glances, no signs of the electricity that flowed between them. It had only been two weeks since they had spent the night together.

Sister Helen explained that they had originally had another priest scheduled, but something had come up and he had to cancel. "We were lucky to find Father Kowolski," Sister Helen beamed. "He'll be great, don't you think, Olivia?"

You have no idea, Olivia felt like saying, and she swallowed her smile. "I'm sure he will. Everyone likes him." Especially me.

They had just talked on the phone the day before. Pete must have known about the retreat and hadn't told her. She figured it was his way of making a joke. Later he could ask, "How did you keep a straight face when Sister Helen said I'd be coming on the retreat?" And he'd probably tell her the only reason he had agreed was that he knew she'd be there.

Two days, two nights. On one hand, it was a dream come true. Being together all that time. On the other hand, it would mean being together all that time but not able to actually *be* together. It would be so hard to pretend she was just the parishioner at St. Andrew's. And would it be hard for him, too? Could he pull it off, the guise of acting as if he barely knew her?

Sister Helen went on to suggest carpools. Olivia found herself raising her hand and saying, "Maybe I could give Father Kowolski a ride. I have no idea where Rehoboth Beach is, and I live pretty close to the church." They'd have several hours alone in the car. She'd get a map, though Pete probably knew the route.

When she did talk to Pete that night, he groaned. "Oh, I wish we could drive together, but I can't come until Saturday. I've got to play assistant coach at a basketball game at St. Bonaventure's Friday night. We'll find a way to be together, though, sometime over the weekend."

As she thought about it over the next few days, part of her wished he wasn't coming. It would just be a lot of tension, pressure to act normal. She would constantly be aware of his presence. That he had just left the room where she was meeting with a group of teachers. That he might come into the room. That he'd be in the room and they couldn't look at each other.

The weekend came, and she drove with Lynette, the biology teacher, and Mylene, who taught French. They took Lynette's car, a hatchback with lots of room for their stuff. Pete arrived late Saturday morning, just in time for lunch. The teachers had been meeting all morning, but they had the afternoon free. Olivia was helping set out the soup bowls when the front door opened, and there he was. She almost dropped the ladle, felt a blush rise from her neck to her eyes. Sister Helen rushed up to welcome him, introduced him to the group. "And, of course, you know Olivia."

"That I do," he said, shrugging out of his coat. He gave a little smile.

Olivia found her voice, hoped it wouldn't wobble. "You're just in time for lunch."

As they filled bowls with tomato soup and picked up toasted cheese sandwiches, Sister Helen explained that Father Kowolski would be available for confession in the afternoon. Confession no longer had to take place in one of those dark booths in a church. "Say, between two and four. He can use my room, and we'll set up a couple of chairs and a small screen." Olivia thought she caught Pete glancing at her. It would be ten or fifteen minutes when they could be alone. Risky, though, because what if she emerged from the room with her hair messed up? With her shirt untucked?

As it turned out, only a few people took up the confession offer, and they were all nuns. Olivia thought it might look funny if she were the only lay person. Instead, she walked the two blocks to the beach and watched the wind-swept waves slap the sand, sending up plumes of spray. She imagined walking there with him, how they'd have their arms around each other, maybe find some shells to take home. Maybe they would even risk a kiss. But he was back at the house, and it was a beach walk they would not take together, at least not this weekend.

The next morning, she was in the living room drinking tea when everyone else straggled in. Pete was staying in the house next door (she wouldn't have slept a wink knowing he was under the same roof), and his group had just come in when Florence, the math teacher who was in charge of breakfast, discovered they had forgotten to bring syrup. "We can't have pancakes without syrup!"

"No problem," Sister Helen said. "There's a small market less than a mile away."

Pete hadn't taken off his jacket yet. "I'll go. My car's right out front, and I want to pick up a paper." He looked around the room. "But I may need a navigator. Anyone want to come along?" His eyes fell on Olivia, who was pretending to read a book. "Olivia?"

Did she? Understatement of the weekend. "Why not? I actually forgot to bring ChapStick." She hadn't, but she congratulated herself on her quick thinking. "Let me get my shoes." She made herself walk slowly to her room, though she felt like doing cartwheels. They'd only have a few minutes to be alone, but it was better than nothing.

"I'll warm up the car," Pete said. "It's the black Fairlane." She loved the way he was pretending that she wouldn't know his car. She told her mouth not to grin.

After crossing the main avenue in town, several blocks from the house, he pulled over on a side street. There were no cars in the driveways, and the houses had that dark look of nobody inside, shades drawn, junk mail sticking out of mailboxes. Olivia couldn't tell if he reached for her or she reached for him, but in less than thirty seconds, their arms were around each other and they were kissing, deep, crushing kisses. "I've been wanting to do this ever since I arrived. You can't imagine how hard it's been." His lips grazed the spot right behind her ear and a shiver ran down to her toes.

"I know," Olivia said, bringing her hand up to his face and leaning in again to kiss him. "I even almost came to confession."

They laughed then, and he put the car in gear and drove to the store.

CHAPTER 27

WINTER DRAGGED ALONG with several desultory snowfalls, snow that looked lovely as it drifted down but turned to gray slush on the ground. The night in the Virginia motel and the staff retreat seemed months in the past as the groundhog's prediction proved true and the temperatures rarely rose above the low thirties. Olivia caught a miserable cold and missed three days of school, staying home drinking instant soup and watching soap operas on TV. Rebecca brought home oranges from the market and dumplings from the Chinese take-out place down the block. Pete had to go to New Jersey for a workshop, and he was away for a weekend. Olivia cursed the weather, her health, and life in general.

Most of the time, when she had been well, it had been too cold for them to meet in his car, and they had to settle for phone calls. Once he mentioned again going to get a dog from the shelter, but then he said he didn't think it was a good idea for them to be seen together, even if it was absolutely innocent. She wondered if he was avoiding being with her, wondered if she had placed too much importance on their night together back in January. To her, that night meant commitment. It had to have been the same for him. Her parents and the nuns at school had stressed "waiting until marriage," and while she didn't accept that as a hard and fast rule, she also was not about to sleep with someone with-out the assurance that he was serious about her. That they were serious about each other. She and Pete had not talked about that in so many words. The magnetic pull they felt for each other overrode a lot of the opportunities for conversation. There were times when she wished they could talk more, but when she was with him, her rational mind shut down. And he did still call, and he sounded like his old self on the phone, so she told herself to stop worrying. He told her how much he missed being with her. And at Mass, when he walked up and down the aisles shaking hands at the Kiss of Peace, she thought he held her hand a beat longer than the usual few seconds, sensed his green eyes resting on her face. There was a mission project meeting, and she felt the electricity between them, even though he was across the room. But not being able to touch was torture, and she was afraid to look at him lest her eyes give her away. So she folded flyers and stuffed cartons and tried to keep her hands from shaking.

And then one night, at the end of February, he called and said, in a voice that sounded husky and low, "We need to see each other." A thrill ran through her like an electric current. The phone calls were good, but not a substitute for actually being together. Just seeing him at church, maybe exchanging a few words at the coffee hour, made her feel distant and lonely, even though he was right in front of her. He explained that he'd been busy writing college recommendation letters, and had that trip to New Jersey, and had been roped into helping with the confirmation class at St. Andrew's. She felt his voice go straight into her, and she sank down to the living room floor, winding the phone cord around her hand, as if she could feel the vibrations from his voice.

She looked out the window, where a dark rain fell. As much as she wanted to see Pete, she didn't want to go out in the cold rain and risk getting sick again.

As if he read her thoughts, he laughed. "Surely not now, but I had a better idea."

Rebecca was down the hall in her room, with the door open. Olivia kept her voice low. "Not going to see the planes land at the airport again, I hope."

He rushed ahead, as if he hadn't heard her. "How about going to Annapolis this weekend?" He said he knew some great seafood places, there was a motel right on the water, and the town would be pretty much deserted. "Even the Naval Academy is closed for some sort of late winter break." Annapolis? He proposed leaving early Saturday and spending the whole day there as well as the next day, because there was a mission at the parish and he wasn't on the Mass schedule.

She told Rebecca she was going to visit a college friend who had moved to Baltimore. She packed that midnight blue nightie again, along with a warm robe. He told her where to leave her car, on a street where Rebecca wouldn't see it, and they met early in the morning before it was even fully light. She brought peanut butter cookies and some granola for snacking.

This was something she had wanted for so long. To be with him out in daylight. To be an ordinary couple. Pete was right, and most of the Annapolis streets were empty. It was still raining lightly, and they walked beneath an umbrella through the drizzle, looking into shop windows. They found a maritime museum and they wandered through the quiet rooms, holding hands, sometimes pausing to kiss behind a pillar. At first she didn't know if they should be so open, but he assured her it was perfectly safe. They were an hour away from D.C. As they meandered over the cobblestone streets, looking for somewhere to eat lunch, she felt just like the other couples they saw, though there weren't many of them. Did they look like an ordinary couple? She in her turquoise ski jacket, he in his khaki parka. An ordinary couple walking down an ordinary street ducking into an ordinary café for a sandwich. Was that what people would see?

And yet she felt strange, as if she were acting in a film. Because as much as she enjoyed it, as much as she liked seeing their reflections in the mirror of the restaurant where they ended up for lunch, she knew this wasn't their real life. Tomorrow afternoon they would go back to their public lives, where he wore a Roman collar and she answered to Miss Prescott, the single woman who taught tenth graders how to write an essay. She told herself to enjoy it, to make the most of every moment, but she felt like she was watching colored sand pour through an hour glass, knowing what made her so happy was so temporary.

After lunch, in his car, he nuzzled her neck and said, "I've had enough sightseeing for a while. Let's go to the motel."

And they did, and they made love, and outside the rain increased. After, he kept himself folded around her, where to her all that mattered was their breathing together, the warm truth of his skin. They fell asleep to the drum of rain on the window.

Later, they drank chianti and ate spaghetti with clams in a dimly lit restaurant. He acted like any date would, holding the door for her, pulling out her chair, passing her the basket of rolls before taking one himself. But that feeling of play-acting returned, the realization that in less than twenty-four hours she would be back in her apartment and he would be in the rectory, and maybe it would feel as if it had never happened.

CHAPTER 28

MAYBE IT HAD been the drizzle in Annapolis that had dampened her spirits, because in a few weeks her misgivings disappeared and it became a spring she would never forget. If she made a list of everything that was good, she would cover sheets of paper front and back. Sometimes she had to shake herself to see if it was really true, if she was really this happy. Was this what it was, to be in love? She had never felt this way before. Certainly not with Trevor, who was so straight-laced and practical, whose idea of making out was just deep kissing, which she liked, but nothing more. And not with any of the other guys she went out with in college. She had fun. She enjoyed their company. But she didn't go home and lie awake all night replaying every moment with them.

She didn't know much about Pete's dating life, way back before he went to seminary. She asked him once that weekend in Annapolis. "Tell me about your old girlfriends."

He laughed. "That was all so long ago. I barely remember their names." And then he had mumbled something about her being the only one for him as he put his arms around her and began kissing her.

After the gray winter, spring arrived as on a sudden exhale. By mid-March the crocuses were peeking out of the ground, and the forsythias were thick with bright green buds. Back in Minnesota, there would still be snow, the landscape gray in winter's long grip. As she drove to school. she rolled the windows all the way down, letting her hair blow free.

She met Pete a couple evenings a week, coming home afterward too excited to sleep. Often, Rebecca was working the night shift, and Olivia would wander around the apartment, jumping from one task to another. Ironing a skirt. Alphabetizing the record albums. Inventorying the pantry shelves. Finally, bleary-eyed at two in the morning, she'd set her alarm and fall into a deep sleep. Sometimes she ate lunch in her classroom and allowed herself a nap at her desk. She didn't care. Exhaustion was a small price to pay to be with Pete.

They still met on a side street where she would leave her car and drive with him. They were careful not to have it be the same place every time, because now that the days were growing longer, someone might notice. There were a few more trips to the edge of the airport, a few more times when he showed her the constellations, standing close behind her as she learned to focus the telescope. The nearness of him, his breath at her ear, made her dizzy, and her fingers fumbled as she turned the magnifying rings. Mostly, though, they drove to a deserted parking lot or a street with few houses, and made out in the back seat. He apologized that it had to be this way, that they couldn't meet out in the open. "Someday," he whispered, and she believed him. She often wondered if this was the way it had begun for Greg and Marianne, the couple from the mission project. Had they begun seeing each other while he was still a priest, and she a nun?

They started going to his school classroom. The building, as he promised, was always dark in the evening, and there wasn't a night watchman or an alarm. He let them in a side door that was shaded by trees and led her along a corridor, up a flight of stairs, and down another corridor to his classroom. She couldn't see much without the lights on, but she tried to memorize the shapes of furniture, and she imagined Pete standing at the blackboard or perching on the desk as he taught his history classes.

She was sure he was a great teacher, that all his students adored him. Who wouldn't? She thought it strange that there was a couch in the room, but he explained that it was a great place to have one-on-one conferences, and he confessed that sometimes in his free period he'd close the shade on the door and use the couch for a nap. They lay there in the moonlight that spilled in through the tall windows. She was excited and uneasy at the same time, because even though Pete said no one was ever in the building at night, what if just once someone did happen to come along? What if a teacher forgot an important paper, or the principal remembered a file he needed for a meeting first thing in the morning? And didn't janitors work at night? No one ever came, though, and when she asked nervously, "Suppose someone is here?" he answered, "I'll hide you in the broom closet."

It wasn't just the sex on the too-narrow couch. It was simply being with Pete, the talking, the way he made her laugh. He called her "Olive" to be funny. "My Olive." It thrilled her. She told him why she loved literature and cooking, and he described his passion for history. And if they never exactly talked about their future, she knew that's where they were headed. Why else would he want to be with her so much? Why else would they finish each other's sentences, be so interested in each other's favorite bands, relate so many childhood stories? Why else would he tell her how much he needed her, how being with her on those late evenings made his whole day worthwhile? Why else would he touch her with such tenderness? There were many times that she wanted to ask him more about what had made him want to be a priest, but it seemed inappropriate when he had his hand down her blouse. She'd ask later. Maybe some time when they were looking through his telescope. But the moment never seemed right, and she never asked. He had told her a little about his vocation when they had sat in his office, and she accepted his words, but now that they were so involved, she wanted to know if his thinking had changed. She wanted to know where she was in the picture. If she knew her better, she might have confided in Marianne, but the mission project was on hold in the spring, and anyway, she and Marianne had never spoken that much. And would it have been appropriate to talk about Pete, when he was in charge of the committee?

She couldn't conceive of their not being together. It just felt right. After a couple of hours, he took her back to her car, and she kissed him one more time, and when she drove away, she was already thinking about when they'd be together again. She often imagined them in the same car, going to their home, never being apart again.

CHAPTER 29

IT WAS GETTING harder to explain to Rebecca where she was going when she met Pete. Rebecca wasn't on night shifts at the hospital anymore, so unless she was working at the bookstore, or out on a date, she was usually around in the evening. "Who are you going out with?" she asked one evening in April, when Olivia was about to leave the apartment.

"Oh, just this guy I met at church. At one of the mission project meetings. He's—he works in the admissions office at George Washington University." Last week it had been a meeting to plan the senior prom. The week before drinks with Malcolm, a fix-up arranged by Mylene at school. She had to be careful she didn't get the names confused.

"And he's not picking you up because . . ." Rebecca raised her eyebrows.

"His roommate's borrowing his car. I said I'd meet him at the restaurant."

Rebecca sat at the dining table, playing solitaire. She shook her head and looked at Olivia.

"I think," she said, "that there's a mystery man."

"Mystery man?" Olivia tried to laugh, but her throat felt dry.

Rebecca slapped down two cards. "Those muffled phone calls. Going out with guys who never come here to pick you up. You're hiding some-thing. Or someone." She looked pointedly at Olivia.

Was she being that obvious? She had prided herself on what a good job she was doing at keeping Pete a secret. She constructed the stories of her fake dates with precision, making sure to sprinkle them with enough details. What she had to drink. What the guy was wearing. Something witty he had said. A plausible reason they didn't come to the apartment. And she had to be so careful not to contradict herself. It was exhausting. Rebecca's dates always came to pick her up. She had audible conversations on the phone with friends as she sat in the living room. And after hanging up the phone she'd talk about it with Olivia. "I have to do something about Ben's taste in movies. I've told him I can't stand sci-fi. What's wrong with a comedy now and then?" Sometimes Olivia would slip out of the apartment ("I need Tampax/I have to drop off a roll of film/I need to get something from my car") and she'd run to the corner where there was a pay phone so she could have a brief con-versation with Pete.

She thought about telling Rebecca about him. Rebecca wasn't con-servative, wasn't judgmental. And in the months they had been room-mates they had become good friends. But Pete had made it clear that their relationship had to be kept under wraps. Not only for his sake, but for hers. "If anyone knew, Olivia . . ." he would begin, and frown. "The world is not ready for us." She loved the us part. And while she under-stood what he said, she wasn't sure the world included a roommate who was her close friend. Sometimes the secret felt too big to hold inside, and she wanted to talk about it with Rebecca. So many times she started to, to share this huge thing in her life. Still, something held her back, and she wasn't sure what it was. She clamped her lips down, swallowed the words, changed the subject.

Rebecca's insistence on the mystery man was the only reason that Olivia agreed to go out with Will. She wasn't interested in anyone but Pete, but if Rebecca actually saw her out on a date, maybe she'd give up on the mystery man idea. It would only be one date, and then she'd never have to see this Will again.

Rebecca was going to dinner with her on-again-off-again boyfriend Jackson, and he wanted to bring Will, who had recently started working at the same bank with him. "He's new to town, and he doesn't know anyone but the bank people," Rebecca explained.

"Couldn't you get one of the nurses?"

"I could, but I'd rather have you come along. Unless mystery man is—"

That decided her. How bad could it be?

Rebecca obviously heard the lack of enthusiasm in her voice when she agreed, and she said, "Lighten up, Olivia. It's just one evening. You don't have to marry the guy. And Jackson knows this restaurant where they have Peking duck." Olivia did like the idea of the duck, something she'd wanted to try.

Like that, it was settled, and Saturday evening Olivia found herself standing in front of her open closet looking for something to wear. She felt disloyal to Pete, wondered if she'd tell him. He had never asked her not to go out with other men, but she assumed he knew she didn't. Why would she even think of seeing someone else? She pulled a yellow dress out of the closet and sighed. It made her tired to think of all the effort required to keep up a conversation with a stranger.

When Jackson and Will came to pick them up, Olivia realized this was the first time since she moved here that a man had come to her apartment door to take her out. She had forgotten how to act on a normal date. The exchange of pleasantries, that awkward silence after the introductions. But Will put her at ease, complimenting her on the Andrew Wyeth print hanging over the stereo, saying he was so glad she was free. "I would have felt like the chaperone if I'd had to go with these two without a date." He was wearing chinos and a blue oxford cloth shirt and loafers. His dark brown hair was damp, as if he had just had a shower, and it curled slightly at the back where it touched his collar. Behind his tortoiseshell glasses, his brown eyes looked kind and turned up at the corners as if smiling. When they left the apartment, Will held the door for her.

They drove in Jackson's car, a dark blue Mustang convertible. He had put the top down to celebrate the heady warmth of spring. Olivia had to hold her long hair with one hand to keep it from blowing in her face. There was a lot of "where did you . . ." and "how long have you . . ." Olivia briefly wondered what would happen if Pete were to drive down Wisconsin Avenue at that same time and see her. Would he wave? Be jealous? Will sat casually with his arm out along the edge of the back seat, asking her about her teaching, about her family back in Minnesota, and she let him distract her.

The restaurant was called The Bamboo Dragon, and Jackson had to circle around before finding a space two blocks away. It was pleasant, though, walking down the sidewalk in the half-light between day and night. There were lots of other pedestrians, and bicyclists swerved around the cabs and cars in the street. Olivia was careful to loop her hand through the shoulder strap of her purse, keeping a little distance between her and Will. Rebecca and Jackson were holding hands, and Will seemed like the kind of guy who would do that as a casual gesture, but she didn't want him to get the idea that she was in any way interested. She was only on the date to placate Rebecca.

They passed on the Peking duck because it took too long to prepare, and instead ordered several platters they could share. Eggplant, dumplings, spinach noodles, sweet and sour shrimp, BBQ beef skewers. They drank an Asian beer Jackson recommended. Before they had finished the complimentary appetizer egg rolls, Olivia was surprised to find that she was having a good time. The conversation drew her in, and she laughed at herself when she refused to try eating with chopsticks. Will asked her about her favorite movies and seemed genuinely interested in her replies. He tried the eggplant, though he said he'd never eaten it before. "If you like it, it has to be good," he said, and she was flattered. He confessed that he really didn't like that many vegetables.

At the end of the meal, the waiter poured them small porcelain cups of tea and put a plate of fortune cookies on the table. Rebecca said they each had to read their fortune out loud. Will's said, "Big journeys start with a single step." He glanced at Olivia with a question in his eyes, and she pretended to be busy with shaking a packet of sugar into her tea. She didn't want him to think about asking her out. She only had room in her life for one man.

CHAPTER 30

REBECCA HAD GIVEN up on her mystery man idea, though she still tried to fix Olivia up for dates. Will had called, as Olivia was sure he would, and she went out with him several times, more to quiet Rebecca's teasing than because she liked him. They were daytime dates, and Olivia suggested things they could do that were far from her neighborhood and far from St. Andrew's. A winery tour, a hike on the Shenandoah Trail, a stroll through the gardens of Dumbarton Oaks. He wanted to take her to dinner, but she put him off. Dinner would be candlelight and wine and the possibility of an intimacy she didn't want. Evenings were for Pete. She met him at least twice a week. Suppose she said yes to dinner with Will and then Pete called at the last minute?

The more she and Pete were together, the more she wanted to be with him. She hated saying goodnight when he left her at her car, and on the ride back to her apartment she felt a rush of loneliness. When she got home, she found herself wondering what he was doing. Was he thinking about her?

She saw what their life together could be like. Finally telling Rebecca, and having Pete to dinner at the apartment, and the three of them laughing about the "mystery man." "No mystery here," he would say as he wrapped his arms around Olivia. And Rebecca, remembering the first time they had all met, would shake her head with a smile and say, "I should have known that baseball was a lucky hit."

And then taking him to meet her family, explaining that yes, he had been a priest, but he had put his vocation aside for her. He had, she would tell them, made the decision to join the priesthood when he was so young, before he truly knew what he wanted to do. And just like he charmed the people in the parish, congratulating Cynthia Baker from the choir on her scholarship to Vassar, offering to call a cab for Mrs. Ryersly on a rainy Sunday, inviting the kids in the congregation to gather at the foot of the altar, he would charm her family. They would, after their initial shock, welcome him, especially when they saw how happy Olivia was. Even her father would come around. Who could resist Pete?

It nagged at the back of her mind that Pete never said much about their future. Once she had hinted at it. They were parked on a cul-de-sac in a neighborhood under construction, surrounded by skeletons of houses and the boxy shapes of dumpsters. "Where do you see yourself in five years?" she asked. He had managed to avoid an answer, pulling her to him instead.

"With you," she wanted to hear him say. She took his kisses as a reply, but still yearned to hear the actual words. Later, she would wonder why she had not pressed him to say more, but she had been so sure he was just waiting for the right time.

Sometimes she saw Greg and Marianne at church. Marianne was just starting to wear maternity tops. It was possible. It could happen with her and Pete.

CHAPTER 31

THE EVENING AT the Chinese restaurant reminded Olivia that there was another kind of life. A life where couples were together out in the open, where they ran into friends and made plans to meet later for dinner, where they went to poetry readings in cafés, where they lounged on the grass in Rock Creek Park at a band concert, where they sat on their front steps eating ice cream, where they drove down a busy street in the middle of the day and waved to people they passed.

Pete told her they didn't need those things, that they were enough for each other. And in their early days together she believed that. She had been so captivated by him, so swept away by the heady spin of being in love, that the rest of the world fell away.

She wasn't sure when that ceased to be enough, when she had moved from wishing it could be different to wondering if she could keep going with him if it weren't. It might have been that morning of the staff retreat when she and Pete had gone for syrup. She had seen their reflection in the plate glass window of the store and for a second they were an ordinary couple out to pick up forgotten groceries and the thick Sunday paper. Or maybe it was that day in Annapolis strolling down the cobblestone streets, eating spaghetti in a hole-in-the-wall restaurant. As much as she loved being with Pete, she wanted to be with him in groups, in daylight, to hold his hand and not care who saw. She wanted to introduce him to her friends, to cook dinner for him at the apartment.

How long could they go on this way? It was spring, and ahead was summer and then the next school year and another summer. When she thought about a year from now, she couldn't see herself still making up stories for Rebecca, still meeting Pete on dark streets, still slipping away to cheap motels. Something had to change.

She and Will rented canoes and took them on the C & O Canal. They shopped at the French bakery for sandwiches to take on a picnic. They strolled through the zoo. It felt good to be out in the open with a man, to meander through a park in daylight, to duck into a restaurant on the spur of the moment to have a sandwich. It wasn't that she was attracted to Will, it was that she liked what she could do with Will. She wanted to pluck Will out of the picture and insert Pete. She thought then that she would be happy. Now she felt like she was only half living, and the hiding made her lonely for what she was missing. Pete, however, seemed perfectly happy to keep on with what they were doing. He taught her about the more complicated settings on his telescope, how to bring the stars into greater focus, and he took her to a park on the bank of the Potomac River down toward Alexandria that was always deserted at night. Later, she would remember that these outings always included a flask or bottle of scotch. At the time, she accepted his explanation that it would help them to relax after a long day of teaching teenagers. He insisted that they didn't need other people, because they had each other.

Her summer plans were hazy. She might take a job at an ecology camp in Maine she had heard about (there was an opening for an assistant cook). The camp ran sessions for adults and kids where they could go birding, learn kayaking, and take nature hikes. She might do temp work in D.C. She might apply for a job at the bookstore where Rebecca worked. Holy Redeemer had summer sessions, but she needed a break from teaching. When she asked Pete about his plans, he said he was teaching summer school, coaching a diocesan Little League team, maybe visiting the mission in El Salvador. He didn't say anything about what they could do together, and she assumed it would be more clandestine meetings. Reluctantly, she accepted that they wouldn't be sitting together on a beach or feeding the seals at the zoo. But the more she thought about it, the more she added to her list of what they couldn't do, and the more she knew she wanted those things. She felt cheated out of what everyone else had.

It came to a head for her at a wedding shower. Annette, the music teacher at Holy Redeemer, was getting married, and her sister Lisle was throwing a shower for her. Lisle lived in a row house in Georgetown, and the guests gathered in the tiny walled garden in the back. It was a May afternoon, the azaleas were blooming, and they sat drinking champagne cocktails and eating finger sandwiches and the heart-shaped cookies Olivia had brought.

Annette's mother had come from Toledo, and Olivia saw how happy she was. Her daughter getting married—every mother's dream. Olivia thought of her own mother, how thrilled she'd be if she were mother of the bride. Years ago she had bought several yards of Belgian lace. "For your wedding veil," she said as she packed it away in tissue paper. Did she take it out of the dresser drawer where she stored it and finger it every now and then, daydreaming about Olivia as a bride?

It was time to open the gifts, and Annette carefully removed the wrapping from each box. Lisle kept the bows; they would form the "bouquet" Annette would carry at the rehearsal. There was a stand mixer, pale green placemats, a spice rack. Olivia envied her friend, wishing she were the one opening the boxes. Not that she wanted the things. It wasn't about the mixer or the hand-embroidered towels. It was about knowing her life was settled, that at the end of every day there was the man she loved and that they were creating a home together, raising children, going to PTA meetings. She had grown up with two brothers and a gaggle of cousins. Children were part of the equation. Mostly, it was about believing in a sure future. It was about belonging. She couldn't imagine being single her whole life, like Aunt Mamie. She wanted to create a family and have the house where everyone came for Thanksgiving dinner.

Annette was exclaiming over wooden salad tongs. Olivia plucked the strawberry out of her wine and let its sweetness dissolve on her tongue. In three weeks, school would be out for the year. She had to make a decision about the summer. And beyond the summer. What then? Pete brushed her off every time she tried to bring it up, and he silenced her with kisses, but she couldn't keep on the way they were without knowing they were going somewhere. They had slept together. To her, that meant commitment. He had to know that, and she couldn't believe it didn't mean commitment to him as well.

When she allowed herself to consider that it might not, she grew cold with fear. And then she swatted the idea away. Of course, he loved her. And didn't loving her mean he wanted what she wanted? Didn't loving her mean knowing how she felt and what she needed? She put her glass down on the flagstone patio. The champagne had grown flat and warm. She realized she had been making a lot of assumptions. He had never actually *said* forever, or *said* marriage, or even spoken about the two of them in the future tense. It was always the moment, where they were right then. That had been fine for a while, but she didn't think she could continue this way for years, even months. Now without knowing about their future.

She would talk to him, not let him change the subject. She'd have to rehearse her words carefully. She didn't want to nag, to be insistent, to make ultimatums. She'd never been that way. But gently, tactfully, she would steer the conversation. And he would respond saying hadn't she known he loved her, hadn't she known he was just waiting for the right time to talk about their future?

CHAPTER 32

THEY MET AT a bar just beyond the airport. It was the kind of place where you'd never see anyone you know, a place frequented by travelers unwinding after a long flight or people with time to waste before departure. The neon sign in the window, blue letters supposed to spell out "cocktails," was missing the first C.

Olivia arrived first, and she waited in her car in the parking lot. Pete had a dinner meeting at his school, but he promised to be there by eight. She rolled down the window, listening to the whine of jets overhead, wishing her car had air-conditioning. It made her remember that first night with Pete watching the planes land. That was so long ago. It was quarter after eight when his Fairlane nosed into the space next to hers.

When she saw the way he unfolded his lanky body from the car, a sizzle of happiness ran through her. It was like this whenever she saw him. He locked his car and hurried over to open her door, apologizing profusely for being late. They stood together for a moment, and he trailed his fingers through her hair, tucking it behind her ear. She leaned into his shoulder, her 5'6" frame a perfect fit to his almost six feet. She inhaled his scent of spicy aftershave and clean cotton.

Inside, Pete led them to a booth away from the ceiling speaker coughing out twangy country music. There were two men drinking from long-necked beer bottles at the bar and a middle-aged couple at a table across the room. The bartender leaned on the counter, watching a baseball game on the muted wall-mounted TV. It wasn't the romantic setting she had hoped for. But they slid in next to each other, and he leaned over and gave her a quick kiss. It tasted faintly like garlic.

As soon as they sat down, Pete shook a cigarette out from the pack he carried in his shirt pocket. He was wearing a red and blue plaid sport shirt, the sleeves still sharply creased. Flicking his cigarette lighter open, he held the cigarette to the flame and took a long, slow inhale. Out of reflex, Olivia waved the drifting smoke away.

"I know," he said. "It's a filthy habit, but it was a really long day." As if sensing her displeasure, he stubbed it out after four more deep draws. She didn't know that for years the smell of cigarette smoke would bring his face back to her.

A waitress whose gray roots were showing through her blond ponytail wandered over and took their order. Scotch neat for Pete. Campari and soda for Olivia. She didn't really feel like drinking. She was nervous about what she planned to say. Nervous about how he would react. She had rehearsed her words, imagined his reaction. It would be fine, she had told herself. He would say just what she wanted him to say. They talked for a few minutes about inconsequential things. Her students' fixation on the coming prom. His dinner meeting with the dean. She hardly knew what she was saying, and she barely heard him when he made quiet humorous remarks about the couple across the room staring into their glasses and not talking. Pete put his hand on her thigh.

She turned so she could look at him. "Pete," she said, "there's something we have to talk about."

"Uh-oh. Not the old 'we have to talk' line. That's never good." He stretched his arms out across the back of the booth. He seemed relaxed, and he let his fingers play through her hair again.

She forced herself to laugh. She wanted to keep it light, at least in the beginning. "No, nothing like that." Though, really, wasn't it?

He reached toward his pocket for his cigarettes, stopped, and took a long pull on his drink. "Shoot," he said, his eyes twinkling. His hand went back to her thigh, and her skin felt warm under the denim of her skirt.

"So, I've been thinking."

"About?"

"About the summer." Take it slow. Lead in with this.

"Right. Is your plan still to go to Maine?"

She hadn't made a firm decision yet. On the one hand, D.C. was hot and humid during the summer, and temp jobs would be boring. She'd done that already. Plus, part of her reason for moving east had been to see new parts of the country, and she'd always heard about Maine lobsters. But it would mean not seeing Pete for over two months. "I thought I was, but I haven't told them yet. And I'm not sure. I'm—I'm thinking it will be a long time for us to be apart."

"Two months. How will I get along without you?" His tone was playful, and he moved his fingers in circles on her thigh. She wanted him to say more about how much he'd miss her, because if he did, maybe she would take those temp jobs.

"Ten weeks, actually," she said, "and it's almost six hundred miles away." She waited for him to say something more, and that song about "500 miles" started to spool through her head. At first, she thought that maybe he could come to visit her, but when she looked at a map and realized the distance, she knew it would be too far. He'd never be able to get the time off from summer school.

He nodded and ran his finger around the rim of his glass. "You're not worried about that, are you? About being in a new place, like you were last fall. Because, really, you'll be fine."

Did he really think it could be about being in a new place? She was long past those panic attacks, long past feeling insecure about where she was. In fact, she could barely remember what that felt like. Traveling to

Maine was no more intimidating than going to a different grocery store. She had done so many new things, been in so many unfamiliar places. There was something offensive about his assuming she was still the insecure person she had been back in the fall. She wanted him to hear that she wanted to be close to him, and she wanted him to echo her feelings.

"Of course not. I'm not worried about going there, and I'll be an apprentice cook. I've just been thinking about the time away and about what it will be like for us after the summer."

He swallowed the rest of his drink. "I will be dancing in the streets with joy and everyone will be wondering what got into Father Kowolski. After the summer, we'll have a passionate reunion, and I'll find someplace we can go for three days where no one will be able to disturb us."

The image made her want to grin, but it didn't answer the question that was brewing in her head. And it sounded like he was joking. "It's just—it's just that I don't know where we are."

He tilted his head to look at her. "Where we are?"

Was he being deliberately obtuse? "Maybe who we are. Who we are together."

"I think we're just about perfect," Pete said, picking up his empty glass and setting it down again.

"We are. But the secrecy, the sneaking around. How long can we keep doing that?"

Pete sighed deeply. "I've explained that, Olivia. You know we can't let anyone know. What it would do to your reputation, to mine—"

"I know, and it's fine for now. It's been fine. But it's not enough forever. At some point we have to—"

"We have to what? Tell the world that Father Kowolski and Miss Prescott are having an affair? Can you imagine what the good ladies of the altar society would say? Or what that laced-up-too-tight Sister Helen would think? Do you want to be a headline in the *Catholic Standard*?" He shook his head as he chuckled, but she heard a bitter tone under his words.

Olivia stopped listening after the word "affair." If that was how he saw it, it made her feel cheap. Affairs were flings. Affairs rarely ended in marriage. Affairs were fodder for scandal.

"An affair? What we have is more than that, isn't it?" She hoped her voice didn't reveal the trembling she felt.

"What we have is all we can have," Pete said, gently.

Was that true? She watched the future she had constructed start to crumble. Surely, he didn't mean it. Surely, he meant to add the word "now." Surely he wasn't discounting their whole future. He made it sound like they were at a dead end.

"But I thought we—" She thought they were going to be together for life. Sex to her meant commitment. How could they not be going somewhere?

He interrupted her. "Don't you know I wish it were different?" He turned to look directly at her. Across the room, the bartender changed the music to something more blues-y, and the drawn-out notes of a saxophone snaked through the bar.

"I thought I did." Because if he really wanted it to be different, he would make it different. Was Pete really saying that this was all there would be? She had let herself hope for so much more. She had seen what their life together would look like. Moving to a new city. Getting an apartment. Starting a family. Years of being together. A lifetime. That Belgian lace fashioned into a long veil.

Pete put his arm around her. When he spoke, his voice was low, close to her ear. "I'd give anything to turn back the clock. To have met you in another life, in college, say, or grad school. To have taken you to dances and ice-skating and to movies. To have met your family and introduced you to mine. But we can't do that. We're right here, in this moment, and we are who we are now."

Olivia found her voice. "But it doesn't have to be this way." She thought again about Greg and Marianne. "There are choices."

"I made my choice. Four years ago when I took my vows."

The room hollowed out around her. She inched away from him, folding her arms around herself. If he never intended to leave the priesthood, why did he do all those things with her?

The couple across the room left, he dragging a wheeled suitcase. A low flying plane shook the windows, and the lights flickered. Olivia looked at Pete and saw a stranger. She could almost count her heartbeats as she waited for him to speak. She noticed little things she had overlooked earlier. White rings on the table where glasses had sat, the blue neon light making the room look as if it were underwater, a jagged tear in the vinyl seat covering. The silence stretched out, a taut string. Would he see how upset she was, how much his words were bruising her?

Finally, he spoke. "It doesn't mean things have to change. We're not like other people. We can make our own rules."

That was what they had been doing, but those rules weren't going to work anymore. Those rules had been fine when they were temporary, in the first days and weeks they had been together, but she couldn't live the rest of her life this way. She had assumed the sneaking around would stop, that he would declare himself for her, that he would leave the priesthood. That was the main reason she had kept seeing him. It wasn't a fling. It wasn't an "affair." Anger and hurt flooded through her. He had known all along that it wouldn't be anything more. When they kissed in his office, when they went to buy the Christmas tree. The whispered phone conversations. The weekend in Annapolis. He must have known, because he professed to know her so well, that she would have seen all those things as signs of commitment. Hadn't she shared enough about her life for him to know that she came from a conservative background, that she didn't take her actions lightly, that even their first kiss had been a big deal for her? And yet he had chosen not to say anything to her. He had assumed she would go along with this. Thirty minutes ago, he had been the man she loved. Now she felt like she didn't know him at all. Or more importantly, that he didn't know her. Her throat was dry.

And she was angry at herself, too, for putting so much faith into something that wasn't going to work. Why hadn't she asked him months earlier how he saw their relationship? Not allowed him to silence her tentative questions with passionate kisses? How could she have been so naïve? Had she wanted him so badly that she could not see he misled her? She had devoted months of her life to a man who could so casually refer to their relationship as an affair. He might have been joking about that, but none of it was amusing to her.

Finally, she shook her head. "I can't do that." It was all she could say. And then she slid out of the booth, rose on unsteady legs. The twenty-two steps to the door of the bar was the longest distance she had ever walked.

CHAPTER 33

OLIVIA MOVED ON automatic pilot through the last days of school. June clamped down with heat, and the students were restless, already tasting summer. The senior girls chattered about college, about boys, their minds a million miles away from school. Had it only been six years since she had been like that? Six years since she had seen her life mapped out in clear steps? College, yes, and then a career (she hadn't known what yet), love and marriage and a future secured. It seemed like sixty.

Every time the phone rang in the apartment, her heart jumped. It would be Pete. He had changed his mind. He wanted to talk. He couldn't live without her. But it never was. It was for Rebecca, or it was her mother ("Will you be home at all this summer?"), or it was someone from school. An invitation to an end-of-the-year barbecue. A reminder from the dentist. She'd sink down on the couch, chiding herself for hoping.

Aubrey called to tell her about the baby (pregnant after only five months!) and Olivia tried to sound excited, but she zoned out and cut the call short, making some excuse. *Rebecca needs the phone. We'll talk later.* It wasn't that she was envious, or that she wished any less happiness for her friend. She just didn't know how to absorb someone else's joy. Her own sadness made her feel too heavy to move.

Everything sucked the energy from her. Writing report cards. Putting gas in her car. Getting out of bed in the morning. Smiling. Even eating. All day all she wanted to do was sleep, but when she fell into bed at night her eyes wouldn't close. She kept seeing Pete. His iridescent green eyes. That small scar across his nose. The way he drove with his elbow resting on the door.

And then there was the final half-day, the seniors in their white dresses, the handing out of diplomas, the reception in the gym with ginger ale punch and bite-sized chocolate chip cookies. *You must be so proud of Denise/Cheryl/Andrea.* In her classroom, airless with the closed windows, she checked that the textbooks were stowed in the closet, the staples removed from the bulletin boards, the desk drawers empty. She turned in her room key and grade book to the office. *Yes, it was a wonderful year.* She forced a smile on her face as she said good-bye to the teachers heading to their cars, to Sister Helen, as she gave a cheery wave. *See you in September.*

She knew she shouldn't, but she drove by the rectory on her way home. What would she do if he happened to be on the street or coming down the front steps? She wasn't sure she could talk to him, should talk to him. Why was she there, then? And would he recognize her car and flag her down? It had been two weeks since that night at the bar. Surely, he hadn't put her out of his mind. Surely, he missed her as much as she missed him. How could it be otherwise? But it was early afternoon, and she was relieved and disappointed that the street was deserted except for a woman pushing a stroller, a college student on a bicycle.

CHAPTER 34

OLIVIA WAS IN her room, intending to pack for camp. Her enthusiasm was tepid at best. Driving all the way to Maine. Hanging around birdwatchers and kayakers held little appeal. The only draw was getting away from D.C. Her suitcase was open on the bed, and she had put in a pair of jeans when she picked up her favorite necklace, the one with the turquoise and silver beads, and noticed the clasp had broken. And then something came over her, a sense of futility. What did it matter whether she took the khaki shorts or the madras? What did it matter how many pairs of socks she packed? Suddenly, it was all too much, and everything from the past two weeks rushed over her, and she was throwing T-shirts and jeans, nightgowns and sweaters on the rug, yanking dresses off their hangers with so much force the wire bent. She sank down on the rug, shaking, and that's where Rebecca found her when she came home from her hospital shift.

"Olivia, what is—" She stopped as she looked around the room.

"I'm packing," Olivia said, and then she began to cry. Not the kind of silent crying she usually did, tears leaking from her eyes, but all-out sobbing. Her shoulders shuddered. Snot dripped from her nose and she didn't care. She was only half aware of Rebecca hunched down beside her, one arm encircling her. Once her tears started, she didn't know if she could ever stop.

"It looks more like a hurricane struck in here," Rebecca said in a gentle voice. "What's going on?"

Olivia had no words to explain it. One minute she had been wondering if she should take more than one sweatshirt, and the next she was angry at every single piece of clothing. She still held the necklace, and she took a breath and lifted it up. "The clasp is broken." That started her tears again.

Stroking Olivia's back, Rebecca looked puzzled. "We can fix that. I have those tiny tweezers. But is that all?" She tried a quiet laugh. "I know you said you were packing, but shouldn't the clothes go *in* the suitcase?"

Olivia drew in a long, ragged breath.

Rebecca stood, kicked off her shoes, and began picking up T-shirts. "What is it? You've been moping around here for the past couple of weeks. I've been worried about you."

Olivia shook her head, wiping her cheeks with her fists. "Don't worry. I'm fine." But she was anything but fine. Food had no flavor. She hadn't washed her hair in three days. She had driven over a curb parking her car because she thought she saw him down the street.

"I don't think so. This isn't what fine looks like." She set aside the purple T-shirt she was folding and sat on the floor next to Olivia, reaching over to take her hand.

Something in Rebecca's voice opened Olivia, and she told her. The whole story. Everything from last fall and the counseling and her growing friendship with Pete. The first kiss and the wine in the rectory and the meetings in his car. She told her about the trip to Annapolis and the motels and how Pete showed her how to work his telescope. She told her how it had to be a secret and how they had a special phone code and how they met in out-of-the-way bars. She said he loved her but he loved being a priest more and she had thought he'd leave the priesthood. When she stopped, the silence was loud with the echo of her words.

And then she started to cry again, picking up a scratchy white sweater to blot her eyes.

Rebecca wrapped her arms around Olivia. "I'm so sorry, so sorry. I wish you had told me. I wish I had known. All those months, and you kept it to yourself. And Pete—the baseball guy—I never would have guessed." She shook her head. "And all the jokes I made about the mystery man—"

Olivia sniffled, took in a big wobbly breath of air. "How would you have known? I wanted to tell you, I did, but Pete said it had to be a secret. He said if anyone knew—"

"That they would have talked some sense into you." Rebecca clapped her hand over her mouth. "I didn't mean to say that. It's just that there's a difference between putting an article in the paper and telling your best friend. It wasn't fair of him to demand that of you."

Olivia had never considered this. Pete had made it so clear that it was for her protection, that it was to protect her reputation. She had had misgivings, mostly at first, but even when they started sleeping together she had wondered if she was in over her head. That was when she should have talked to someone. She remembered starting to tell Aubrey at Christmas. But it was all right, she had told herself, because he loved her. And didn't love trump all the rules? Would Rebecca have helped her see it differently? Or would she have assured her what she was doing was fine, that love was fine? If Rebecca had voiced her objections, would she have even listened to her?

Rebecca went around the room, picking up the nightgowns and dresses and T-shirts. "Well, you've told me now, and now I'm going to take care of you. You just sit there. I'll clean this up. We'll worry about all this stuff tomorrow. I'll help you pack. You still have three days until you leave."

She brought Olivia a cold washcloth for her face. "Come on, I'll make a salad. There's an open bottle of wine in the fridge. And if you want to talk some more, fine. If you want me to go throw raw eggs at Pete's door, fine."

Olivia managed a tiny smile. Inside, the fist of hurt loosened just a bit. She allowed Rebecca to take care of her, even managed a few bites of salad, and fell asleep on the couch to the sound of water running in the kitchen sink.

CHAPTER 35

A SMALL BIRD with rosy feathers landed soundlessly on the railing of the porch where Olivia sat late one afternoon. She'd been in Maine for ten days and had not had time to learn the names of the birds that perched and flew around the small island. Grayson, the camp director, had given her a tattered bird book, but so far, she'd been too busy to look at it. Busy, or asleep. Because when she wasn't working, she burrowed into her narrow bed. She spent her mornings working in the camp office, a small cabin right up the path from the dock, sorting mail, handing out extra towels, answering the phone, arranging boat trips, doling out maps of the island to the campers. A new group came from the mainland every week—birders, kayakers, and people who just wanted to enjoy a few days in a quiet, peaceful setting. In the afternoons she helped Noah, the cook, with dinner prep. After the evening meal, there were usually activities for the campers like slide shows, lectures, or night kayaking. She might take a walk down by the water or retreat to her room to read. Her light was out by nine. She thought sleep might help her forget.

Before she left D.C., she talked to Pete once on the phone. He called and asked her to come by his office, to "sort things through," but she refused. It would be too hard to see him and know he would be on his side of the desk, she in a chair on the other side. It would be the same chair she had sat in all those Tuesdays, and she didn't want to be reminded of where they had begun. It would only underscore the distance they were now required to keep. And more, what would it accomplish? They had each made their decisions. The phone conversation lasted less than five minutes. She had no more words for him, and it hurt too much to hear his voice.

Today the mail brought a letter from him, and it lay on her lap, unopened. The camp was quiet, almost everyone on the other side of the island looking for osprey. The mail arrived before noon, but she set the letter on the corner of her desk, telling herself it was because she had to report to the kitchen, but knowing she was afraid to open it. What could he say that he hadn't already? And did words matter? Would words make her feel better? Or, and she dared to hold on to a strand of hope, had he reconsidered? And if he had, what would she reply? She made herself clear that night in the bar, and she was afraid he would ask her to compromise somehow. She wouldn't do that.

She spent the afternoon shucking corn for chowder, dicing potatoes. Now she had a free hour, and she looked at the unopened envelope. The sun was warm on her shoulders. The bird tilted its head toward her, as if encouraging her to read the letter. She slid her finger under the flap and pulled out three sheets of white stationery with boxy cursive written in blue ballpoint.

Dear Olivia,

You made the right decision to leave this hot, humid city. I hope you are staying cool up in Maine and enjoying some of those lobsters you talked about.

I'll get to the point. You asked me why I got involved with you. I've given this a lot of thought since you left, and I hope my answer will help you understand. I thought I could be a different person. I thought I could be a priest and also share my love with you. I fell for you that first day on the baseball field, and as I got to know you better through the mission project, I saw a beautiful young woman I admired so much.

And then, you came to me for counseling, having those panic attacks. I wanted to help you, to get you back on track. And all those conversations we had—it just felt like we clicked. I would wake up every Tuesday morning knowing I'd see you that afternoon, and it made the whole day brighter. Your smile, your stories. As we became friends, I knew it was ok. Why not be friends with you? Who wouldn't be?

But before long, I realized that it was more than friendship. I was falling in love with you, and I thought I could handle it. I could do both. Because one didn't feel like it had anything to do with the other. I could say Mass and hear confessions and teach high school and show up for social events at the church and I could also see you, be with you. They were two separate things and both were very real. Both were so important to me.

I never thought you would see anything more to it than what it was. You always seemed happy with the way things were, you always seemed to accept that I had this other life. After all, we had so many of our meetings in a church rectory.

There were so many times that I thought about leaving the priesthood, about being with you for the rest of my life. But then something would happen. A late-night phone call about a parishioner needing last rites, and that drive through quiet neighborhoods bringing Christ to her. Being the voice and hands of the church at the bedside of a dying man. It's too powerful for words. Or I'd be standing at the altar saying the words of the consecration over the bread and wine, and they did become not bread and wine but the body and blood of Christ. Through my hands. The word sacrament began to have new meaning to me, and I saw so much of what I did in my priestly role as truly holy.

I realized I couldn't revoke those vows I took, even in the face of such deep love for you. They had to take precedence. They were my life. They had been my first choice, and I had to stand by them.

I don't say this without pain. You can't know how hard it's been for me. And to see your disappointment, your sadness, is like a knife turning in me. If I could do anything to make this easier for you, I would.

Please let us continue to be friends. I know we can't go back to where we were. But you will always be in my heart, and I can't imagine my life without you in it in some way.

Pete

Olivia hadn't realized she was crying until the ink blurred in the last paragraph. She wiped her eyes with the back of her hand. In the next few days, she would reread the letter so many times that there would be phrases she'd memorize. She would keep the letter for years, pushing it to the back of a drawer, unwilling to let it go.

When she finally folded the letter and looked up, the little bird had flown away.

CHAPTER 36

IT WAS DAY sixty-five. Olivia had been counting the days since she had broken up with Pete. At first, she thought that as the numbers grew it would get easier. Maybe once she made it to thirty she could start counting by months instead of days. But she had arrived at the one-month mark (June 20) and had kept going one day at a time. Thirty-one and thirty-five and forty-eight. His letter had arrived on day forty-five. And now on day sixty-five, she still felt raw.

It seemed that the smallest thing could bring him back. Words from a song overheard from an open window, a roll of Lifesavers, the scent of lime. One day soon after she arrived she rode the ferry over to the town on her afternoon off, wandering down the streets, window-shopping. There was a dark Fairlane outside of the drug store, and her breath stopped. But it had Vermont plates. Of course, it wasn't Pete. She had told him she didn't want to see him.

On this morning in late July, she was sitting in the office sorting the mail she collected from the eleven o'clock ferry. Since she had been here, Rebecca had sent her a couple of postcards, and her mother sent hometown newspaper clippings she thought Olivia would enjoy. And of course, the long letter from Pete that was now nestled among her T-shirts. Today there was nothing for her, just a camp bank statement, an electric bill, a few letters for campers, and the latest issue of *Yankee* magazine. She put the letters in a pile to take over to lunch, set aside the official pieces for Grayson, and thumbed idly through the magazine. An article about an artist who made jewelry from feathers, a recipe for pineapple upside down cake, scenes of mountain hiking trails.

The sun fell in wide drowsy swaths over the wooden boards of the office floor. The door was open to catch breezes through the screen, and it brought in snatches of birdsong. She really should sweep the porch and straighten the bookshelves, but she felt too lethargic. Half-reading an article on lighthouses, she was aware of a subtle change in the light. A long shadow fell across the floor, and she glanced up at the screen door and saw him backlit on the porch. Her breath caught in her throat. She would know those shoulders anywhere.

Had he changed his mind? Had he come all the way to Maine to tell her he couldn't live without her? Her hand reached up out of habit to push her hair behind her ear, and she rose from the chair so quickly it almost toppled. All of the sadness that had dragged her down lifted up and swirled away, and her mouth opened in a wide smile.

And then the screen door opened, and he stepped out of the sun.

It wasn't Pete.

It was Will.

He was grinning and holding out a bunch of white daisies wrapped in lavender tissue paper. Olivia couldn't think of a thing to say because he was the last person she expected to see. There were the obvious questions she could ask, like what was he doing here and how had he known how to find her, but her voice had dried up. A group of people walked by the cabin, laughing. The bell on the dining hall porch clanged to announce lunch.

Will didn't look anything like Pete. He was shorter, and his shoulders were not as broad. He had that hair that erupted into curls if he didn't tame it with gel. She had believed it was Pete because she wanted it to be Pete.

He broke the silence. "Surprise!" he said. He seemed almost boyish standing there holding the flowers. He was wearing a Red Sox T-shirt and cut-off jeans, and his unruly hair showed comb tracks, like he had stopped to freshen up before coming to the island.

Surprise was an understatement. "What are you—I mean—how did you—" She was so flummoxed that she couldn't get a whole sentence out. All she had told him was that she was going to an ecology camp in Maine for most of the summer, and there had been no need to provide details. She didn't think they'd be in touch. Their casual dates had been just that, and she thought the chances were slim that they'd see each other when she returned in the middle of August.

Will grinned. "I came to take you to dinner. I asked Rebecca where you were, and I looked it up and got a map and here I am." He explained that he had been visiting his family in Boston for a few days. "Maine isn't that far from Massachusetts." The way he was speaking sounded like they had just seen each other yesterday, and that it made perfect sense to drop in on her like this.

But it didn't make sense. She and Will were casual friends, and casual friends didn't drive 600 miles to stop by with flowers and go to dinner. How long did he plan to be here? Where was he going to stay? It was three hours to Boston, so she could hardly say thanks for the daisies and send him on his way.

It wasn't just that he wasn't Pete. It was that it was Will, and they barely had what you could call a relationship that warranted driving all the way from Washington, D.C. She had no energy for small talk, for Will's smiling enthusiasm. Since she had been at the camp, she had managed to keep her distance from everyone. She worked in the kitchen, doing the menial tasks assigned to her, and Noah the chef left her alone to chop and stir, while he listened to opera music on the radio. In the office she answered the phone and handed out schedules, and she doubted that any of the campers (they rotated every week or two) even knew her name. She liked that. Her only goal was to make it through each day and add another to her distance from Pete. She neither needed nor wanted company or social entanglements.

Still, Will was here, and she couldn't hand him a ferry schedule and steer him to the two o'clock. She had to be in the kitchen (it was baking day) all afternoon, but she could give him a pair of binoculars and a map of the island. Maybe they could slip over to the mainland for an early dinner and he could find a motel or B&B for the night. And then in the morning he'd go back to Boston and make his way south to his life in D.C. She wouldn't even give him a chance to say anything about staying longer.

She forced a smile on her face as he extended the flowers to her. They were drooping in the midday heat. "Let's find a vase and some water," she said.

CHAPTER 37

THE LAST WEEKS of camp wound down, and the third week in August she was on the New Jersey Turnpike, heading south. It gave her lots of time to think as she left the island behind and grew closer to D.C. She stopped at a rest stop to buy ice cream (strawberry) and had a déja-vu flash. It was a generic fast-food place like any of the ones where she had stopped a year ago when she drove through Illinois and Ohio and Pennsylvania, a low stucco building next to a bank of gas pumps. There was the same rush of cold air as she opened the door to the restaurant. She was buying the same flavor. But the person she was now was transformed by everything that had happened. She was standing at the counter handing over her money to a teenaged boy with chocolate stains on his shirt just as she had the summer before, but she had traveled miles between those summer afternoons, miles that couldn't be measured on any road.

It was day eighty-six, but she was almost ready to change the counting to months. She liked the idea of months, they were solid and grounded, stayed where you put them, whereas days cluttered like leaves, like flitting moths. Three months. A whole season. She felt the weight of it. She thought maybe she should feel free, feel the benediction of distance, but she didn't. She was going back to the city where Pete lived, and she both feared and desired seeing him.

Will had sent her one postcard since their dinner in Maine. It featured a photo of the D.C. skyline at night, with the simple message, "Looking forward to your return." The dinner was pleasant, but she wasn't ready to get into a relationship. She heard nothing more from Pete, and she didn't answer his letter. What could she say? There was no way she would try to dissuade him from his vocation, not after reading the impassioned tone of his words. He loved her, but he loved God more.

School would start in a couple of weeks, and she would spend those weeks revisiting lesson plans, reading the stories in the new anthology Sister Helen had sent her. She was glad not to be returning as the "new" teacher, feeling more confident. Originally, she had planned to take a grad course or two because Sister Helen had strongly suggested she pursue a master's degree if she wanted permanent certification, but after her summer in the camp kitchen, had decided to look into cooking classes. She needed to keep busy, and learning to make bouillabaisse was more appealing than taking education courses.

What would it be like knowing Pete was only a couple of miles away? In time, and it might be months and months, she might be able to speak to him and not feel her heart lurch in her chest. Maybe a single summer wouldn't be distance enough. She could start going to a different parish, because if she stayed at St. Andrew's, chances were good that he'd be saying the Mass she attended. If she did stay, she'd make sure not to join the queue to shake his hand at the back of the church, slipping out the side door instead. She would not get in his line for communion.

Rebecca was in Ocean City for the week, and Olivia opened the door to an empty apartment. It had that closed-up feel, hot and thick with dust and silence. The first thing she did was open the windows, throw her bags on the living room floor, and open the fridge for a soda. There was a bottle of pineapple juice and empty ice-cube trays. Beyond that, the fridge held a couple of yogurts, a jar of organic peanut butter, and three Chinese take-out containers. Evidently Rebecca's cooking skills hadn't broadened over the summer. She sniffed the cartons, wrinkled her nose, and pitched them in the trash can. She opened cupboards, hoping for a can of tuna or a box of spaghetti. There was tuna, but no mayo. A box of rigatoni but no sauce. Getting in the car and going to Safeway was the last thing she wanted to do. After over ten hours in the car, her back hurt, she was hot and sweaty, and she didn't care if she drove again for a week. Sighing, hunger winning over fatigue, she picked up her car keys, and was startled by a knock on the door.

And there, grinning and holding two paper grocery bags, was Will. Again? Was surprise his middle name? She didn't feel like socializing, was desperate for a shower and about fourteen hours of sleep. She scrabbled around for ways to politely tell him this wasn't a good time. But then she caught the aroma of garlic and basil.

"Did anyone order take-out here?" He lifted the bags up by their handles. "I thought you might be hungry."

Starving was the word, but she was embarrassed by her travel-rumpled clothes, her sweaty hair escaping from its ponytail. And hungry as she was, she was also exhausted and not up to any of Will's cheerful conversation.

Without waiting for her reply, he continued, "Rebecca said you'd be home today, and I know she's at the beach and probably didn't do any grocery shopping, so I stopped by that Italian place on Wisconsin Avenue. I remembered you said you like basil, so I got pasta with pesto."

They had eaten caprese salad when he was in Maine, slices of ripe tomato drizzled with olive oil and layered with fragrant basil leaves. She told him it was her favorite herb. Amazing that he remembered that. Pete probably had no idea about her food preferences.

"But how did you know when I'd get here?"

He shrugged. "I figured about ten hours. I've been driving around the block for forty-five minutes." He must have sensed her hesitation, because he set the bags down by the door. "Look, it's all ready, and you can eat whenever you want. I'll just leave you to it." He started to turn away.

She couldn't let him just drop off the food. Tired as she was, she knew he had gone to a lot of trouble, even looking for something with basil. She stepped back from the door, shook her head. "Of course, you'll stay." She picked up one of the bags. "This feels like enough for half a dozen people. And I've been alone in my car all day and can really use the company." That was a lie, but it seemed kinder to lie than to send him away. She peeked into the bag. "And you brought wine! That settles it."

She led him to the table, and he unpacked the bags while she brought out plates and glasses and silverware. He pulled out a chair for her, insisted he serve. "I'll be your garçon," he said, and then he laughed. "That's about all I remember from my high school French." In spite of her fatigue, she let herself relax as she inhaled the scent of garlic shrimp, basil pesto on shell pasta, and a salad of watermelon and honeydew. The wine was crisp and cool (he had brought it chilled!) and there were double-chocolate brownies for dessert.

This was the first time she had eaten dinner with a man in the apartment. She wondered if Pete would even have thought of bringing an impromptu meal. There was that one time when he had a grease-stained bag of McDonald's burgers and fries in his car, but that was because he had missed dinner. Will had done it for her. She speared a cube of watermelon, savoring the flavor of summer.

After a while, she noticed her fatigue had dropped away, and she was enjoying the conversation with Will. He was an amateur photographer, and he told her about his short trip to the Chesapeake Bay where he shot three rolls of pelicans in flight. She dug out the photo she had taken on the island, a fishing cabin where the editor of Emily Dickinson's poems had stayed. She planned to use it when she taught Dickinson's poems. She marveled that he was so interested in the story, even though she was pretty sure he never read poetry. She noticed how he smiled with his whole face.

The light outside started to fade, and she was about to search for a candle when he glanced at his watch.

"Oh! It's almost nine. You must be exhausted. I didn't mean to stay so long." He stood and gathered the plates to clear the table.

She suppressed a yawn, took a sip of wine instead. "No, it's fine. I had a good time. And the food was great. Leave the plates. I'll get them later."

But he was putting the leftovers in the fridge. "You've got enough for lunch tomorrow," he said, wiping his hands on a dish towel. She thought he probably brought extra on purpose.

At the door, she started to thank him again, but he put his finger on her lips. "I wanted to do this," he said. "I wanted to see you again." She noticed the deep brown of his eyes. Surprised at herself, she tilted in and kissed him, and when he left, she leaned against the closed door for several minutes.

CHAPTER 38

THERE WERE SO many times that she found herself saying, "This time last year." Driving to church and circling the block for a parking spot, she'd be back at that first coffee hour. Standing in the front of her classroom she would see a sea of other faces, last year's freshmen, and she'd have to blink to bring this class back into focus. It could be anything. Rebecca surrounded by a sea of fabric. A pyramid of pears at Safeway. Thunder on a Sunday afternoon. A kaleidoscope of sounds and images blinded her at random moments, and she would shake herself and return to the present, though sometimes like a stubborn dream the images would haunt her for an afternoon, an evening, a day. And always Pete. Pete behind his desk. Pete in his car. Pete turning the key in the door to the motel room. So much had happened in that year, and she wondered what her life would be like today if it were erased.

She forced herself to push that year into the past and focus on the here and now. And *here* was her second year of teaching at Holy Redeemer, feeling more settled. *Here* was going to the early Mass when she knew Pete would not be the celebrant. *Here* was the Wednesday evening class she had found on pastry-making. And more and more, *here* was Will.

She couldn't help liking Will. There was something contagious about his enthusiasm, his cheerfulness. He was at the apartment one day when Rebecca complained about the broken sash in her bedroom window and said she was going to leave a note for Mrs. Trimble. "Don't bother her," he said. "I can fix that." And he did. And he unclogged the drain in the bathroom sink, took care of the squeak in the front door. Mention anything that was stuck or broken or out of alignment and he'd jog out to his car and return with a tool. Finally, Olivia told him she had a tool kit of her own and why not use that? He picked up a couple of the tools and said, "These look brand new." She confessed that she had never used any of them, but she kept them because they were a gift from her dad. He laughed and said, "You have to love a girl who has her own adjustable wrench."

She had never planned to have him come around that often. After he brought her dinner her first night back, she thought it only fair to repay him, and she invited him over for lasagna, sending him home with leftovers. It was a little awkward because she thought about how she had kissed him but didn't know what it meant. If it meant anything. She certainly wasn't going to get involved with him, not so soon after Pete. The kiss had just happened because she had been so moved by his generosity. She doubted he would have initiated the kiss, and she was shocked that she had. Maybe, she thought, it had been the wine.

He seemed to think they could pick up where they had left off last spring, when they had casual daytime dates. He didn't pressure her, but he'd either call or show up with an "I was in the neighborhood" excuse and propose going to the farm market or taking in an early movie. Once he said he wanted to go to the zoo to photograph giraffes, and though she had no particular interest in giraffes she went along because it was a sunny Saturday afternoon and she had nothing else to do. She found herself fascinated, and more so when he told her that giraffes had a special substance in their saliva that healed the cuts in their mouths from chomping on the acacia trees. He constantly surprised her with these weird little-known facts. They bought paper bags of peanuts and cups of overly-sweet lemonade.

Before long he was coming over every Saturday and called at least once during the week. He started to kiss her at the door, a light, friendly kiss, and she was okay with that. "No," she told Rebecca, who gently teased her, "there's nothing going on between us. We're just friends."

And Rebecca had countered with, "Are you blind? The guy is crazy about you."

Olivia didn't want anyone to be crazy about her. It was too soon for that. Pete was still a loud echo in her heart. She wanted someone to go with to an outdoor concert, or for walks on the canal. Will was a welcome distraction. They went to a rathskeller one Friday night shortly after school began with a couple of the other teachers and their dates, and that was good. It made her realize how much she had missed this, the normalcy of being out on a casual date. It turned out that Alice's date Sherman had also gone to Penn State, just a year before Will, and the two guys traded stories about professors and the basketball team. Will took over the ordering, since he had been to Germany and knew all about German beers. He held her hand under the table.

So, they went on in this way through the fall. Olivia continued to keep count, though, of her time away from Pete, and in mid-October it was five months. Right before Halloween she read Pete's letter again, but she found that she was skimming a few of the paragraphs.

CHAPTER 39

REBECCA'S SCREAM MADE Olivia drop the book she was reading in her room. She rushed into the kitchen where her roommate was standing cradling her hand with blood oozing between her fingers.

"What did you—" Olivia grabbed a dish towel from the side of the sink and wrapped it around Rebecca's fingers, feeling light-headed. She had never been good around blood. Rebecca's eyes were wide with surprise or shock or both.

"I was chopping an onion, and the knife slipped." Rebecca peeked under the folds of the towel. "I think it's deep." The knife had fallen to the floor, and the onion lay on its side on the cutting board, speckled with red. Olivia opened the cabinet over the stove and reached for the box of Band-Aids. "It's beyond a Band-Aid," Rebecca said. "I think we have to go to the ER."

It was the day before Thanksgiving. Rebecca had insisted on making the stuffing to go with the turkey breast Olivia was going to roast the next day. Olivia was happy that she wanted to do something besides open a can. Maybe she should have given her an easier task, but what could be easier than chopping an onion? "How are we going to get there?" Olivia asked. Her car was in the shop for a tune-up, and Rebecca drove a VW with stick shift. Olivia had never learned. It wasn't an ambulance call, but maybe a cab?

Then Rebecca blinked and sank back on to the kitchen stool. She looked a little pale. She could be around other people's blood with no problem, but evidently hers was a different matter. "Will?" Will had decided to stick around for the holiday instead of driving to Boston to see his folks. He only lived twenty minutes away.

He made it to the apartment in fifteen.

Two hours and five stitches later, along with jokes from the E.R. nurses ("third knife-chopping incident this afternoon"), they were back in the apartment, and Olivia fixed the three of them scrambled eggs and toast.

"What are you doing for Thanksgiving dinner?" Rebecca asked Will, scooping up a forkful of eggs, resting her bandaged hand on the table.

It turned out he was doing nothing special. He said he'd probably get take-out or "heat up something frozen." Olivia reflected that he and Rebecca would be a disastrous pair in a kitchen.

"Then you absolutely must come here," Rebecca said. "After filling in as an ambulance driver, it's the least we can do. As long as you don't mind being surrounded by women. I invited two of my nurse friends."

Olivia echoed the invitation. "Of course! We won't take no for an answer." She watched a smile spread across Will's face, imagining his relief at being spared the loneliness of frozen fried chicken. She thought about the turkey breast thawing in the fridge, hoping that with the sides the nurses were bringing, and the stuffing (she'd have to finish it tonight), there would be enough. Men ate a lot. Oh well, she could always run out for some rolls.

Will leaned against the refrigerator, smiling. "I'll bring wine."

They ate around two, because Chloe and Rachel were on duty at five. Will had brought a desk chair (Olivia and Rebecca only had four dining chairs), and they crowded around the table, while Rebecca assured them the stuffing had been restarted from scratch, and everyone praised Chloe's cranberry relish and Rachel's squash casserole. It was just what

Olivia had imagined when she had first come to D.C. Friends gathered around her table, the warm sound of conversation, elbows jostling over serving dishes. This, she thought, is what home feels like. The sink was piled with pots and pans, but they were out of sight, and on the table in front of them was the golden-brown turkey breast. Even though it was early afternoon, there were four off-white candles circled around a small pumpkin as a centerpiece. For a split second, she closed her eyes and smiled inside. The room smelled like nutmeg and thyme.

After dinner, when Chloe and Rachel had left and the dishes were washed and put away, Olivia and Will went for a walk. It was that time of day when the light glowed purple with the coming dusk and windows gleamed golden with lamps. The neighborhood was quiet, everyone inside their houses watching football and snapping wishbones. It was mostly row houses, pastel painted brick, aluminum storm doors. "I love going by houses and making up stories about the people who live there," he said, taking hold of her gloved hand. He pointed to a dark gray house with Christmas lights outlining the door. "Like those people—they put their tree up in the middle of November." And in front of a house with peeling white paint and no lights on, "A widow lives there, and she's gone to her daughter's house for the weekend."

Olivia entered into the game. "Clearly a bunch of guys," she said as she pointed to the trash can filled to the brim with pizza boxes and empty beer cans in front of a duplex with a bright red door. She could hear the thump of a bass from inside.

They continued as they walked, inventing people and their lives. The bachelor college professor who didn't own a TV and listened to opera on the radio. The newly married couple using their wedding china for the first time. The hairdresser who worked in her kitchen giving haircuts without a work license. With each story, Olivia laughed harder, and when they found themselves in front of her house again, she pointed to the door and said, "And what about here?"

"A beautiful woman who turned what could have been a lonely

afternoon into a feast." And with that, he kissed her. It was a different kind of kiss, and his lips were warm and tasted like wine and pumpkin. He cradled her face in his hands, and she felt electricity for the first time.

Later, when Rebecca had taken a painkiller and gone to bed, Olivia was putting laundry away in her room. There in the sock drawer she saw Pete's letter. She took it out, started to open it, and put it back. It occurred to her that today was November 26. The six-month mark had come and gone without her noticing. It had just been a regular day.

CHAPTER 40

ON A FEBRUARY Saturday, Olivia watched Will as he stood on the stepladder in her living room changing the burned-out ceiling bulb. He angled his hip against the rungs and untwisted the bulb with one hand. She liked to watch the ease with which he fixed things, how it never seemed to be an effort. It was just one thing she was learning about him. Over the months they had been dating, she had grown to know him in all those little ways that make up a person. She knew how he whistled under his breath while he drove, that he disliked most vegetables except peas, that he wished he'd gone to grad school. She knew why he was a democrat (and why this rankled his parents), that he read the comics section of the newspaper first, and that he had an irrational fear of hypodermic needles. And she was pretty sure he was in love with her.

She wanted to let herself be in love with him. She wanted that fire-in-the-heart feeling, that sense of missing him five minutes after they parted. But something held her back, because wanting felt too much like being vulnerable, too much like risk. There were many times when she still cried when she was alone, not thinking about Pete, but because she felt something was missing and because she was reluctant to take another chance. She was afraid to trust another man, and she was afraid to trust herself.

He climbed down from the ladder, tossed the old bulb into the trash. They had planned to walk along the waterfront and find someplace to eat, but it had started to snow, fat wet flakes that turned to slush as they hit the ground. So they sat on the couch, debated seeing a movie, and out of the blue, he said he wanted to go to Sunday Mass with her.

She knew he had been brought up Catholic, and he admitted that he "kind of fell away" during college. A lot of her Minnesota friends had given up church after high school, and there had been times when she wondered why she hadn't. In college, especially, when Sunday morning was often the only day she had to sleep late. But if she happened to go home for Sunday dinner someone would be sure to ask if she had been to Mass. Not so directly, but just leading questions regarding the sermon, or "Did you go to the noon Mass again?" Religion, organized religion, had been ingrained deeply in her, and she held on to the prayers and rituals, a comforting tie to the familiar. Once she moved to D.C., she would have felt something was missing if she had not attended Mass. For a while last fall, she had considered finding another church, but it was convenient staying at St. Andrews. Pete had said they would still be friends, but she had no intention of speaking with him. The weekly bulletin had started publishing the names of the celebrants for the next week, and she avoided his Masses, settling for mediocre sermons and often having to go to the very early service.

So far, she had managed not to run into him, and that was amazing considering she lived so close to the church. If there was a schedule change, and he was the celebrant, she left by the side door. She knew he shopped at the Peoples Drug on Wisconsin Avenue, so she went to a different drug store. She avoided the coffee hour. Once or twice, when he was giving a sermon, she thought he looked directly at her, but she couldn't be sure. She had lowered her eyes, feeling heat suffuse her face, but then reasoned that surely, he couldn't pick her out in such a congregation of over four hundred people. Or could he, with her auburn hair?

Taking Will to church with her was no problem. She was touched that he had asked. The problem was having Pete and Will in the same space. Because if Will started attending Mass with her, eventually Pete would be the celebrant. And Will, outgoing as he was, would want to go right up to him and shake his hand and thank him for the great sermon. How would it feel to be standing with the man she had loved and the man who loved her now?

In the meantime, Will said he'd pick her up the next morning at ten-thirty, and after Mass they could go to brunch. She opened the newspaper to the movie section, and they talked about how to spend the afternoon.

CHAPTER 41

WHEN WILL AND Pete met, it was by accident. Will and Olivia had been to the eleven o'clock Mass the second Sunday in April (Will was a regular now) and Father Walker, the pastor, had been the celebrant. It was a chilly day, and a drenching rain fell, so Olivia led the way through a covered passageway between the church and the school to get closer to where they had parked. Will had his arm looped over her shoulder, and they were debating whether to go to the Irish place for eggs benedict or to the diner for French toast. Olivia didn't hear footsteps, but the voice stopped her short.

"Olivia! I thought that was you!"

Her mouth went dry. She spun around to see Pete, wearing a raincoat over his black suit, leaning against a doorway and grinning. That same smile. Those same green eyes. His words echoed in the empty hallway. It felt like Will disappeared and it was just she and Pete in the watery light from the windows.

She had known it would happen, that someday they would run into each other. It was amazing that it had taken this long. All fall, all winter, and now it was spring. Unbelievable. She had prepared herself for a chance meeting, telling herself she would smile, she would be friendly, she would not show how she felt inside. Definitely awkward, she thought, and bittersweet, but they would exchange a few words and then part.

Mostly, she didn't think about him. She was busy with school, was taking a class Thursday evening in Italian cooking, was seeing Will every weekend. The annual staff retreat had been at a lodge out in the Shenandoah Valley, and the chaplain had been a Franciscan monk. She still kept Pete's letter in her sock drawer, but she hadn't read it since October. Mostly, she forgot it was even there.

But seeing him standing in front of her, with that shock of hair falling over his eyes, was a rush of memory so strong she had to grab Will's sleeve. The words she had memorized evaporated, and she was at a loss for what to say. A simple "How are you?" seemed so banal, so thin. She said it anyway, squeezing the words out from a throat that had gone dry.

"It's so good to see you," Pete said, smiling. "How have you been?" He spoke the way you would to an old classmate, someone you had worked with but had lost touch. There was no hesitation in his voice, no sign of the awkwardness she felt. He pulled a cigarette out of his pocket, seemed to realize where he was, and put it back.

She wanted to be anywhere but here. She wanted to be in Will's car splashing through rainy streets to the diner. She wanted it to be yesterday, she wanted it to be tomorrow. How did you talk to the man you had loved when that man hadn't loved you enough? And how did you do it when you were with another man, another man you were sure was falling in love with you? A roll of thunder rumbled outside, and the rain slapped against the flagstone path.

Clearing her throat, willing herself to be calm, she said, "Fine." She was intensely aware of his eyes and intensely aware of the nubby texture of Will's jacket. Moments slid by. "This is Will. Will, this is P—Father Kowolski."

Pete held out his hand. "Pete," he said. "Only my high school students call me Father Kowolski." They shook hands, smiling in the casual camaraderie men can exhibit when they've never met. "Are you—I don't think I've seen you in the parish."

"I'm a recent recruit." Will nodded toward Olivia. "Olivia has brought me back to the fold."

She knew Will would stand there chatting for an hour, and she just wanted to get away. Pete didn't seem the least bit disturbed at seeing her, while she felt clammy and hot at the same time. Almost ten months. She counted them in her head. And his voice and his face brought it all back, just when she thought she had buried it. She forced herself to smile, looked at her watch. "It's good to see you too, but we—we're late for brunch." She wrapped her fingers tighter around Will's arm.

Pete looked like he was going to say something else, but she didn't wait to hear it. She steered Will toward the parking lot, and when she looked back, Pete was pulling up the collar of his coat, and she could barely make out his face in the shadows.

CHAPTER 42

IT WAS SUMMER again, and Olivia had a job teaching remedial English in summer school at Holy Redeemer. It was mornings only, and in the afternoons she worked as a baker's assistant. She had taken a baking class back in the fall, and Carlo, the teacher, told her she had a knack for it. He owned his own bakery, and he offered her the chance to help out three afternoons a week. "I can't pay you," he apologized, "but I can guarantee that by August you'll be making croissants and pie crusts like you've never tasted." Will bought her an apron with her name on the pocket in magenta script. He told her he was proud of her and offered to lend her money if she needed it while she had only a part-time salary over the summer. "I've saved enough, but thanks," she told him.

It wasn't the offer of money, or the apron, but Olivia sensed a shift in her feelings toward Will. It had started in May when he had to go to Florida for a training conference. The apartment felt empty, even though Rebecca was there. Olivia kept expecting Will to knock on the door, saw him in her mind sprawled on the couch, his shoes off, reading the sports section of the paper. When the phone rang, she brightened, thinking it would be him. And when it wasn't, she sank in disappointment. He was gone over a weekend, and on Friday night she went out with some friends but felt alone, even in the midst of their chatter.

Rebecca noticed. "That man better get back here quickly," she commented on Saturday afternoon. "You look like you lost your best friend."

Olivia hadn't realized it showed, but she did feel that way. It wasn't just that she was used to having Will around, it was that there was a hole when he wasn't. She kept having that feeling that she had forgotten something, or had lost something, and until Rebecca spoke, she hadn't realized it was Will. When he wasn't around, she looked for him. When he was around, she felt complete. Before that weekend, she hadn't realized how much she wanted to be around him, to hear his voice, to feel his hand on the small of her back when they crossed a street.

More and more, he had begun to speak of them in the future tense. Nothing huge, but phrases like "We'll have to go to the zoo again when the weather warms up," or "When I show you . . ." or "Someday, we'll . . ." She rarely gave it much thought, but when he called from New York, on another business trip, he said, "I wish you were here, Liv." That, too, was new. His nickname for her. "I'll bet you've never been to Lincoln Center." She'd never been anywhere in New York. "We'll have to go there together, and I'll take you to a funky little bar I like in the Village." There it was, that future tense again.

Something shifted inside of her with that phone call. It was as if her heart ticked an extra beat while she spoke with him. Holding a mug of tea and inhaling hibiscus and mint, she understood that Will was not just that easygoing person at her side, fixing leaky faucets and bringing her humorous gifts and bags of take-out. She hadn't seen this coming. She hadn't expected to see his deep brown eyes when she heard his voice on the phone. She hadn't expected to find herself thinking of him at odd times of day, to smile as she recalled something he had said. She hadn't expected her whole body to tingle when he kissed her. She hadn't expected that as important as his presence was starting to be, it was his absence she felt the most.

She loved him.

On the fourth of July, he proposed. They had taken a picnic supper to a deserted park, spread out a quilt on the grass. Olivia had brought cold chicken and a salad and strawberry tarts. Will had brought a bottle of wine. They ate and talked and complained about the heat. Then, when the tarts were reduced to crumbs, he told her to close her eyes. She heard the sharp strike of a match, smelled the faint trace of sulfur, and when he said, "Open your eyes," the looked up to see a burst of fireworks streaking up to the sky. Sparks fell around them, and he was reaching his hand toward her with a ring, a sapphire surrounded by tiny diamonds. She felt no hesitation as she said yes, and they lit sparklers and waved them around overhead, the tiny pinpricks of fire swirling around them like fireflies. Then they lay down in the grass, holding hands and looking up at the wide sky, where light-years away the stars blinked in and out.

She left Pete where he was, in her past. She turned on her elbow and looked at Will, trying to find his eyes in the dark. This time last year she had been on a small island in Maine listening to loons as they flew over the pines in the lavender evening sky. This time last year she had been so deep in sadness she couldn't imagine a future. Now she looked at Will, saw he was looking at her, and that whole sad summer disappeared. She'd never have to go there again.

CHAPTER 43

THEY PLANNED AN April wedding. It would be two years since they'd met, and spring in D.C. was radiant with azaleas, redbuds, and dogwoods. Her parents, of course, wanted the wedding to be in Minnesota, but Olivia argued for D.C. because all their friends were there. She'd lost touch with most of her high school and college friends, and Aubrey had moved from Chicago to Dallas and was expecting twins. Will's parents, who lived outside of Boston, said they hadn't been to D.C. in years, and they hoped the cherry blossoms would be in bloom.

They had a long to-do list (Will was a believer in lists) and one Saturday afternoon in early January she and Will were in her living room checking things off. A thin, persistent rain fell outside, and she wished it were snow. She still missed the Minnesota winters. She'd turned on all the lamps against the gray light outside, and they were sitting on the couch with mugs of tea and a plate of chocolate marshmallow brownies. Will kicked off his shoes and picked up the sheet of paper.

A lot had already been done. Order invitations. Choose bridesmaids (Rebecca, Olivia's cousin Betsy). Church (St. Andrew's). Reception place (inn in Chevy Chase). Hotel rooms for out-of-town family. See bakery about cake (Carlo).

Will chewed absent-mindedly on a brownie as he scrolled down with his finger. "Ah," he said. "Officiant. Father Pete?"

Olivia paused mid-sip. Inevitably, now Pete often said the Mass they attended. She had given up trying to steer Will to other services, and with only three priests in the parish (including one who was senile and didn't say Mass very often) there was a 50/50 chance that Pete would be on the altar. Will loved his sermons, said they were so much more relevant than the ones he remembered from his earlier church-going days. "He makes Jesus seem like a real person," he commented, "and I love the way he often brings in modern references like films." Will always wanted to stop and say hi at the back of the church after the service. Olivia had grown used to that, but she tried to cut the conversations short. She still felt uncomfortable around Pete. She knew he wouldn't (couldn't) say anything, and she was sure Pete didn't have feelings for her anymore. So much time had gone by, and he had seemed genuinely happy when they told him they were engaged. She could tell from announcements in the church bulletin that he was very busy with committees and clubs at St Andrew's, fully involved in his priestly life. Still, memories of their year together were quick to surface, and she wanted them to disappear. Her life was with Will now.

Maybe, she thought as she wrapped her hands around her mug, this was the time to tell Will. "You know, there was a time when—" or "There's something I think you should know." If she explained it the right way, Will would understand. After all, it had happened before she even met Will. The two of them had talked briefly about past relationships (Olivia's college boyfriend Trevor, Will's girlfriend Lucy who was married and lived somewhere in Rhode Island). High school romances, prom dates, a woman named Brenda who still called Will periodically asking him out. But Pete was in a whole other category. It had been no ordinary romance. He had been, and was, a priest. And he was a priest whom Will knew. Still, difficult as it would be, she knew she should tell him. She worried, though, about what Will would think. Worried that he'd judge her, think what she had done was wrong. And there was Pete to consider. He had always insisted that their relationship be a secret. Would telling Will now be unfair to Pete, reveal something he wanted, needed, to keep quiet?

The apartment felt cozy in the gray, rainy afternoon. There was a John Denver record on the stereo, the rich aroma of chocolate, lamps warming the corners of the room. If she were to tell him now, she was afraid her words would break the spell of the moment, the easy intimacy. And when Will put the list aside, and circled her with his arms, she told herself it wasn't the right time.

CHAPTER 44

REBECCA WAS GOING to make Olivia's wedding dress. "It will be my gift," she said. So on a chilly Saturday in late January, they sat on the living room floor with splayed-open bridal magazines, clipping out pictures. For Olivia, it was like when she had played with paper dolls as a kid, cutting out paper dresses and folding the little tabs onto the cardboard figures. "Look," said Rebecca, pointing to a dress in one of the magazines, "here's that neckline you like."

"Yes, but I don't like those sleeves." She got up and changed the record, putting on Carole King's *Tapestry*.

"That's why I'm making the dress. I can use that neckline and the cap sleeves from that other one you like. And where's that picture of the one with the empire waist and the lace insets?" She rummaged around the pile, drew one out. She had a piece of foam board where she pinned on each of the parts Olivia had chosen. The board was a collage of sleeves, bodices, trains, and veils. As soon as she made a drawing, incorporating all the parts Olivia liked, they were going to go to the fabric store. Rebecca was the only one Olivia would trust with her wedding dress. During their time as roommates, she had seen how she could transform a length of fabric or a thrift store find into something wonderful. A handful of scarves into a skirt, a pair of denim overalls into a sundress. Now a thrill zinged through her as she imagined the scattered sections on the foam board actually coming together to be the beautiful, perfect dress she would wear when she walked down the aisle. Rebecca promised to use the Belgian lace Olivia's mother had kept, carefully wrapped in tissue paper. Just last week Olivia had asked her to mail it.

Rebecca pushed her glasses up on top of her head. "So, have you and Will decided who will marry you?"

"Uh-huh. Pete."

Rebecca stopped cutting out the dress with the neckline Olivia had chosen. "Pete? Pete as in the priest you were going out with?"

"Why not? He'll do a great job, and we really don't know any other priests." Seeing the expression on Rebecca's face, she added, "I know what you're thinking, but all that with him was over a long time ago. We're just friends now, and he's really happy for us."

Rebecca shook her head. "And Will is okay with it? Even knowing that the two of you were involved?"

Olivia paused, pretended interest in a photo of a wedding cake. "He . . . doesn't know."

"Really? You haven't told him?"

Olivia shook her head.

"But you're going to tell him? Right?" Rebecca frowned as she picked up the scissors again.

Olivia fished the marshmallow out of her cocoa, popped it in her mouth. "I was going to, back when I knew it was more than casual between us, but I just didn't know how to bring it up. 'Before we get serious, I think you should know that I was dating a priest last year.' It sounded like it would be so out of the blue. And then the more time went by, the less important it seemed."

"And now?"

"Well, it's a little late now."

Rebecca shook her head. "Olivia, he has to know. You have to tell him." Her voice sounded uncharacteristically serious. Urgent, even. She sat back on her heels, frowning. "It's just not fair to keep something so important from him, especially since he's going to be the one performing the ceremony. The thing with Pete has been over for a long time. What's the problem?"

"I can't. He'd just be mad that I never told him before. He'd think I was keeping something important from him on purpose."

"Will? Mad? Not the Will I know. I'm sure if you explained—"

"No. Pete's back to his life as a parish priest, and I'm in love with Will. I never even think of Pete that way anymore." She pointed to the dress parts tacked to the board. "And I'm getting married. And my best friend is making my dress." She wanted to change the subject.

"But, Olivia, suppose he does find out some day? Wouldn't it be better for you to tell him now and work through it and then be done with it?"

"He'll never find out. There's no reason he would. Look, can we just focus on the dress?" Olivia was growing annoyed at Rebecca's insistence. It was *her* decision. Carole was singing that song, "So Far Away." Yes, those days were so far away, so far in the past.

For a few minutes there was just the snip of scissors and the sharp rasp of tearing paper. Then Rebecca spoke. "And how do you feel about it? About Pete being the official?"

"Officiant." Rebecca often got church terms mixed up. "Oh, it's fine. In fact, it feels like a real closure, like he's giving us his blessing." She did think that. There had been a bittersweet feeling when she and Will had gone to see Pete in his office, to ask him about it. She couldn't help but remember all the late afternoons she had sat on that couch, all the times she and Pete had drunk wine and made out. But she also saw those times now through a haze, seeing the two of them as shadowy figures not quite in focus. Will was the real, breathing, solid man with her. She thought for a moment that Pete looked a little sad, but then he grinned and told them how happy he'd be to marry them, asked them questions about the ceremony, about where they'd be living. Olivia saw that there was still a roll of lime Lifesavers on his desk and the checkers game still over by the window. But then Will took her hand, and it felt so warm and familiar that she stopped noticing those things. She detected a hint of distance in Pete's voice, and his eyes only lingered on her for a second before he looked away. He shook both of their hands when they left, and his touch was brief and businesslike. Yes, Pete had moved on, back to just being a parish priest.

Rebecca made a humphing sound. "Or maybe he will be realizing everything he gave up."

CHAPTER 45

AND SUDDENLY, IT was a clear, sunny day in April. Olivia stood at the back of the church, holding on to her father's arm. She felt him tremble through the smooth gabardine of his tuxedo sleeve. He was more nervous than she was, she mused, as the organ music trickled down from the choir loft. The bridesmaids and the groomsmen were already standing in front of the altar, Will with his brother George, the best man. Pete stood in front of the altar holding an open notebook. She thought he was looking straight at her, but she ignored it, glanced instead at the backs of heads in the pews, found her mother in her turquoise dress. She felt the muscles in her father's arm tighten as the organ swelled into "Trumpet Voluntary," and then she fastened her eyes on Will as she and her father started down the aisle.

After the ceremony (a full Mass), after the vows and the ring exchange, after the kiss (she smelled jasmine), she and Will turned to face the guests. He had his arm through hers, and she reached over, holding his hand and her flowers (hydrangea, baby roses, lily-of-the-valley) with the same hand. Aunt Mamie had her handkerchief to her eyes. Will's father beamed as he flashed them a muted high five. Her nephews were tugging at their neckties. Olivia looked over to Rebecca, who winked.

And then they were walking quickly down the aisle, toward the sun that splashed through the door from the street. They turned to wave to everyone, and she saw Pete halfway raise his hand. Then she looked up at Will and down to their hands, wearing shiny gold bands, and she thought she'd never stop smiling.

PART THREE
1990

CHAPTER 46

"SEXUAL MISCONDUCT." THE words broke the room in half. Olivia had one ear on the TV but most of her attention was on the book she was reading, when she heard the phrase and the name together. "Father Peter Kowolski." She looked at the screen in shock. It had to have just sounded like his name. It couldn't be Pete.

But how many people had that last name? And there was his face on the screen, and she blinked hard as she saw the grainy photo of a man in a clerical suit. Pete would be about 50 now. The photo showed a man older than the one she had known, slightly overweight now, but she couldn't mistake the shock of hair that fell over his forehead, the intensity of his eyes. It was him.

She reached over and turned up the volume, hearing the newscaster complete a sentence. ". . . former priest of St. Andrew's parish." Pete? How had he— She missed most of the words, because Will came in the front door then, dropped his briefcase on the floor by the coffee table, and leaned down to kiss her. "Hi babe, I'm—wait! Is that Pete?" He stared at the television, then looked at Olivia as the program switched to the weather.

Olivia's head was reeling. She hadn't gotten many of the details. There had been something about "allegations" and "accusations." Will's hand on her shoulder brought her back to his presence, to the nubby texture of the couch where she was sitting, to the scent of meatloaf from the kitchen. "It was." She wished there were instant rewind on the TV so she could see it again.

"Why was he on TV? Is he back in D.C.?" Pete had moved to Philadelphia several years after Olivia and Will married, and for a while he sent them Christmas cards, from there and later from Scranton and Baltimore. And they had sent him cards, with photos of Brent and Lindsay as infants and toddlers, and then as they entered school. But they hadn't had a card from him in years, so that tenuous bond frayed into threads. She rarely thought of him. Only when she'd open the album of wedding pictures and see him raising his hand in benediction. But then she was always more focused on her and Will, and Pete was only a face in the background, a part of the life she had left behind. Now the news had brought him into the middle of her living room.

Olivia spoke through a dry mouth. "It said he was accused of sexual misconduct." What did that term even mean? "Misconduct" didn't sound that serious, but if it wasn't serious then why had it made the news? Was it the same as abuse, and did it mean that Pete had been accused of some kind of sex abuse? It didn't add up. Not the Pete she had known.

"Pete? No way." He peppered her with questions, but she hadn't heard enough of the story. She waved the questions away, her mind reeling. "I didn't hear it all. It has to be a mistake." But his face had been real, and the phrase "sexual misconduct" kept spooling in her head. She'd stay up to catch the eleven o'clock news. Maybe the story would be repeated.

"Let me know if you hear anything more," Will said, shaking his head in disbelief. He loosened his tie, shrugged out of his seersucker jacket, said he'd drag Brent away from his video games and go shoot some baskets before dinner. "Something smells good," he said, as he headed upstairs. The channel switched to national news. Olivia turned off the TV and went to the kitchen to make the salad.

Brent loved the meatloaf, and Will had seconds, and Lindsay was chatting about her friend Keisha, whose dog Zelda had just had puppies. It was background noise for Olivia, who ate without tasting, nodded occasionally, and kept hearing the phrase "sexual misconduct" in the same sentence with Pete's name.

CHAPTER 47

THERE WASN'T ANYTHING about Pete on the late news, so the next morning, after dropping Brent off at soccer camp and Lindsay at her piano lesson, Olivia went to the 7-11 to buy a newspaper, since they only had home delivery on Sundays. She didn't wait to get home to read it, but sat in the parking lot and spread it out over the steering wheel. And there it was on the front of the Metro section—the same photo she had seen on the news. The headline—*D.C. Priest Accused of Sexual Misconduct.* Despite the growing humidity of the morning, she felt goosebumps prickle her arms. It wasn't a mistake. Pete really had been accused.

Accusations weren't proof, though, and accusations could be wrong. She skimmed the article, too keyed up to read slowly, and then she went back and reread it. It was there in black and white, and she didn't know if her dizziness was from the July heat shimmering on her car or from the words in the article. She had read occasional pieces (was it in the Sunday *Post* just a few weeks ago?) about Catholic priests accused of abuse. In Ireland. In Chicago. She hadn't paid much attention. They were, she surmised, isolated incidents. She never dreamed she'd read about it and it would be someone she knew. Much less, knew well. Much less, someone she had loved.

With shaking hands, she turned to the second page where the article continued, and the words swam on the paper. When she had heard the story on the news, she had assumed that whatever it was had happened after she had known him. But no. The dates given were from before they met, while they were together, and after she married Will. Boys who had been in his high school classes, altar boys now grown up, and two women. Had they been girls when it happened? Or were they adults? There weren't any details beyond phrases like "inappropriate touching" and "sexual advances," so she didn't know what had really taken place. Nevertheless, thinking about the possibility of Pete doing anything that might be labeled sex abuse was enough for her to feel sick, like a cold hand was squeezing her stomach. None of it fit the Pete she had known.

She stopped reading. Her world shrank to the front seat of the car, to the hot steering wheel, the vinyl upholstery that stuck to her thighs, the staccato of the DJ on the radio. And then even those things faded, along with the traffic and the customers on the sidewalk in front of the store. She couldn't register anything but the words in the article. Sexual misconduct. Pete in rehab somewhere. Who or where were the accusers?

As she stared at the words, images blurred in and out. Pete behind his desk, Pete reaching for her in his car, Pete guiding her hands to focus the telescope. His eyes, his lips, the set of his shoulders. The seduction of his voice on the phone, the laugh that rose from deep in his chest. Pete guiding her through the exhibits of the museum in Annapolis. The images came and went like jumpy slides from a projector, and always her eyes returned to the phrase on the paper in front of her. Sexual misconduct. What exactly did these people say he had done?

She drove home in a fog, needing to be inside the house where it was cool and quiet and she could think. In the kitchen, she moved automatically, stacking the bowls in the dishwasher, brushing toast crumbs off the table. She sat and read the article again, hoping she had missed something. But the words were the same, and the dates were the same. And one of the years had been the time he was with her. While he was telling her he couldn't get her out of his mind, was telling her how beautiful she was, he had been fondling his students? Teenaged boys? He had been calling other women on the phone, seeing them? None of this could be true. She felt a headache spiral over her right eye, and she tossed the newspaper on top of her kitchen desk, next to a recipe she had cut out for fried chicken.

CHAPTER 48

TWO NIGHTS LATER, Olivia and Will were in the kitchen eating blueberry pie. Lindsay was at a sleepover and Brent was up in his room watching a baseball game on his portable TV. To be exact, Will was eating. Olivia was pushing a blueberry around on the yellow plate with her fork.

"Great pie," Will said, scraping his plate to get the last of the sticky juice. He took a sip of his iced coffee. "Why aren't you eating?"

"Here, you can have mine," Olivia said, sliding her plate across the table. "I'm not hungry."

Will never turned down seconds of anything. "There's a hint of something I can't put my finger on," he said, lifting a forkful to his mouth.

"Lemon."

"Ah, I wouldn't have guessed." He always loved anything she cooked, even the disasters. He often hung around her in the kitchen, wanting to help, though mostly he was a distraction because there would be too much to explain. Now he tilted back in his chair, smiling, in one of his "all's right with the world" moods when a simple slice of pie could fill him with contentment.

Olivia tuned him out. She couldn't think about pie or fried chicken or other mundane things like when she'd take the car in for the oil change it needed. All she could think about was Pete, and what he had supposedly done. Outside, a toad croaked under the azaleas, and the copper wind chimes clinked on the porch. It was almost ten-thirty, not too early to go to bed. She hadn't slept well since seeing Pete on TV. Even though she went to bed exhausted, thinking she'd sleep for nine hours, after an hour she was wide awake, staring at shadows on the ceiling, thinking about Pete, questions reeling through her mind. If it had happened so long ago, why was it suddenly in the news? How old were those boys now, and what had made them come forward with their accusations? And the worst one—what did it mean for her? Who was the man she thought she had known so well?

Will looked over at her as he licked his fork. "Are you okay? You've been distracted all evening. Surely you're not worried about that big catering gig?"

No, it wasn't the catering job for the Knights of Columbus. She could make salmon croquettes in her sleep. It was that she couldn't get the photo of Pete out of her mind, couldn't erase the allegations. She pulled her napkin into her lap, wound it around her palm. She shook her head.

"Then, what's wrong?" Will paused as he collected the plates.

"It's—Pete."

"Yeah, what a shock." He took their plates over to the sink and turned on the faucet. "I mean, I thought we knew him pretty well." He shook his head, squirted dish soap into the sink. "Did you find out anything more?"

Will only scanned the paper at work, and not even that every day. Obviously, he hadn't seen the story. Olivia hadn't had time to tell him about what she had read. As he rinsed the plates, she told him about the boys at his school and the women and the allegations. Her voice shook.

Will turned. "So there were several accusations? I thought maybe it was just one, and you were sure it must be a mistake."

"I was. But the newspaper article made it clear that there were over a dozen. Over a lot of years."

Will turned off the water, came over to sit at the table. "Were any of them at St. Andrew's?"

"There weren't any specifics. But it mentioned altar boys, and he had only been at two parishes when we knew him. So maybe." She remembered him out in the schoolyard after church services, shooting baskets with the altar servers.

Will came back to the table and sat. "So, while we were going to Mass there, and you were on that mission committee, he was doing that stuff?"

She nodded, miserable.

He slapped his palm on the table. "Jesus, Olivia! He married us! We sat in his office and planned the ceremony with him, and he stood at the altar in his vestments and pronounced us man and wife! And all the while he was diddling around with the altar boys? How could he think he could be a priest and do those heinous things? Boys, Liv, boys!"

Here it was. Almost two decades telescoped into this moment on a hot summer night.

"There's more."

Will raised his eyebrows. "He did something else?"

She couldn't put it off any longer. She had to tell him. All those years when she thought she could keep Pete a secret, thought her time with him was over long ago and didn't matter anymore, thought time had healed any hurts from the past—roared in and landed right on the gingham placemats on her kitchen table. She wished she had listened to Rebecca. Will might have accepted it then, when they all thought Pete was innocent and just a short-term romance. It would have been hard to admit to Will that she had been in love with a priest, but he would have come around. After all, Will knew Olivia loved *him*, and he would see that it was all in the past, nothing that could come between them. She drew in a breath, rolled and unrolled the edge of her placemat.

"I—he was my counselor."

"Counselor? You never said anything about that." Will frowned, tilted his head as if he was trying to make sense of it.

"It was before we met. I was kind of overwhelmed in a new place and was having panic attacks. He really helped me. And then, we became friends, and then we were—more than friends." There. In just three words, she said it. More than friends. Would Will make the leap to what that meant? She watched his face for a reaction.

He still looked puzzled, and then his eyes widened slightly. She felt the silence open up, waiting for him to fill it.

"More? What do you mean?"

"We were—involved." She reached for her napkin, folded it and refolded it, smoothing out the wrinkles.

Will shook his head slightly, as if to clear it. "You were involved, as in romantically involved?"

Olivia's throat felt tight. She couldn't speak.

"Wait! Did he hurt you? Take advantage of you? Oh, I could—" He clenched his fists and stood, pushing his chair back so violently it almost fell over.

"No. It was nothing like that."

Pete had not hurt her. Pete had loved her. She would explain that to Will, tell him how it happened, and then he would see why she was so upset, and he would do anything he could to help her. That was Will—her greatest support person. He would be shocked at the idea of her and Pete being romantically involved (who wouldn't?) but once she told him how it happened, he'd understand. Or if he didn't completely get it at first, she'd be able to help him see how it was. And he would know why Pete's story on the news was such a shock. The faucet dripped, plinking drops of water into the half-full sink. Will's cheeks were pale, and he went over and pulled the stopper, letting the water gurgle out into the drain.

After a long minute, he came back, dragged the chair out and sat. "Tell me."

And she did. The story she should have told him almost twenty years ago. She left out the parts about going to motels, and she decided not to tell him she had wanted to marry Pete. It might look like she had chosen Will on the rebound. And that wasn't true. She had always loved Will for himself. As much as she wanted to share her past with her husband, she also wanted to avoid hurting him. He would accept her reasons for keeping it a secret. That it had nothing to do with the two of them. Didn't everyone have at least one secret? And were secrets necessarily bad? Later she would question why she had kept it from him for so long, would see how secrets could fester, but now it seemed like it had been the right thing to do. At the time, it had been no more than an innocent omission.

Somewhere during the telling she started crying, but stopped, wiping her eyes with her napkin. She felt more settled, her voice stronger, and it felt good to bring it all out in the open. But then she saw his face. His lips formed a tight line. "Why," he asked, "didn't you ever say anything?"

CHAPTER 49

WILL LEFT THE kitchen, and his question hung in the humid air. She didn't have an answer, at least not one that would satisfy him. Or her. All she had was a huge lapful of regret and more questions than could possibly have answers. Water rushed through the pipes, and she knew he was upstairs in the bathroom getting ready for bed. She should go up and try to explain, but she wasn't sure he even wanted to listen to her. And she didn't know what she could say.

Instead, she went into the dark living room and turned on the TV. She dialed down the volume and sat in the corner of the couch near the open window. There was thunder far away, but it was probably only a heat storm. She'd welcome the comforting sound of rain; maybe it would even lull her to sleep.

She had never seen Will look hurt before, but that was what she saw in his eyes, in the defeated curve of his shoulders as he left the kitchen. And it was her fault. He always shook off annoyances, always found something positive to say. His walking away from her was surely a sign of the pain he felt. Of course, they had arguments, but they were always about simpler things. Should Brent be allowed to take shop instead of Spanish II? Could Lindsay get her ears pierced? Who would take off work to wait for the plumber? He had never walked away from her like this.

The thunder moved off, and she lowered her head onto her arms on the back of the couch, closing her eyes. She wanted to rewind the whole last week, wanted to go back to where they had been before they saw Pete on TV. Back to Will coming home to shoot baskets with Brent, back to chopping onions for meatloaf, back to the worst of their problems being where to go for vacation or whether or not Lindsay could wear a bikini swimsuit.

She wondered if he was sleeping. What would happen if she slipped into the bed next to him? What could she do to make it right? Maybe it wasn't possible. And then she shook her head. Will would come around. He was just surprised. Tomorrow they would talk again, and it would all be fine.

At some point she fell into a deep trough of sleep. When she woke up in the morning the *Today* show was on the TV and Will had left for work.

CHAPTER 50

OLIVIA SPLURGED ON a special dinner for the two of them. Herbed rack of lamb, rice pilaf, an arugula salad with fresh peaches. Lindsay was at a pool party, and Brent had gone camping for the weekend with his friend Todd and his family. When Will came into the kitchen where she was slicing peaches, he said he expected their usual Friday night pizza. The lamb stood on the counter, ready for the grill. "What's the occasion?"

"Well, the kids are both out, and I got these great peaches at the farm market, and I found a recipe for an herb rub I wanted to try, and—" She was speaking too fast, and he had just asked a simple question. Maybe the dinner had been a bad idea. It wasn't that she thought she could bribe him with food, she simply wanted to do something just for the two of them. She knew it would take more than lamb chops to heal what was wrong between them. But maybe it would be a start. It had been four days since she told him about Pete, four days of awkward conversations and more words unspoken than said aloud. Will shook his head the several times she tried to begin a conversation about it. "Will, can I try to explain?" He just wasn't ready yet.

Will went off to light the grill, and later they ate on the patio. She had put a bunch of daisies in a blue jar in the middle of the table, and had set out the clear glass plates and blue and white napkins. Would he remember that time he had brought her daisies all those years ago in Maine? They made casual conversation, and it almost felt like the old days, their solitary dinners before Brent and Lindsay were born, or when they waited to eat until the babies were tucked in their cribs. He sat back in his chair and his face seemed to soften from the hard lines she had seen lately. He ate seconds of the rice and insisted on clearing the table. She relaxed a little. The sun was setting, spreading coral across the sky as they dipped into dishes of raspberry sorbet and she lit a candle.

"Will," she said, "I am so sorry."

He put his spoon down and looked over at her. She noticed the slight wrinkles in his brow had returned, and she saw the dimming of the smile he had worn a second before. He sat silent, and she saw a hardness in his eyes.

"I should have told you about Pete a long time ago, before we were married. But I didn't think it would matter. It was over between him and me. And I was afraid."

"Of what? That I couldn't handle the truth?"

"No. That you would think badly about me. That you wouldn't understand."

"Olivia, you could have told me you had robbed a bank or that you cheated on your taxes. I loved you for who you were, not for anything you had or hadn't done."

She knew that now. Why hadn't she known it then? She saw him sitting across from her at the table as the generous-spirited man he was, had always been. He was never critical or judgmental. Hadn't Will's openness to everything, his acceptance of everyone, been one of the reasons she had fallen in love with him?

He drank the last of the wine in his glass. "What hurts is that you didn't trust me. That you didn't think enough of me to know that I would have accepted anything you'd done, anything you said." His words sounded flat, and he slumped in his chair as if all the energy had drained out of him.

She stirred the melted sorbet in her dish. Tiny seeds floated on the surface. An apology seemed as ineffectual as a slight breeze on a steaming day. Still, it was all she had. "I'm sorry."

Lindsay poked her head out the kitchen door. "I'm home!" She disappeared inside, heading for her room where she would be on the phone for hours rehashing the party.

They sat in silence for a few moments, the humid air thick with tension. As if looking at a film collage, she saw images of their life together. His broad smile when she walked down the aisle at their wedding; him holding Brent moments after his birth, tears glazing his eyes; the two of them and both kids crammed on to one long sled sliding down a snowy hill, no one steering; him coming in from raking the yard, yellow leaves stuck to his legs. She saw them doing the Sunday crosswords together, painting the nursery, digging out the flower beds, going to wine tastings. She wanted all of that back.

He spoke first. "Look, I know you never meant to hurt me. It's not about you intending anything. It's that you kept it to yourself all those years, and maybe if we hadn't seen that news story, I never would've known. And you let him marry us. We were on the altar at our wedding, and Pete knew, and you knew. And there I was, the odd man out. Don't tell Will, he doesn't deserve to be let in on the secret. Don't tell Will, he might freak." His voice had risen, and it shook with the intensity of his words. "Do you have any idea how foolish that makes me feel?" There was a bitter tone to his voice that she had never heard, as if every word brought a bad taste to his mouth.

"It wasn't anything like that. I didn't think any of those things. And it was over between us. I had ended it."

"The point, Liv, is that I deserved to know that this huge thing had happened to you. You can't possibly think that being romantically involved with a priest wasn't a huge thing."

SILENT

"It was, but I told you it was over when I started seeing you. I—"

"If he had moved away, if he was somewhere in California or Florida, then maybe I could see it, but he was still at St. Andrew's, and you went along with asking him to marry us. Don't you think you should have said something then?" He waved his hand over the candle where a small gray moth was hovering, its striped wings dangerously close to the flames. The sun had disappeared below the trees, and the patio beyond the candle had fallen into darkness.

Olivia didn't know what to say. Will was right, of course. And now she knew, too, that things you bury that shouldn't be buried have a way of rising to the surface. If only she had listened to Rebecca when she told Olivia she had to be open with Will. If only she had stopped worrying about it and just told him. It wasn't that she didn't trust him. It was that she was afraid of losing him, afraid that he would leave her if he knew.

"If I could turn back the calendar, I would. I'd tell you everything. But I can't do that, and now, besides saying I'm sorry, I don't know what else to do."

Will moved his empty wineglass in slow circles on the table. "I have to ask. What do you think? Did he do those things? *Could* he have done those things? The news didn't spell it out, but I can only imagine. Is he gay? I mean, going after the boys. And how could he be gay if you and he—if you were together?"

Olivia shook her head. It was a question that had been plaguing her. How could he have wanted to have sex with her and also do things (she still didn't know what) with boys? When she thought about that, she felt dirty imagining his hands all over so many others and then on her. She pushed that thought away, grabbing on to what she wanted to believe. He had loved her.

"No," she said. "He couldn't be. None of this can be true."

Will frowned, used his thumb and index finger to snuff out the candle. The darkness breathed around them, and crickets chirred in the grass.

209

He pushed back his chair. "I just need time to think, to take it all in." He picked up their wine glasses and headed for the back door.

Maybe after he thought for a while, his hurt would subside and he would see that she needed him, that this was something they could face together. She lingered on the patio listening to the neighborhood settle into night. The Weschlers' dog whining. A wave of music from the open window of a passing car. The clunk of a door closing. When she went inside, the only light was the lamp over the stove. The plates and glasses were put away, the dishtowel folded neatly over the rim of the sink. She curled into a corner of the living room couch and let the house settle in silence around her.

What she wanted, as she sat in the dark living room, was for Will to come down, his hair rumpled from his pillow, and sit with her. She wanted to hear him say he had been shocked at first, but he was on her side, had always been on her side. She wanted to feel his arm on her back, pulling her to him, until they sat nestled against the cushions, his leg brushing hers, her hand on his chest, feeling the steady reassurance of his heartbeat, breathing in his scent of grass clippings and Ivory soap. If she couldn't go back and undo the past, she wanted the present to welcome her, to be the place where she belonged. Because right now, she didn't feel like she belonged anywhere.

But there were no footsteps on the stairs. Upstairs, Will and Lindsay slept spooled in their dreams, and she sat downstairs hugging her knees, with too much space around her. What, she wondered, did Will want? Was it to have things as they were before they saw Pete on the television? Basketball in the driveway with Brent, singing off-key while Lindsay played the piano, planning for that "second honeymoon" trip to Barbados? She knew it was what she wanted, but it couldn't be that simple. She also had to make peace with the past. Did Will think if he ignored the past it would disappear?

She had no idea what spun inside his head, because he wouldn't talk to her about it. And now, more than ever, she needed him. Not to reassure her that everything would be okay; she knew it wouldn't. But to reassure her that he was still with her. She wanted him to ask her to massage his neck at the end of a workday. She wanted him to rub her back when she had been out gardening all morning. She wanted words, the sound of his laugh, a phone call in the middle of the day to see if she could meet him for lunch. She wanted him to sit beside her to watch a movie on tv, she wanted him to offer to run to the store when they were out of paper towels or mayo. She wanted him to bring home take-out because she'd been prepping for a catering job all day. What she didn't want was what she had. His silence. His leaving for work extra early and staying late. His asking with annoyance, "Are we out of peanut butter?" as if it were her fault.

It wasn't about things. It wasn't about the peanut butter or the phone calls or plane tickets to Barbados. It was about presence. She didn't pretend that he could fix any of it, that he could make Pete disappear, or that anything could make her forget. It was about Will being by her side, sensing her need for him. Answering that need. Loneliness swilled around inside her, and she burrowed deeper into the couch.

CHAPTER 51

OLIVIA AND REBECCA had kept up their friendship through multiple moves and life changes. Her old roommate was the first person Olivia told after Will when she had the pregnancy test and she knew Brent was on the way. Rebecca insisted that 8 months pregnant or not, Olivia had to be in her wedding. Rebecca and Steve had hopped from city to city (Dallas, Omaha, Boston, and now Baltimore), and Olivia and Will had lived for thirteen years in Richmond. Regardless of where they were, though, one of them would pick up the phone to announce a new job, a new baby, or just to chat. They never talked about Pete. Most likely, Rebecca saw him as a figure in the distant past. Their conversations revolved around whatever crises or joys populated their days now.

So it was no wonder that two days after the dinner, Olivia knew Rebecca's was the voice she needed to hear. When Rebecca picked up the phone, she broke into laughter. "It must be ESP," she said. "I just burned a batch of peanut butter cookies." Evidently, her prowess in the kitchen hadn't improved over the years.

Olivia wound the cord around her hand. She dispensed with chatting and blurted it out. "I found out something, and I made a huge mistake."

"Whoa, Olivia, slow down."

It was hard to know where to start, so she just began with "I saw Pete on the evening news. You know, the priest."

"Father Pete? Your Father Pete?"

"One and the same."

"Why would he be on the news?" Olivia could hear Rebecca's stereo in the background, Creedence Clearwater. Then silence as she turned it off. "Did he do something to get famous?"

"Not exactly. Or yes, kind of." She paused, swallowing. Her throat felt tight. "He's accused of some kind of sex abuse."

"No! Are you sure?"

"There was a photo and his name. And there was a story in the paper that mentioned St. Andrew's." She told Rebecca about the accusations from the students.

"Wait! Kids, like grade school kids?"

"I think high school. Where he taught. And college guys."

"What did it say he did?"

"Nothing specific. Just phrases like 'inappropriate touching.'"

"And you had no idea?" She paused, and Olivia imagined her shaking her head. "I didn't mean that the way it sounded. Of course you didn't. And anyway, it must have been after you were with him. He's not still at your old church, is he?"

"No. I mean, yes. I mean, he's not still at St. Andrew's. The news story said he's somewhere in Georgia. But no, it wasn't after I was with him. It was—before. And—" She paused to swallow. "It was while he was with me."

"Wait. He was seeing you and he was molesting his students?" There was a moment of silence. Rebecca's words echoed in Olivia's ears. "I only met hm at those baseball games, and of course, at your wedding, but he seemed so—normal. Nice." She paused. "Even if he did break your heart that summer."

"That's just it. He was a nice guy. I can't wrap my head around it."

There was a pause, and Olivia imagined Rebecca twirling an earring the way she did when she was thinking.

Finally, Rebecca spoke. "So what does Will say about it?"

"That's the other part. Will is furious."

"Well, he should be. If what the paper says is true, he must feel terrible for those boys. I'm furious. Just thinking about how they must have felt makes my blood boil. I've read other stories in the news about priests abusing children. It's sick. And the priests always make sure they bully the kids into not telling. And he's probably devastated for you, that this happened to you too."

"Not just because of Pete." Olivia plopped down on a ladder-back chair, tucked her feet around the legs. "He's furious with me. Because I never told him."

"How could you have? You just found out."

"No, I mean about the two of us. How I was seeing Pete."

"Even after you were married?" Rebecca's voice rose, astonishment in her tone. "I thought you—"

"I kept meaning to. But then time went by and it never seemed to be the right time and then it didn't seem to matter." She had pushed Pete to the back of her life, a memory that had nothing to do with Will and the two kids. Had nothing to do with her catering and family vacations and being on PTA committees. When they returned to the D.C. area, they attended another church. Holy Angels. She hadn't even known where he was until she read the article.

Finding out about him felt like standing on an outcropping of rock and hearing cracks start to open. It was why she had phoned Rebecca; her long-time friend could always stabilize her. Above all, she wanted Rebecca to help her sort it all out. Between hearing about Pete and having Will so angry with her, she felt like those cracks were widening under her. She thought she heard Rebecca sigh.

Rebecca spoke. "I guess I can see that Will would be upset. He probably feels, I don't know, left out? Like you were keeping something really important from him." She paused, and Olivia hear her sigh. "Is that it?"

"He thinks I didn't trust him enough. He thinks I deliberately hid my relationship with Pete, that I thought he'd, in his words, 'freak out' if I told him. And I know I should have told him. I don't know why I didn't."

"Look, I know Will," said Rebecca, her voice softening. "He'll get over it. Just give him some time."

"I don't know, Rebecca. I've never seen him like this."

"Again, give him time. But, what about you? It must have been beyond shocking to find out about this."

Olivia didn't know how to put it into words. None of it fit. The guy who played baseball in neighborhood pick-up games, the guy who loved her oatmeal cookies, the guy who loved looking through a telescope at the stars, was secretly touching teenaged boys? "I just can't make sense of it. He wasn't like that when I knew him, and yet these men are saying he was. I'm not sleeping well, and I keep seeing his face and wondering if I knew him at all."

"I can't even imagine. Do you want me to come over?"

Olivia knew she would come if she asked. But she lived over an hour away, and Olivia had shopping to do for a catering job. "I'm fine."

CHAPTER 52

THE NEXT DAY, she rose early, planning to work in the garden before it got too hot. It would calm her, the easy repetitive motions of loosening the soil around the plants, pulling out weeds with their thready roots. She could envision the rose bushes breathing around her, unfurling their delicate petals. Sometimes (she wouldn't admit this to anyone) she even talked to the zinnias and the marigolds. Yes, the garden was the place to be on this morning. The house was quiet, the kitchen still cool from the night air that had come in from the open windows. She was looking for her sunglasses amid the clutter on the desk when she saw the folded newspaper. She picked it up and looked at Pete's photo. How could it be?

She had believed in him as the dedicated priest who had been the first person to welcome her to the parish, who spent hours preparing a Sunday sermon, who knew all the parishioners by name. He had been the originator of the mission project, had suggested reading out children's birthdays at the popular nine a.m. Sunday Mass. She had loved his contagious laughter, his patience showing her how to use his telescope, his intuition in knowing just from the way she sat in a chair that she had had a bad day. She had loved the way he was so self-assured and how his words of advice were always sound. And maybe most of all she had loved him because he loved her.

The shift from gratitude and admiration into deeper feelings had been shocking to her, but she had trusted him, and the two of them had felt right. But now, after reading the news, she wondered if there were signs she should have seen, what she might have overlooked. Yes, there had been times he said he'd call and didn't, or a few evenings when he was late showing up at their secret place, but he always had a good reason. A last-minute faculty meeting, a request for a priest to take communion to a sick parishioner. That could happen to anyone. Who wouldn't have believed him? And there had been no reason to doubt him when they finally met and he gathered her in his arms and whispered that he had been waiting for this moment all day. It had felt so good to be loved.

But what if he had been late because he had been trying to seduce a student he had kept after school? What if he had given an altar boy a ride home and had touched him and made him promise not to tell? There wouldn't be signs of that, would there? How could she have known? Or was she just too trusting?

She thought she knew so much about him, things he had told her and things she had observed being with him. She knew about his family, how he wanted a dog, that he drank scotch and smoked Winstons. But really, the list of what she knew was so small compared to what she didn't know. What music had he listened to as a teenager? Had he voted in the last election? Who had his best friends been when he was growing up? Did he use ketchup or mustard, or both, on his burgers? What was his favorite time of day? Did he read the magazines he had fanned out on the table in his office, or were they there just for show? Had he ever traveled out of the country, and what places did he wish he could visit? Was he ever afraid?

Little things, all of them, and maybe they didn't matter. What mattered were the huge questions, the most important being had he only pretended to love her? Had something clicked in him the first time he saw her? Did he have a plan then? Was that why he didn't tell her he was a priest? And had the rest of it been a sham? His concern when she cried in the classroom after the meeting? His furrowed brows when she admitted she was having those panic attacks? The way his eyes filled with longing? All the times he told her he couldn't get her out of his mind, that being with her at the end of the day made the rest of the hours bearable? Had none of it been real? She couldn't accept that. Accepting that would also be to blame herself for falling for him.

She spiraled back to that first year. Without Pete, maybe she would have met those law students and senate staffers Aubrey had talked about, maybe the stories she told her family would have been true. It was an accident that she happened to be at that ball field and at the coffee hour the next day. Suppose she and Rebecca had gone to a museum instead, suppose she had chosen a different church? St. Andrew's had been the closest, but she could have driven just a few miles more and attended Holy Angels, or Sacred Heart, or St. Francis Xavier. She had never been a believer in fate or predestination, but Pete had said so many times that it had been no accident that she had landed in his parish that she nodded in agreement, feeling so fortunate, accident or no accident. Yes, it had to have been authentic, just what he said. She would have known otherwise.

But if the article were true, and it was still an if in her mind, then she had given her heart to a man who wasn't who he said he was. Who, instead of being a pillar of the church community, was living a dark and disturbing lie. She didn't know what to think. Folding the newspaper into a smaller and smaller square, she stuffed it back in the bottom drawer of her kitchen desk. She stood for a moment listening to the thrum of the fridge, goosebumps prickling her arms, and then she went into the mud room to collect her gardening tools.

CHAPTER 53

A WEEK LATER, Olivia was again in the garden, dead-heading the rosebushes, when a pea-green VW chugged into her driveway and Rebecca stepped out. She was wearing a paisley skirt and a purple striped top, and it made Olivia grin. Only Rebecca could get away with an outfit like that. Olivia glanced down at her own outfit—cutoffs and a faded tank top with the logo of one of Brent's soccer teams.

"Surprise!"

"What are you— I mean, I'm glad to see you, but—"

"Can't a good friend just stop by?" She picked up one of the fallen roses and plucked off the petals. "These make great potpourri. Mind if I take some?" She was already putting them in the oversized pocket of her skirt.

"Rebecca, you live in Baltimore. You don't just 'stop by' from Baltimore."

"Yeah, I know. Steve has the day off, and he and Sarah are having a father-daughter day. Petting zoo." She dropped down on the grass beside Olivia. "I've got the whole day free." She reached over and enfolded Olivia in a hug. Olivia smelled lavender. As they drew apart, Rebecca patted her purse. "And I have something to show you."

"It's getting hot out here," Olivia said, putting down her shears. "Let's go inside."

They sat on the screen porch with glasses of iced coffee, and Olivia brought out a plate of almond cookies. After a few minutes of chatting ("Why don't my cookies ever turn out?" Rebecca complained), Rebecca reached into her bag and brought out a folded section of newspaper. "There was an article in the *Sun* about Pete."

"Was it the same story?"

"I guess. It says just about what you told me was in the *Post*. There was just one thing I noticed that you didn't mention." She held the paper out to Olivia. "The church is looking for people to give more information about him."

Olivia scanned the article. It was, as Rebecca had said, the same as the one she had read, but the final paragraph leapt out at her. "*Church officials are asking anyone who has more information about Father Kowolski to step forward.*" She had read that in the *Post* but it hadn't registered. There were the names and phone numbers of the Washington and Baltimore bishops. She put the paper down in her lap.

"What kind of additional information? Don't they have enough?"

"Well," Rebecca said, "maybe if some of the accusations prove false, they want others to fall back on."

Olivia shook her head. "Do you really think someone will read this article and head to the phone to call the bishop? Would you? Don't you think most people would like to forget about it?" Her head swirled with questions. Who were the people who had come forward? If it were altar boys, they'd be grown men now. What had made them break the silence of almost twenty years? Had they just come forward recently or had the list of accusers been growing over years? And how many accusations did it take for the church to remove a priest from a parish and put him in rehab? That's what the article said about Pete. He was in rehab somewhere. The information was sketchy. It referred to "several credible sources." Several could be three. Several could be a dozen. Several, she mused, could be wrong.

Part of her held on to the thread that said the whole thing was a mistake. She wanted to believe that the Pete she had known was the real Pete. "Suppose," she said now to Rebecca, "that this isn't true at all?"

"You mean, that Pete didn't do any of it?" Rebecca's voice had risen a few notches. Then she knit her brows and shook her head, speaking more gently. "Olivia, I get how you wish it wasn't true. It must be a nightmare. But does it really make sense that people from different places and different years would make up the same story?" She pointed to the paper that lay on the glass-topped table in front of them. "Boys from St. Andrew's, from Baltimore, from that high school where Pete taught in Philly. Women from we don't know where."

"I know, but I—"

Rebecca finished her sentence for her. "Wish it had never happened. But, and I don't want to sound blunt and cold, it did. And it happened to you."

Olivia didn't say anything. She picked up a cookie, but she wasn't hungry. Despite what Rebecca and the news said, she prayed they were both wrong.

Rebecca reached for the paper. "They're talking about you."

"Me? What does that article have to do with me?"

"You can be one of the people to come forward."

Olivia felt hot blood rise in her cheeks. How could Rebecca even think she could do that? Would do that? What would she tell anyway? That she had loved Pete and he had loved her? What business was that of the Church? "That's not going to happen."

"I know it would be hard, but you don't want him to get away with it, do you?"

"You don't get it." Olivia picked up the cookie again, broke it in half. Broke the halves into smaller pieces, littering the table with crumbs.

Rebecca sighed and seemed to be measuring her words. "Liv, but what he did was abuse. To them. To you."

"No!" Olivia's voice startled her, the word shattering the quiet morning. "What's in the paper has nothing to do with me. I'm disgusted about what the boys say, though I'm not convinced it's true. You didn't see how it was with us. He loved me. What we had was good."

"Olivia, he had no right. That's what it comes down to. What I know about the Catholic Church you could fit in a thimble, but I do know that priests have no business having a sexual relationship with anyone, and that includes women."

Olivia was livid. Rebecca had barely known Olivia when she started seeing Pete. How could Rebecca presume to understand what it had been like? She looked over at her, and in a flash saw not her good friend but someone who was judging her. She wanted Rebecca to take her pot-pourri-filled pockets and drive back to Baltimore. They couldn't have any kind of conversation if Rebecca had this ridiculous idea that Pete had abused her. She gathered the glasses and the plate of cookies and stood. "I think you'd better go. I'm sorry you drove all the way over here, but I can't do this. I need to be alone."

CHAPTER 54

BEFORE SHE LEFT, Rebecca apologized, saying maybe she had been too harsh. "It's just that it makes me so mad that he did that to you." Olivia faked a smile, watched the green VW pull away, and went back to her gardening. For a while she snipped at the wilting flowers with sharp snaps of the shears, but soon her energy waned, and she sat on the grass, idly taking petals off the pink rose she had just removed from the bush. Its edges had already started to turn brown.

He had loved her. She knew that. What they had together had been true. Part of her wanted to call him (if she had known where he was) and ask him to explain. Listen to him say yes, it was all a mistake. The boys had made up the stories. He would never do anything like that. Didn't she know that? And she would relax, say, yes, of course she did. And he'd say something like, "Look, when this all blows over, let's get together for dinner. You and Will and me." It had been almost twenty years. She wondered if he still sucked on those lime Lifesavers.

But then she remembered what Rebecca had said about reporters having to check and double-check their sources. The newspaper article had three names in the by-line. It wasn't just one reporter's work. And there were probably others behind the scenes. A story this big (it was on the front page of the Metro section) must have taken months to research. Could three separate reporters have reached the same wrong conclusions? But she wondered if the reporters had actually spoken with the boys (some of them men now). Had any of them even spoken with Pete? Of course not, she realized. He was somewhere in rehab.

All afternoon, a thought itched at the back of her head. She pushed it away, made herself focus on shrimp salad and strawberry tarts. In the kitchen, she sifted and chopped, rolled out dough, measured the ingredients for her favorite spice mix. She was calm when she cooked, and was usually totally wrapped up in what she was doing, but today something nagged at her. She tried to focus on the aroma of paprika and chili flakes, but her mind was elsewhere.

She was rolling out the dough for the tarts when the doubt grew more insistent. Over twenty years of allegations. Four parishes, two schools. And in addition to every accusation reported, how many had been lumped together in the "several other credible sources" phrase in the newspaper? Two? Five? Fifteen? What she had called coincidence wasn't that at all. She couldn't deny it any longer, and the knowledge moved through her like a wave of sickness so that her hands shook and cold sweat beaded on her forehead.

The dough sat unfinished on the floury board, and she sat down hard on the high wooden stool. The man who abused boys had touched her with the same hands. Questions ricocheted around in her mind and seemed to bounce off the bright yellow walls of the kitchen. Had he constructed this whole fantasy about being a man who just couldn't help himself from falling in love with her? If so, then he hadn't been in love with her at all. She was just one more object to him. She was no more important to him than the altar boy had been, or the high school math student, or the college guys who had gone to him for counseling, or the basketball players, or any of the others who had not spoken up. Because if ten had said something, maybe there were thirty who didn't. And he had maybe been touching a fourteen-year-old at five in the afternoon and then met her three hours later in his car, saying he had been thinking about her all day. He had touched her with those hands, and she'd thought he only wanted to touch her, that he would do something that priests shouldn't do because she was so damned special. But she wasn't. She was someone willing to get into his car with him.

Three hours ago, she had been defending Pete, and now she knew she was only defending herself. She shook her head, remembering how she had pictured them married, with children in strollers and a front yard with azaleas. She had seen them as another Greg and Marianne, that happy couple at church who had left their religious lives for each other. She had believed with her whole heart that he loved her, and that his love for her went deeper than the love of his vocation. And even when he chose that vocation over a life with her, she had admired him, thought him noble, unselfish.

But it had been a lie.

She felt clammy and weak. The smell of strawberries in their sweet syrup turned her stomach. She dumped them in the garbage disposal, gathered up the half-rolled-out dough and fed it bit by bit into the grinding gears, a hard stream of water from the faucet forcing it down through the pipes.

CHAPTER 55

SHE DIDN'T KNOW why she kept the news articles. Her first instinct had been to throw them away, but maybe she'd find an error, a place where the writers expressed doubt. Or maybe when she had doubts, she could reread the words and know yes, it was true. Whatever the reason, she had crammed them in the back of the bottom drawer of her desk. The desk was where she kept the kids' report cards, medical and dental records, files of recipes and household repairs. The articles defied classification, so she pushed them in behind the hanging file for car repairs.

She knew they were there, but she didn't want to touch them. There was no need to read them because their words were etched in her mind. Credible sources. Sexual misconduct. High school students. The dates jumped back and forth. Before she'd known him. While she knew him. Since she and Will had married. The last time she had touched the papers, the day after Rebecca's visit, when she pushed them to the back of the drawer, she had gone directly to the sink to wash her hands. It wasn't just the ink smearing on her fingers. It was the words themselves. She couldn't get all the ink off. It lingered like a shadow on her skin.

Pete had abused his students. Pete had not been honest with her. Pete had abused her. Had he charmed the others the way he had charmed her?

Had he told them how special they were, had they been beguiled by the light in his green eyes, the earnestness of his words? Like her, had they misinterpreted what he said and did, blind to what was manipulation masquerading as genuine affection? Or had they been cajoled against their wills, drawn into something they feared but didn't know how to escape?

Rebecca had encouraged her to write a letter, but she didn't think she could do it. She didn't want to call attention to herself, and she hoped by not doing anything it might all go away. She threw herself into her work. A lunch for the women's auxiliary at the fire house, two dinners, a small wedding reception in the park gazebo. She minced and chopped and sautéed. She crimped pie crusts and made raspberry purée and cold asparagus soup. She tried not to think about Pete, but he was right there in the bottom drawer of her desk over in the kitchen corner. Trying to forget about it was like trying to silence a song that replayed itself in your head and kept you awake at night. She played music on her tape player with the volume set on high, trying to find distraction in other songs. Crosby, Stills and Nash. The Beatles. Barbra Streisand.

She tried to talk to Will again, but he pushed her off. He still avoided talking about it. He had merely shaken his head at the idea of her writing the letter. "Do you really want to expose yourself that way? What in hell do you think this will accomplish?" It felt like he wanted to act as if it had never happened. She didn't take the time to try to analyze his reaction, and it would be years before she would understand that he was speaking from his own pain, that the whole thing was too much for him to deal with. Now she only felt the span of the rift between them. It felt like he was mad at her all the time for things that had nothing to do with Pete. One day she vowed to write, even got out a box of stationery. The next she dismissed the idea. It went back and forth like that for a week.

Finally, it was Lindsay and Brent who decided it for her. Watching fifteen-year-old Brent reach for another pancake at the breakfast table made her think about Pete's students. Listening to her daughter chatter about which boys would be at the pool party accentuated Lindsay's innocence. Olivia had a fierce desire to protect them.

She would write the letter.

She was still not convinced it would make a difference. One letter. One priest. She wondered if any other people had read the news articles and come forward. Maybe there had been dozens, and her voice would be just that, one voice. How could that matter? But if she didn't write the letter, would it be the same as condoning what he had done? She looked around the kitchen table, at the spray of freckles over Brent's nose, the way Lindsay's dark lashes framed her eyes. They became, for an instant, the other teens Pete had hurt.

But it worried her, the actual writing. It would be a big risk, exposing herself this way. Her name at the bottom of the letter. Her return address on the envelope. The news article had said the church promised anonymity, but how anonymous would it be when her name was right there in blue ink? Someone would know, and not a trusted someone like Rebecca, but a stranger unfolding the stationery. She would address the letter to the bishop, but she had no idea how many hands it would pass through before it landed on his desk.

Rebecca was away on vacation with her family, and since Will refused to even talk about the letter, she was on her own. She waited until one hot afternoon when the house was empty and she had no catering excuses. She retrieved the newspaper articles from the drawer, ripped a few pages out of an old spiral notebook (this might take several attempts), uncapped a pen, and sat at the patio table. She put the words on the paper slowly, read them over, ripped it up, and began again. After an hour, she saw how, as she wrote, the tip of the pen had torn the paper, but she kept going through four drafts, until she had it the way she wanted. With great care, she wrote the final version on clean sheets of pale blue stationery.

CHAPTER 56

IT WAS ONLY five days after she sent the letter that someone from the chancery office called and asked her to come in so they could "look into" the situation. She was surprised at how soon she heard from them, but figured it meant they believed she had something important to say. When the secretary said she'd be seeing a monsignor, she was disappointed. What about the bishop? The bishop was out of town. But the monsignor was also important, and the chancery secretary had said he was in charge of "this situation."

She kept a copy of the letter. The night before the meeting she took it with her into the bathroom, turning on the shower so she wouldn't be disturbed.

Dear Bishop McLaughlin,

I am writing in regard to . . . knew Father Kowolski . . . counseling . . . became friends . . . made advances . . .

At the time I thought . . . now I know . . . stepped out of bounds . . . never should have . . . deep hurt . . .

Want to make sure . . . young people he might . . . if this helps . . .

When she told Will, he shook his head and said only, "I wish you hadn't done this. Do you really want to go to the bishop and talk about it? Let it go. It happened a long time ago. But since you did . . . good luck. I hope it goes okay." He looked sad, and he opened his mouth as if he was going to say more. Then he shrugged and took the hedge clippers out to prune the forsythia. Discussion over. He refused to discuss it anymore, and he didn't ask to see the letter. He didn't seem angry, just resigned. In another life he might have offered to go with her.

It was different with Rebecca. She was back from vacation, and when Olivia phoned her, and she could hear the smile in her friend's voice.

"Yes! You're doing the right thing. I know it'll be hard, but you can do it. Just tell the truth." And Rebecca insisted on going with her. "I'll buy you a drink when it's over."

The day of the appointment dawned rainy, and the streaming water on the windows only intensified her nervousness. She turned lights on in every room, sat staring at the bowl of cereal she couldn't swallow. Brent and Lindsay were moping around the house complaining about having nothing to do, so she gave them enough chores to last a week. Will left for work as if it were an ordinary day, saying nothing about the appointment. She had told him the day, but maybe he had forgotten. Later she would realize what an asset it would have been to have him with her, to show that he was supporting her in her claim. She would also understand that hers was a solitary battle.

She and Rebecca arrived ten minutes early for her eleven-thirty appointment. The chancery building was red brick, rising high above the street, with a big parking lot where most of the spaces had "reserved" signs. She had chosen a conservative navy dress and had even worn pantyhose and heels. She'd had to search through her closet for the shoes. The office was chilly, and they sat on a small Naugahyde couch in the waiting room, and Olivia nervously picked up leaflets scattered around the coffee table. *You and Your Faith. Finding Christ in the Workplace. Catholicism in the Modern World.* She was too distracted to read them. Their words had nothing to do with her. The words she would say were churning around in her head, too many words, maybe not enough words. It was all she could do not to stand and run out the door. She thought she might throw up.

At precisely eleven-thirty, a young overweight priest appeared, introduced himself as Father Vincente, and asked her to follow him. Rebecca stood, too, and he said, "And you are . . ." When she explained she was the best friend, the priest shook his head. "I'm sorry, just Mrs. Simpson." He pointed to a table by the door. "If you'd like coffee . . ." Olivia cast a last glance at Rebecca as she followed the priest through a door that made no sound when it opened or closed. If she had been unsure before, now she desperately wanted her friend with her. She didn't know if she'd be able to speak at all. As they walked down the carpeted hall, Father Vincente explained that she was the one making the accusation, it wouldn't be appropriate to have anyone else there. Olivia didn't understand that, but before she had a chance to object, the priest was opening a door and gesturing her inside. After she entered, the door closed silently and Father Vincente disappeared.

The monsignor and another priest were seated at a wide mahogany table when she entered the room. She knew the monsignor because he was at least twenty years older than the other man and was wearing a cassock with magenta piping. She recognized her handwriting on the paper in front of him, and he and the priest each had a yellow legal pad. There was a chair in front of the table for her, an upholstered armchair like her grandmother had in her living room. The monsignor rose and shook her hand, and the other priest nodded and fiddled with a tape recorder. "You don't mind, do you? We want to be sure of accuracy in case we have any questions." Olivia didn't like the idea of being recorded, but what could she do? She draped her raincoat on the back of the chair and sat. Her feet felt damp in her shoes. She was torn between what she was afraid to do and what she wanted to do. She wished Rebecca had been able to come with her. The room felt way too big for the three of them.

The monsignor summarized what she had said in her letter. His voice was non-committal, and he kept his eyes on the unfolded paper, smoothing it down with his fingers. Then he looked at her, and she saw no expression in his dark eyes. She had thought he might start with something like, "I am so sorry you—", but there was nothing like that. He said they would be asking her questions "for clarification." And they did. In the beginning the questions were easy—dates and circumstances. Why had she sought counseling? Had anyone seen them together? She answered easily. These were the parts she had rehearsed in her head.

And then the questions shifted. More personal. What had she been wearing when she went to Father Kowolski's office? Had she given him any signals? Why had she gone back after the first time he touched her? The tape recorder whirred. Occasionally the monsignor or the priest wrote something on his legal pad. Olivia felt sweat drip down her ribs. These weren't the questions she expected. They all seemed to be about her and not about Pete. Her mouth was dry, and she wanted a glass of water. The rain beat on the window and the squares of glass bloomed with steam.

Had there been penetration? Orgasms? How many times? She began to feel like she was in confession instead of making an accusation, and she was embarrassed at the questions and the answers she had to give. Talking to a monsignor about orgasm? She begged her skin not to blush, and she forged ahead. Told herself they were just words. They asked. She answered. "Yes, he did those things. Yes, I did that, but—" What was the purpose of this form of inquiry? Why did they need these details? The monsignor had no expression on his face, no eyebrows raised, no hint of a smile or a frown, and Olivia had no sense that he saw her as a woman telling a difficult story. She wished Rebecca was with her. Or Will. Would Will's presence have made a difference to the monsignor, helped to convince him that she was a responsible, married woman who was telling the truth?

Finally, there was a long silence, and the priest clicked off the tape recorder. Without the whirr, there was only the spit of rain on the windows. The monsignor seemed to be thinking, and he tented his long, skinny fingers to his chin. The minutes ticked by. She wondered what the next step would be. In spite of having to answer the graphic questions, a feeling of relief replaced her nervousness. Now something would be done. She could see the blur of green trees outside, hear the whine of a siren.

Finally, he spoke. "You know, Mrs. Simpson, sometimes a young woman can send signals by her clothes, the way she sits." Olivia looked down at her lap, the hem of her dark blue dress. "A tight blouse, a short skirt." What her clothes have to do with any of this? "We know Father Kowolski was a young priest when you knew him. It is very possible that he was . . . distracted." He smiled, but his smile looked like ice. "Not that he should have done what he did, but . . . well, he was only human, and you—"

What was he saying? That she had made Pete touch her? That he could be forgiven because he was young and she was a distraction?

"Did you go to a Catholic school?"

She thought it an odd question, but she nodded in a daze, feeling that the conversation was going in a whole wrong direction. This wasn't why she had come. The relief she had felt five minutes ago turned to confusion. Hadn't she made herself clear? And what did her education have to do with any of it?

"Then you know, I'm sure, because I'm sure that the nuns taught you this, that there are different messages given by clothes and posture and even words. And you were a grown woman. You knew the difference between right and wrong." Every sentence was laced with judgment. Her stomach twisted.

He was saying it was her fault. He was saying she had tempted Pete. She found it difficult to listen because the words started to whirl around her. The rain at the window was too loud, the room too cold with the air-conditioning blowing from a vent over her head. He was folding up her letter, sliding it into a file folder. She wanted it back. She wanted to take her words back, if this was what he thought. The younger priest had ejected the tape from the recorder and was wrapping the cord around the machine. The cassette went in the folder with the letter.

"Certainly, we will take what you told us into advisement. Thank you for coming in."

The meeting was over.

CHAPTER 57

SHE SHOULDN'T HAVE gone to see any church officials. While she hadn't expected the monsignor to jump up and clap his hands and tell her she had given them the missing piece they needed, she hadn't anticipated his patronizing attitude or what felt like a dismissal. Of course, she had no way of knowing what was in his mind, or if what she said would impact what happened with Pete. The monsignor wouldn't have revealed any of that. But her overall reaction was that it had been a waste of time, since he had turned her story around, implied that she had been the temptress. She thought she had made it clear that Pete had initiated all of it. In his implication that she had been flirting, it felt like he was protecting Pete.

Rebecca dragged her to lunch after the meeting, and Olivia refused to talk until they were seated in a booth at the Irish pub and she had a Manhattan in front of her. When they left the chancery, she just shook her head at the fusillade of Rebecca's questions, her heels tapping furiously on the wet sidewalk. She was afraid any words that came out of her mouth would spark with fire. Rebecca had an umbrella, but Olivia barreled ahead of her, oblivious to the rain dripping beneath the collar of her slicker.

She hadn't gone to the Church just for herself, but for anyone who hadn't the courage (and she had struggled to find hers) to come forth. She had been thinking about those others, knowing that someone had to speak up and what it meant to stay silent. There had been that incident in New York City where the girl was being attacked on the sidewalk and the people in the apartment houses just looked down and watched it happen. It wasn't their problem. But maybe there was no such thing as an innocent bystander. If she didn't speak up, if she saw something wrong and turned her head, wasn't she condoning the wrong? The church had asked for additional information, and she had given it. Shouldn't it have been received with more gratitude? With more professionalism?

"I told him everything," she explained, after taking a long swallow of her drink. "And he had the nerve to ask me if I had been wearing a short skirt." Anger seethed around every syllable. She told Rebecca about all the personal questions, the tape recorder, and the insinuation that she had tempted Pete by her clothing.

"He's full of shit," Rebecca said, her dark eyes wide. "I would have told him to go to hell."

That made Olivia smile a little. All five foot three of Rebecca standing up to the monsignor in his black cassock and stern eyes. She would, no doubt, have bristled at the personal questions and refused to answer or had some no-nonsense retort. But Rebecca didn't understand how it was with Catholics and priests. You didn't talk back to a priest. And a monsignor? He was next in command to a bishop, and then a cardinal, and a step above that, the pope. No. You might think a priest was full of shit, but you kept that to yourself. Sitting in the restaurant, her drink almost drained, taking tentative bites of her roast beef sandwich, Olivia couldn't see herself talking back or refusing to answer any of the embarrassing questions, but she felt in every cell in her body the indignation at the way he had treated her. And what would talking back have accomplished?

She knew how it looked to others. That she had been an adult, that she had not been forced. And the monsignor must have wondered why it took her so long to come forward. Why didn't she say anything when it happened? He hadn't asked her that, though it had been implied when he said, "And now, all these years later, you've decided to speak up." How could she explain that in all those years she had never seen it as abuse? That she had only good memories of her time with Pete? That it was only when the story surfaced of what he had done with his students that she had reluctantly put two and two together and seen herself in the mix?

Rebecca helped herself to Olivia's French fries. "Would you consider trying again? Say you want another chance to explain?"

"Sure. That's a great idea. I can go through the same interrogation again, and maybe wear a mini-skirt and too much make-up." She shook her head. "And what would it accomplish?" There was nothing else she could say, and one morning of humiliation was enough.

"So, this is it, then?" Rebecca grabbed the check and pulled out her credit card.

Olivia picked up the Styrofoam box with the leftovers of her sandwich. "What else can I do?" The news article said Pete was in rehab. Maybe they'd keep him there. Her testimony may not have had any impact, but maybe there were others who were believed. She hoped that would be enough to keep him from ever serving in a parish or a school again.

CHAPTER 58

OLIVIA STOPPED GOING to church.

It was not an easy decision, and she fell into it at first without intending to. First, there was that Sunday when she had a catering job. She had refused all such jobs before, because going to Mass with Will and the kids had been a priority. That weekend, she went to the Saturday evening service. But the same client called again, praising her scones and the frittata, and she weakened and said yes. That time, she hadn't been able to go to church Saturday because Brent had a soccer game. She told herself it was just a one-time thing.

That second Sunday morning, she was busy with made-to-order omelets, and before she knew it, it was one in the afternoon, and she was packing up her pans and the leftover fruit salad, and there was still half a day in front of her. She realized she hadn't even missed being at Mass, and was more surprised that she didn't feel guilty. It shocked her, as she stood in the September sun by the open trunk of her car. She would have expected to feel remorse, a clutch at her heart, a wash of guilt. Hadn't she gone to Mass just about every other Sunday of her life? Shouldn't she feel that something was missing? But all she felt was calm. Plus, several of the guests had asked her for her business card. Good. More work and less time to think.

Ever since she found out about Pete, when she went to church with her family she couldn't help but look at the other priests with jaded eyes. They all looked so decent and above-board, but so had Pete. No one would have guessed that the man who gave such relevant sermons (and whose examples often drew laughter) had been having sex with a string of women and had been fondling his male students. She knew now that his vestments were only a covering, a costume, and she didn't trust the other men who wore them. Oh, she knew there were good priests, but how could you tell? She found herself losing track of the service as these thoughts intruded and the words on the song sheets blurred as if they were in another language.

She had grown up in the church, nurtured by the prayers and rituals. She had even been in a Catholic Girl Scout troop. Her mother kept a string of pearly rosary beads (blessed by the pope) in a china dish next to her bed, and her father had led them in grace before meals, even if they ate out in a restaurant (she had found that mildly embarrassing). She hadn't even had any non-Catholic friends until she was in college with twelve years of Catholic education behind her. She remembered all those years ago when she moved to D.C. and her Aunt Maisie's dictate that she "find a church right away." It had been in following that advice that she had met Pete. Maisie had been dead for six years, but what would she have said if she had known? Would she have echoed the monsignor's view?

On the Thursday after her second time missing church, she drove past Holy Angels church with its sign out front listing Mass and confession times. As if she were in the building, she saw the way dust motes floated in the sunlight decanted through the tall windows. She smelled the hint of incense and snuffed candles, heard the wheeze of the heavy door, felt the cracked red leather of the kneelers. But when she braked at the corner and looked back, she felt apart from it. In a blink, she knew she wasn't going back. How could she pray in a space where the celebrants reminded her of Pete, when she suspected them all? How could she profess allegiance to a church that had turned its back on her? She kept seeing the condescending smile on the monsignor's face when he suggested she had tempted Pete. Her eyes prickled with sadness and anger. Sadness at what she was losing. Anger that this had to happen.

She had always valued being part of the church. After returning to the D.C. metro area from Richmond, the church was one of the first places where she and Will connected with people. Brent and Lindsay went every Tuesday afternoon for CCD, and Will helped with the finance committee. The two of them went to the monthly film discussion group, and she supplied the cookies for coffee hour the second Sunday of each month. The Catholic community had, as it had when she had been growing up, gathered her in, made her feel at home. And now she would lose all that. She wanted all the good parts, but she couldn't have them and also live with the betrayal. There was no choice but to leave it all.

Sitting in her car, with leaf shadows making sunstruck shadows on the window, she could hear Will's arguments. Pete wasn't here. Pete belonged to her past. The parishioners were good people who wanted her with them. One monsignor didn't make up the whole church. And the worst, "I knew that letter was a bad idea." As if it were the letter's fault. Will still didn't understand.

Back home, as she unpacked the grocery bags, she saw signs of the parish everywhere. The wilting palm branch behind the calendar hanging in the kitchen, each month a scene of Holy Angels parish life. The September page showed a classroom, children sitting at their desks, heads bent over books. The church bulletin from last week on the coffee table. Lindsay had drawn a red circle around the announcement for the teen group's car wash. The phone number for the rectory on the list on the fridge, along with numbers for the police, the pediatrician, poison control, and her parents.

Lifelines.

But not the church. Not anymore.

CHAPTER 59

THE KIDS WEREN'T stupid. They knew there was something going on for Olivia to suddenly stop attending Mass. Every Sunday when they left, they gave her questioning looks that she pretended she didn't see. Finally, one Sunday morning, while she sat in sweats in the kitchen drinking coffee and Will was upstairs shaving, Brent spoke up.

"What is it with you and church, Mom? Are you becoming Jewish?"

Olivia almost choked on her coffee. "Jewish? Why?"

"Well, Rebecca has been around a lot lately, and she's Jewish." Did Brent think she and Rebecca were having theological discussions? Or did he think that Olivia, in not going to the Catholic church, was looking around for another one?

She put down her mug, picked at the top of a cranberry muffin. "No, Brent, I'm not becoming Jewish."

"Then what, Mom?" Lindsay twirled a strand of hair around her finger, a sign that she was nervous. "Why don't you come with us?" Olivia heard a slight quaver in her voice, and the word that stood out to her was "us." She should have known that they, and Lindsay especially, might take it personally. Might think she didn't want to be with them.

Olivia busied herself with the coffee pot. She didn't know what to say.

Except for Will and Rebecca, Olivia hadn't told anyone about Pete. It wasn't something you blurted out in the coffee shop or on the sidelines of a soccer game. There were still questions she couldn't answer, and Brent and Lindsay were sure to have a lot of them. No, she decided, she couldn't even think of telling them until she had unraveled the answers herself.

"It's complicated," she said, knowing this was not an answer at all. And then she distracted them with plans for a family picnic in the afternoon, asking what kind of sandwiches they wanted, complimenting Lindsay on her new hairstyle, asking Brent if he'd please take out the garbage. Then she disappeared upstairs to shower, waiting to come back to the kitchen until she knew they'd left.

CHAPTER 60

NONE OF IT was supposed to be this way.

She wasn't supposed to have to tiptoe around on the proverbial egg-shells, afraid every word would cause that dark look to curtain Will's face. She wasn't supposed to have to make decisions that would make her children uneasy, or to spend hours trying to find the words to explain those decisions. She and Will were supposed to be able to talk about anything, wrangle the sides of a problem and emerge, if not agreeing, then at least respecting the disagreement. She was supposed to be honest with her kids, to answer their questions truthfully.

The past was supposed to stay in the past.

The four of them were supposed to sit together in church, a family with nothing to hide. Instead, it was a golden day in October, Will had taken the kids to Mass, and she was sitting on the couch in the living room with her sewing basket. Brent had torn the sleeve of his favorite, well-worn denim jacket, and she had promised to mend it. This was easy. Cut a square from a pair of outgrown jeans, attach with the iron-on tape, and carefully stitch the edges. Outside, a cool wind swirled leaves around the yard, and in the corner of the front hall the grandfather clock bonged its brass pendulum. Eleven times. Father Michaels would be processing down the aisle. There would be the rustle of song sheets, the whoosh of the door as latecomers entered. A toddler would bounce up and down on the kneeler, be placated with a Tupperware container of Cheerios. The altar boys with their slicked-down hair would put the tall fat candles into their holders.

As if she were there, she could hear quiet settle over the congregation as the first prayers were over and everyone sat for the readings. "A reading from the letter of St. Paul to the Colossians." When Lindsay was little, she thought it was "the galoshes." "Why was he writing to shoes, Mommy?" Olivia missed those innocent days, but she could still hold on to them and smile. What she missed more now was the present. When her family came home, the kids would be talking about a conversation she had not been part of. About people they had seen. About the "ugly hat Mrs. Bascombe wears every week." About (this from Brent) the boring sermon. She'd love to hear a boring sermon.

Will would go up to change his clothes and say nothing.

She'd love to be the person driving to the deli after church to pick up sandwiches for lunch. She'd love to be the person waving to friends across the parking lot. She'd love to be the person holding her husband's hand as they sat with the music swelling around them. Pulling the thread in and out of the edges of the patch, she made the stitches small and even. She had made her choice. And as hard as it was, she knew it was the right choice.

But it was so hard to stand up for herself when her family was either critical or asking questions she didn't know how to answer. She wanted to hear Will say, "I wish you'd come with us, but I respect your decision. I'm sure it's not easy." Instead, when she told him she wouldn't be going to church anymore, he had sighed deeply and shaken his head. "I just don't get it. What does attending Mass have to do with Pete? Or with the monsignor?" He asked her if this was some sort of crusade, and she bristled at that. His tone had underlined his words. The way he said "crusade" made it sound dirty. For the first few weeks he had asked if she'd changed her mind, but now he never brought it up. He hustled the kids out to the car and left her alone.

The kids, after Brent asked if she were converting to Judaism, didn't say anything, but she knew they wanted to ask. Once, when they were leaving, Lindsay had lingered at the back door and looked at Olivia sitting at the kitchen table swirling a teabag in her mug. Lindsay had opened her mouth as if she were about to speak, but then turned and left. Olivia knew they were confused, and she knew it wasn't fair to wave them off with her blithe "it's complicated." She knew she had to anticipate and prepare for what they might ask if she told them anything. One question answered would lead to a dozen more.

Will said that the kids would come to accept her staying home, and before too long, it would be normal, the way things were. But Olivia knew he was wrong, and she knew she owed them the truth. What she didn't know was if they could handle it. And what she feared most was what they might think of her. Their mother had been involved romantically with a priest? With a priest who turned out to be a sex offender? What kid could understand that?

Olivia folded Brent's jacket. She had taken such careful, small stitches, had matched the fabric so well, that you could hardly see where the tear had been. She ran her fingers over the soft cloth, closed the lid of the sewing basket. She imagined him wearing it, shooting baskets out in the driveway in the falling leaves.

CHAPTER 61

SHE PUT OFF saying anything to them, and then it was the holiday season. Will's sister and her husband and three kids coming from Connecticut and spending Thanksgiving. Christmas a breath away. Wreaths hanging on front doors and Santas in the department stores even before the first of December. Getting out that cardboard chest with all the ornaments and trooping through five lots to find the perfect tree.

It was a family tradition that Will and Brent would set up the tree in the stand and untangle the lights and wind them through the branches. It was Olivia and Lindsay who did the actual decorating. Then Will would come home from work and make a big ceremony out of plugging in the lights and they would celebrate with hot chocolate and popcorn. This year was no different, and Olivia felt the tension between her and Will begin to ease. He seemed like his old self, laughing about those ornaments the kids had made in nursery school, bringing in take-out when he knew Olivia was busy with catering prep (so many holiday parties), suggesting the two of them have an evening out for an early supper and shopping. He even hung mistletoe in their bedroom. Olivia began to relax. They didn't talk about Pete, or her visit to the chancery, but at least they were easier around each other.

Lindsay had joined the youth choir, and they were singing at Midnight Mass. She burst in one day from practice, waving her purple scarf, calling out, "Mom! I have a solo! I'm singing the first verse of 'What Child is This'!" And then she stilled, biting her lower lip. "You will come, won't you?" Olivia had not returned to church.

Of course, she would. This wasn't about her problems with the church, it was about her daughter. She would go and she would smile and she would be proud of her child. She would say "Merry Christmas" to people she had not seen in months, would hope no one would ask where she had been. She would be happy to be sitting next to Will, and if she felt like a stranger there, she would find comfort in the familiar. The creche figures up on the side altar, the hymns ("Joy to the World," "Silent Night"), the smoky scent of candles, the jewel tones of the stained-glass windows). She would fix her lips in a smile and know her presence was a gift to Lindsay.

And it would just be that one time.

CHAPTER 62

THEN, IN JANUARY, she saw Pete in the public library. She was standing in line to pick up a book on hold, four people ahead of her, and she looked over into the reading room where there were shelves of periodicals, a couple of long tables, and half a dozen armchairs. He was at one of the tables, his back to her, turning the pages of a newspaper. She recognized the back of his head, the way he sat with his chin resting in the palm of one hand. Always the right hand, because he was left-handed and sat that way when he was writing. He wasn't writing now, but his left hand held the top corner of the newspaper page. He was wearing a black and brown plaid flannel shirt, the sleeves rolled up. He had always been warm, even when the temperatures dipped down.

The door to the building opened, but something colder than the winter air washed through her. What was he doing here? How had he happened to come to her Chevy Chase library, not two miles from her home? The newspaper article last summer had said he was somewhere in New Jersey in a rehab place. Had he been released so soon? Did he know where she lived? The cold settled in a lump in the middle of her gut, and she folded her arms around herself. She looked down at the car keys dangling from her hand and realized her fingers were shaking.

He was the last person she wanted to see. She had even ripped up the newspaper article with his face on it. Seeing his picture sent waves of nausea through her, tremors of anger. She wanted to erase his image from her mind, an image that kept recurring like a stuck frame on a movie reel. And here he was, not fifteen yards away from her. The shaking radiated up from her fingers, until even her lips were trembling.

Would he, face to face with her, start up a normal conversation? Ask about the kids? Pretend his face hadn't been all over the local news four months ago? Would he think that maybe she didn't know, try to have a light conversation as if they were old friends running into each other? Or would he be embarrassed, contrite? And would she, bruised with anger, be able to hold herself back from slapping him?

She had just about made up her mind to leave without the book (there were still three people ahead of her) when he stood, folded the newspaper, and turned around. And of course, it wasn't Pete. This guy looked to be about thirty-five, and Pete would be in his early fifties. His hair would be gray, and his shoulders would have the slump of a much older man. From the front, this guy looked nothing like the man she had known. He wore a wedding ring, and he had a mustache.

The man in the plaid shirt replaced the newspaper on the rack and headed back toward the fiction section. Olivia felt the floor shift beneath her. Even though she knew it wasn't him, sweat broke out on her forehead. She didn't know how long she had been standing still until a tug on her sleeve brought her back. "Ma'am?" The woman in line in back of her who was trying to keep a toddler from running in circles was pulling gently on her sleeve. "You're next." Olivia looked up to see a wide space between her and the pick-up desk. For a moment she forgot why she was there. What was the book she had come for? She spun on her heel and rushed toward the door.

Outside, she gulped great mouthfuls of the cold, thin air. The sky was streaked with deep purple, and behind her the library windows glowed orange. The cars that passed on the street had turned on their headlights. There was no sign of the man. He was probably browsing in the stacks. Still, she kept seeing the back of his head, the way his shoulders drooped as he leaned over the newspaper. Still, she kept seeing the man he wasn't.

CHAPTER 63

IT HAPPENED A couple more times. One day she was standing in line at the dry cleaner's, and he was over by the message board where the owner posted notes about dog walkers and babysitters. He had his back to her, but there was something about the way he stood, about his hairline. Another time she was waiting on the corner, about to cross the street, when a bus rumbled past and he was in the third seat from the front, wearing an orange cap.

At the dry cleaner's, she had grabbed Will's shirts from the hanger and thrown a twenty-dollar bill on the counter. In the car, she lowered the visor on the front window and slumped down in the seat and watched as the man exited the shop, plastic shirt protectors waving behind him like a flag. It wasn't Pete. It was a man barely thirty, wearing glasses, and he was much shorter than Pete. Pete had never worn glasses, just those Aviator sunglasses if he was out in the bright light. Get a grip, she told herself. And the man on the bus, well, she had only seen him for a split second, and when she blinked, the bus was past. Under his cap, blond hair had fringed out.

She knew those people had not been Pete, but she worried that some-day she might see him. Maybe he had been released. Maybe whoever was in charge of rehab (was it doctors?) decided he was okay now. Would he be? Would a few months of therapy cure him of whatever had made him abuse all those people? Did he promise he wouldn't do it again? And would anyone believe him? Surely it would take more than a promise. Surely it would take years. He might be there for the rest of his life.

Sometimes she'd be in the grocery store, or the movie theater, or at the kids' school for a basketball game, and she'd hear a laugh. A word. The sudden sense that she heard him. Pete had always said "Terrif!" when he especially liked something. And one night, at the game with Montrose High, when one of the freshmen made a foul shot, someone shouted, "Terrif!" and she froze. She excused herself, stepped over people and clomped down the rickety metal stairs of the bleachers, saying she had to use the restroom. Then she stood at the door to the parking lot taking deep breaths. Of course, it couldn't be Pete. Why would he even be at this game?

One day she was having coffee with her friend Elyse. Elyse and her husband Jeff went to Holy Angels, but Olivia mainly knew her from working together on the Science Fair committee at the junior high. Their girls (Lindsay and Marni) were freshmen in high school now, and Olivia and Elyse met from time to time for coffee and to commiserate about being parents of teenagers. Elyse was the quintessential school volunteer, and she was always after Olivia to join this committee or that. Today, it was something about the Valentine's Day dance. Olivia laughed and begged off. She already had three catering events coming up.

Elyse stirred sugar into her cup and looked over at the cashier's stand. "Oh! There's Jeannine!" She shook her head. "No. Just someone who looks like her. Do you ever have that thing where you see someone you think you know but then you look again and it's a complete stranger?"

It was just a week after she had seen the guy at Qwik Clean. Weird that Elyse would bring it up. Olivia nodded, blowing on her coffee to cool it before she took a sip.

Elyse continued, "For a second, I thought that was Jeannine Phelps. You know, she runs the thrift shop? It's so weird. Yesterday, I was getting my nails done, and two chairs over was a woman who I swore was my neighbor Grace from when we lived on Orchard Street. I started to lean over and call her name, and then I stopped myself. 'Elyse,' I said, 'Grace moved to Seattle four years ago.' And anyway, she'd never be in a nail salon. She even cut her own hair." Elyse shook her head. "I felt so stupid. And when I looked again, I thought I was crazy. That woman didn't look anything like Grace. She had freckles." She paused to take a sip. "I must be losing my marbles. It comes from being the mother of a teenage girl who wants to dye her hair pink."

Olivia chuckled, because when Elyse described it, it did sound humorous. It was good to know that this happened to other people. "That's funny you said that, because something like that occurred with me just the other day." She told Elyse about the guy at Qwik Clean.

"Did you actually say anything to him? I mean, before you knew it was someone else?"

"I—left. It was someone I—didn't want to talk to." She felt a little dizzy.

"An old boyfriend?" Elyse raised her eyebrows.

"No. Nothing like that. Just—" Olivia wondered if she should say any more. She was sure she could trust Elyse, even though she seemed mostly amused at the moment. But she knew her well enough to know that she could also be serious and sympathetic. Trustworthy. Maybe it was time to tell someone about Pete. If she kept thinking she saw him, maybe that was a sign. But she had never told any of her friends except Rebecca. Not Aubrey. Not people in the neighborhood. Not any of the college friends she still kept up with. No one she knew now. It was safer that way. Safer not to be exposed. Safer to be the person everyone thought she was. Look what had happened when she told Will.

Still. It might feel good to tell someone. Not the whole story. Just pieces. Something like, "A long time ago I was abused by a man." Plenty of women were abused. Walk down the street, into a department store, a park, a PTA meeting, and there were women who had been abused. You couldn't tell by looking at them, or even by talking with them. She didn't know any, but that didn't mean the woman sitting next to her at a meeting or selling her apples at the farm market hadn't been abused in some way. Not by priests, maybe, but she didn't have to tell that part. In fact, she didn't have to give any details. Just open the door a little bit to herself. It hurt her heart to lock it inside. What she needed most was to feel loved and accepted, and carrying it inside made her feel separate from everyone else. That was the whole problem with Will's reaction. Seeing the way he turned away from her, when all she wanted was to have his arms around her, made her feel empty and alone. It was like that Hopper painting of the people in the diner. One customer sits alone, the brim of his hat hiding the top of his face. There's a couple at the counter and the guy who works there taking orders, but no one looks at the guy with the hat. Outside, the street is dark, but in the diner a strong artificial light accentuates the man's isolation. Maybe he's just gotten a raise, maybe his girlfriend has dumped him. There's no one around interested enough to ask.

On the other hand, it was risky. Suppose Elyse never looked at her the same way again, or suppose she laughed it off ("Oh well, that was a long time ago."). That's what she imagined most people saying. That she should be over it by now. Could get over it. That's what Will thought. "It's all in the past, babe." There was no way to know. She didn't even know if she could get over it. Or if that was even the goal. Maybe she just wanted to change the way she saw herself. Because as much as she had told herself it had not been her fault, there was still that voice that reminded her she had gone with him. She had said yes.

If there was anything that plagued her, it was that. Disillusionment about Pete, anger at Pete, the dirty feeling that she had been used. They were all there. But underneath all of that was knowing she had said yes when she should have said no. If any one of her friends had confessed to getting involved with a religious minister, a rabbi, a priest, she would have grabbed her by the arm and told her to get out of it. Turn her back. Save herself. But she hadn't done that with herself. She had believed in love that wasn't love.

She didn't have to decide today. Maybe, after she thought about it, she could bring it up again, that coincidence thing, and say, "Remember that day when we were talking about . . ." Tell more of the story, explain why she had panicked at seeing the guy with his laundered shirts. Now, she gulped her coffee, felt it burn down her throat. Glancing at her watch, she feigned surprise. "I have to go! I forgot Brent has an orthodontist appointment."

Did Elyse read something into Olivia's reaction to her question? Her eyes seemed to sharpen as she looked at Olivia. "We'll chat again," she said, as Olivia gathered her coat and purse.

CHAPTER 64

HER BROTHER EVAN'S visit was a surprise. He had a business meeting in New York, and that was so close (an hour's flight) so why not come stay with her and Will, see the kids, "get away from all that snow in Minnesota"? With one thing and another, it had been a couple of years since Olivia had been back there, since the summer when Brent was 13 and Lindsay 11 and they had rented a cabin up on Lake Wymar. She knew she should make it a point to get back more often, especially since her father had suffered that slight stroke. So, seeing Evan would be the next best thing.

He was seven years older than Olivia, and the gray on his head told the truth of his nearing fifty. The first morning he was there, she found him in the living room looking through her wedding album. He laughed, pointing at a photo of himself with sideburns and hair grazing his collar. "I sure had a lot more hair then."

"Darker, too," Olivia said, handing him a mug of coffee.

"Oh well, gray hair is a sign of distinction," he said, flipping to the next page.

She set a plate of oatmeal muffins down on the coffee table and sank into the couch next to him with a cup of tea. It was good to share the morning with him. Will was at work, the kids at school. She was worried about her dad and the stroke, wanted to get the full story from Evan. He only lived a few miles away from their parents and was over at their house all the time, fixing something, driving them to appointments. Her mother kept reassuring her that everything was fine, because she didn't want Olivia to worry. Olivia didn't believe her.

"So, tell me about Dad. Is he still using the cane? Mom won't tell me anything."

"He's fine. Not driving much, because he has some weakness on his left side, but he gets around. The main thing he misses is being able to go fly fishing."

They chatted about that, Olivia wondering if it was time for her parents to sell the big house and move to a smaller place. Evan bragged about his son Spence who had accepted a residency in surgery at the Mayo Clinic. He turned a page in the album, put his finger on a photo. "This is such a beautiful picture of the two of you at the altar with those stained glass windows. Remember how Reggie almost dropped the ring? And look, you can just see Aunt Mamie with that crazy hat." They talked about other people in the photo, and how everyone looked so young. They laughed about the fashions of the day—wide lapels on the men's jackets, maxi dresses on the young women. Evan pointed to the members of the wedding party. "Do you still keep up with Rebecca?" He paused. "I can barely see the priest. What was his name? Paul something?"

She took a sip of tea before answering. "Pete."

"I'm sure he has a lot of gray hair now," Evan said, reaching for his coffee. "I think he was about my age."

Olivia didn't want to talk about Pete. She picked up a muffin, peeled off the fluted wrapper. She had sprinkled the tops of the muffins with pecan streusel, and it had toasted to a golden crunch.

"I remember we had a pleasant chat at the reception. He told me about some filters I could use for my telescope when it turned out we were both into astronomy. He seemed like a real friendly guy. He said he thought the world of you, that you had worked with him on some committee."

Evan had a photographic memory, could remember everyone he had met. Olivia flashed back to that mission committee. The stuffy classroom where they packed school supplies. How she had respected Pete for starting the project. How she had looked forward to the meetings. What were the other people's names? There was that married couple. He had left the priesthood to marry, what was her name? Gina? Marilyn? No—Marianne. They had been Olivia's poster couple of how it was possible to leave religious life for marriage. It seemed so long ago, and yet it took only a second to be in the room with the scent of crayons and blackboard dust.

"Whatever happened to him?"

Olivia was annoyed at Evan for bringing up Pete. It was supposed to be a relaxing morning. Sitting next to her big brother, showing off her house, the rooms she had decorated, having him see her as a successful caterer, mother of two teenagers. The thought of Pete tarnished the moment. Of course, he had no idea, but Evan was never one to give up on a topic, so he asked again.

"Do you ever hear from him?"

Olivia folded the muffin liner into a triangle, set it on her saucer. "Not for years."

She should have left it there, but she continued, "He—um—he got into a bit of trouble." A bit of trouble? That was one way to say it.

Evan looked at her, raising his eyebrows. He started to turn the page in the album. "What kind of trouble? Stealing from the poor box?"

She ignored Evan's casual joke. Why not say the truth? He was her brother. If she couldn't tell him, whom could she tell? She had never said anything more to Elyse, but Evan was her family. He was the one who had always protected her, looked out for her, taught her to drive stick, helped her when she got stuck in trigonometry. When he met Will, that time she took him to Minnesota to introduce him to her family, he took her aside when they were both in the kitchen. "You have a winner," he said. "I'm proud of you. You're going to have a great life."

Olivia took a breath, wrapped her hands around the warmth of her mug. "He was accused of sexual misconduct." Why was it that every time she said those words she felt a sinking in her gut?

Evan took a slurp of coffee and closed the album. "What? The priest that married you was a pervert?" He sounded shocked.

Olivia hated to think of that term. Abuser was bad enough, but pervert sounded so—dirty. And when she heard it, she felt dirty herself, as she had so often. A pervert had touched her.

Days could go by when she didn't think about it. When she had lots of catering jobs, she filled the hours planning, shopping, prepping. She could spend almost a whole hour composing a cheese and fruit platter, arranging the items by color, almost like creating a painting. She kept a file of her customers. Evelyn hates mushrooms. The library group praised the gazpacho. She'd put on a tape and turn the volume way up, and Neil Diamond or The Byrds would bounce off the walls as she chopped and sautéed and stirred. She felt the most alive when she was experimenting with a recipe. But now Evan had to open that album and ask about Pete. Oh, it was innocent on his part, but now the air in the room felt stale, and even the aroma of cinnamon made her nauseous. She reached for the album, turned to the page with Pete, and ripped out the photo. Tore it in pieces. Evan was looking at her with a frown.

"What are you—"

"I never want to see his face again." The words were as sharp as thistles in her mouth.

And she told him. The whole thing. From the baseball game to the counseling to the connection she felt with him to falling in love to the insane happiness of that year. She told him about breaking it off and meeting Will and putting Pete out of her mind, thinking he was happy somewhere in a parish, giving those great sermons, singing hymns off-key, sipping scotch in his office at night, maybe finally getting that dog he had wanted. And then seeing him on the television and finding out it had all been a lie.

Evan ran his finger around the rim of his mug. "I just don't understand it."

"I know. It's like one of those nightmares you have, and when you wake up you feel like you're still there in it."

"No—" Evan paused, frowning. "I don't understand why you fell for it."

Olivia thought she could hear the dust motes that swam in the sun by the window. The good feeling of being with her brother dissolved as if it had never existed, leaving in its place an airless emptiness.

Had Evan really said that? Evan—the brother who had always been her champion. The brother who had unsuccessfully tried to hide his tears the day she and Will married. The brother who tried to interview every date she had in high school, saying no one was good enough for her. This brother was voicing his disappointment in her? Saying, in effect, that it was her fault? The bite of muffin she had just taken turned to sawdust in her mouth.

She had no words. She just stared at him, thinking that this gray-haired man was a stranger.

"I mean," he continued, "didn't you think it odd that a priest would be interested in a woman? Couldn't you have seen through him, through whatever it was he told you?" He didn't sound angry, more disappointed. And disappointing her favorite brother was worse than having him mad at her. Last night at dinner he had regaled her kids with stories about them growing up, and she had felt so close to him. Now he was frowning at her.

Olivia couldn't believe he would say this. And he, tenacious as always, wouldn't shut up.

"Were you that lonely? The guy was a priest. Didn't some part of you wonder about his motives? Geez, Olivia, what were you thinking?" His voice softened a little. "I guess he had everyone fooled, but I would have thought you'd be smarter than to fall for someone like that."

This wasn't what she had expected. Anger, yes, but anger at Pete. Not judgment about her. She had just trusted him with the worst that had happened to her. The secret she had held close for twenty years. Didn't he, her older, "wiser" brother, have any inkling how hard it was for her to talk about it? How dare he turn it around and blame her?

He was saying she should have known better, that because she was an adult it was partially her fault. If she had been a child, or a teenager, would he have reacted this way? She didn't understand why her age mattered. Was this why the monsignor had dismissed her account? Was it only abuse if you were under 18? Evan was fiddling with the cuff of his shirt. He wouldn't meet her eyes, and a frown darkened his face.

It was Tuesday. He was leaving Thursday morning. The two days would feel like a month.

CHAPTER 65

OLIVIA FOUND OUT about the support group when she was in her doctor's office in February for her annual check-up. Dr. Embrow was running late as usual, and Olivia had forgotten to bring a book. Even so, she didn't mind the wait; it was one of the few times she could honestly say she had nothing to do, and she relished the fifteen minutes. There were the usual thumbed-over magazines on the tables, *Good Housekeeping* and *Today's Health*, but they didn't tempt her. Then she spied the rack of pamphlets next to her chair. Information tracts on breast self-exam, diabetes, high blood pressure, menopause. Menopause was a good distance away, and she never gave any thought to diabetes. But one title jumped out at her. *Support Group for Sex Abuse Survivors.* Something hummed in her like a low buzzer, and she reached out for it. It wasn't the words "support group" as much as "sex abuse survivors." Was she? She tended to think of herself more as a victim than a survivor, but she did wonder what the purpose of the group would be. The turned-around conversation with Evan the month before still ate at her, opening up old wounds.

She looked around the waiting room before she picked it up. If anyone saw her reach for it, would they assume she had been abused? Not that it was anything to be ashamed of, but she also wouldn't want to pick up the one about skin rashes and have people think she had something contagious. The only other person there was an older woman scribbling something in a notepad. Maybe she was just overly sensitive. Still, it was something she had mostly kept a secret for a long time, and she was careful to keep it that way. She had just glanced at the cover, hadn't had time to read any of it, when the nurse opened the door to the exam rooms and called her back, and she stuffed it in the side pocket of her purse and went in for her appointment.

Laetitia Embrow was nothing if not thorough. That was why she was always late. She refused to give a quick clinical exam and send her patients off with a prescription or an appointment card. She was mainly a gynecologist, but many of her patients ended up seeing her as their GP. "I'm a specialist with a specialty in everything," she joked. Olivia had first seen her for an annual Pap test, but now she consulted her for everything, though she was rarely sick. There was the time she cut her finger with her pruning shears and needed stitches and a tetanus shot. And the time she had the ear infection. Mostly, though, it was just her annual GYN exam. Laetitia took the time to listen, never seemed in a hurry, and she wrote down everything in her patients' charts, even non-medical notations. The first time Olivia saw her do this, she had just mentioned taking a class in Asian cuisine, and she asked the doctor why she wrote that down. "I treat the whole person," she answered, "and this is part of your whole person." Olivia loved that about her. She loved that her chart recorded more than just her blood pressure, height, weight, and mammogram results.

Today, after she stripped off her gloves and Olivia sat up on the exam table, Laetitia wheeled back on the rolling stool and crossed her legs. "So, what's happening with you these days? How's the catering business?"

Olivia gave her a quick rundown, glancing at her watch. She had to pick up Lindsay in a half hour. She started to slide off the table when Laetitia pointed to Olivia's bag.

"I see you've been perusing our wonderful collection of information pamphlets," she said. "What caught your eye today?"

Olivia looked at her bag. "Oh, that. It's just—"

"Isn't that the one about the support group?" Her eyes softened, and she leaned forward slightly on the stool.

"I guess. I was just looking and then Marnie called me in, and I didn't have a chance to put it back." She didn't want to reveal why it had caught her eye. What would she say? Laetitia, she had discovered over the years, was very tuned in to people. She probably knew it had been no accident that Olivia had chosen that particular pamphlet. But here, in midafternoon on a Tuesday, she didn't think she wanted to talk about it.

"Did you read it yet?" Laetitia put Olivia's file down on the counter next to the sink. She seemed in no hurry to leave the room.

Olivia was pretty sure the doctor knew the contents of all the pamphlets displayed in the waiting room. She was also pretty sure Laetitia's question wasn't just a casual inquiry, that if there were a problem she'd want to help. She might think Olivia knew someone who had been abused, or she might guess that it was Olivia herself. And Olivia knew Laetitia wasn't being nosy; she would be genuinely concerned. But Olivia didn't think she wanted sex abuse to be a notation in her chart next to "studying Asian cooking" or "husband has new job."

It had been eight months since she learned about Pete, and it wouldn't leave her alone. Apart from Rebecca, and Will, and the monsignor (who had rudely dismissed her), Olivia had told no one the whole story. Evan, yes, but just the bare bones. Laetitia's gentle blue eyes and her earnest, accepting manner tempted her. It might feel good to tell someone, someone not so close to her. She was tempted, but then Olivia checked her watch again. Lindsay would be waiting.

She had no intention of actually going to a support group. She couldn't imagine telling this to a group of strangers. And while Laetitia would probably be supportive and non-judgmental, she didn't know if she could tell her either. How would she squeeze such a huge story into a small window of time? And how far did non-judgmental go? Even though it was something she thought about all the time, even though it caused her to turn away from the church, even though she wanted to think of herself as a survivor (as the title of the pamphlet implied) and not just a victim, she didn't know if it was possible. She didn't feel like a survivor. Deep down, though she couldn't say the word yet, what she felt was shame, that nagging thought that part of it had been her fault. And because of that, she didn't want to tell anyone. What would people think of her? She had kissed him willingly, had gone to bed with him willingly. She had opened her heart to him willingly. The phrase that she kept repeating to herself, that wouldn't leave her alone, was "Why did you let him?" She had thought they would have a life together, that was why, but would anyone think that could even be possible?

Laetitia crossed her legs as she sat on the low stool, with a relaxed look that said she had all the time in the world. "You know, Olivia, you can tell me anything," she said. Olivia wanted to believe her, and she almost wished she had the time now. More, she wished she had the courage. But Lindsay would be standing outside the school, and the February afternoon was cold. At least, that was what she told herself as she stood and hooked her bag over her shoulder.

CHAPTER 66

IT WASN'T UNTIL two days later that Olivia looked at the pamphlet she had picked up from Laetitia's office. She felt its presence all the time, as if it had grown bigger than the purse that contained it. She told herself family and work kept interfering, and she had no time to herself. Brent sprained his ankle in a basketball game, resulting in a trip to the ER. She had that vegetarian lunch to cater. But a part of her was afraid to look at it. Afraid to encounter that word "abuse" and all its implications. Finally, it was Friday evening. They had eaten the leftover potato samosas for dinner, Brent was (grumpily, she assumed) sitting on the sidelines at the high school game, Lindsay was spending the night with her friend Leila, and Will was in the den watching "The Great Escape." He wouldn't budge for a couple of hours. No excuses, she told herself.

She had tucked it down at the bottom of the purse (she carried a bag almost as big as a tote bag) where she was sure it would be out of sight, but that morning when Lindsay had reached for the purse to get lunch money, Olivia had snatched it back in a panic.

"What's the matter? I'm not robbing you! I just need two bucks for lunch."

"I don't want you messing up stuff in here," Olivia answered as she fished out the money.

Lindsay had looked at her with a quizzical expression, because she went in her mom's purse all the time, to get money, to use her ChapStick, to rummage for a pen. And then she shrugged and went off to school.

Olivia asked herself what she was afraid of, why she had avoided looking at the pamphlet. What happened with Pete was always with her, so it wasn't as if it would bring up something she had hidden away. Who he was and what he had done to her was like that low buzz from a ceiling bulb you're always partially aware of but learn to live with. She functioned. She responded to people. When the phone rang and it was a catering customer, she quoted prices and gave menu suggestions. When she met a friend at the supermarket or the hardware store, she answered "Fine" to a casual "How are you?" There were clean sheets and towels in the linen closet, meals on the table, bills paid, gas in the car. But she often felt that she wasn't really there, like she saw the world through a pane of glass that kept her apart and yet visible to everyone else. No one could guess how that glass protected her. No one could see it, not even Will.

Will. She doubted he'd ever understand. They had mostly stopped arguing over little things, and he had stopped trying to get her to go back to church. There was a careful truce between them, and he seemed happy with their life together. He was almost like his old self, teasing her on occasion, bringing her little unexpected gifts, holding her in bed. And if there were fewer times when she responded to his desire to have sex, he didn't say anything. She cursed her reactions, because she had never said no until she heard about Pete, and she had loved having sex with Will. Now even sex had become tainted because she kept remembering Pete touching her and the very thought of that made her cringe. It didn't matter that it was Will. She kept seeing Pete.

Will had always been good at filing things away, though she suspected it was for his own protection. She thought he wanted to forget how deeply he had been hurt when she kept Pete a secret all those years. She figured that was why he no longer pushed her in anything, why he did his best to keep everything on an even keel. He wasn't comfortable with confrontation, with too many questions. So even with him, she was behind that pane of glass. He saw her as he wanted to see her, and if she were to rap on the glass, he would prefer not to notice. So, she never brought it up, hadn't since back in the fall when she stopped going to Mass, and she wondered if Will thought she had, in the words of that phrase she hated, "gotten beyond it." She doubted she ever would. Maybe that was why she had picked up the pamphlet.

When she opened it, words on the paper leaped up at her. Validation. Connection. Healing. Empathy. Hope. They were all good words, but what did they mean? Validation of what? That she was a good person? And connection. Connection with other people who had also been hurt? Did she want to connect? Would telling her story bring up parts she was trying to forget? Would it force her to shatter that glass protection? And could she even tell her story to strangers? She hadn't been able to tell Elyse or even Dr. Embrow. Why would it be any easier with people she didn't know?

The group that sponsored the support sessions was called Circle Space. The opening paragraph described the mission of the group as "fostering connection and support in a safe space." It spoke briefly about boundaries, about welcoming everyone, of "endings and new beginnings." There was an affirmation from someone who had attended the sessions. "Circle Space gave me hope." Olivia wasn't looking for hope. She just wanted to be rid of Pete. She just wanted the door that opened to their time together to be double-bolted. She couldn't go on thinking she saw him or heard his voice.

Olivia had been brought up to keep personal things to herself. "No use airing your dirty laundry," her mother had quipped so many times. And this was the epitome of dirty laundry. If she went to one of these meetings, would she have to speak or could she just listen? She couldn't see herself opening up right away. Suppose the other people there were all victims of rape or incest or violence and saw her twenty-year-old story as not the same thing as they had gone through? Suppose they questioned, as the monsignor had done, her part in it? Some might question why it had taken her so long to come forward. Why she hadn't said anything at the time.

The meetings were Thursday evenings, in a conference room at the Presbyterian church. If she went, and it was still a big if, what would she tell Will? She knew he wouldn't approve, knew it would open up the anger he had managed to tamp down. He had always been anti-therapy, liked to make fun of "shrinks." Things happened, he insisted, and then you moved on. What was the point in dwelling on unhappy or tragic times? He wouldn't understand how she would even think of telling her story to a room full of strangers, or worse yet, that there might be people there whom she knew. Or people that he knew. She had considered that, how she'd feel if she went into the room and there was the mother of one of Brent's friends, or the young Asian woman who shampooed her hair at the salon. Would it make her feel closer to those people or would she be embarrassed? "All discussions are confidential," she read in the pamphlet, but still, people would know. Would she see it in their faces every time they met? And would they, in turn, also be embarrassed, to the point that they might feel awkward being with her?

She didn't know anything about how a support group worked. Laetitia would probably know, and now Olivia wished she had stayed a little longer with the doctor, to ask. It was free (donations accepted), and there would be eight meetings. If she didn't like it, she wouldn't have to go to all of them. That made her feel better.

The brochure was a tri-fold, and in the center panel was the word healing, written in large, bold script. This, the text explained, was the ultimate goal of the support group. Not forgetting, not fixing, but healing. Being well, being whole. That's what she thought about healing, and feeling whole again was what she wanted.

But at what cost? She didn't know what was worse—holding her terrible secret inside or letting it out for others to see.

CHAPTER 67

THE MEETING WAS at seven-thirty. She had decided on grilled cheese for supper, and was pulling slices of Swiss and Havarti out of the fridge, when Will came in the kitchen. He had his parka on, and the car keys dangled from his finger. She had told him about the meeting, and as she expected, he had frowned and shaken his head. Things had been going well between them, but the thin set of his lips when she mentioned the support group told her the two of them were still on shaky ground.

"If that's for us, don't bother," he said. "I'm taking the kids out for Chinese."

"Oh? You didn't say anything. I thought we'd have—"

"We just decided. Lindsay had a craving for sweet and sour chicken." He zipped up his jacket. She felt a chill in the air that had nothing to do with the lingering snow outside.

Just like that. The three of them were going out for dinner. She knew why. Will didn't want to be in the house when she left for the support group meeting. It was his way of saying he was against it. She squared her shoulders, determined not to let it shake her resolve, but felt a sinking around her stomach. The thought of melted cheese suddenly seemed revolting.

Brent came in and grabbed his jacket from the kitchen chair where he had dropped it after school. "Mom? Are you making a sandwich? Aren't you coming with us?"

Will glanced over his shoulder. "Your mom has something else to do tonight." He rattled the keys impatiently. "Come on, Lindsay's already in the car."

"Want us to bring you leftovers?" Since a brief lapse into teenage rebellion back in the fall, Brent had turned himself into Considerate Young Man. Olivia suspected that it was because he wanted to be allowed to get his driver's license, but she'd take the attitude for whatever reason.

"Sure. And don't forget a fortune cookie." She put the cheese back, decided to just heat up some mushroom soup. She wondered if it was her imagination, or if Will closed the front door just this side of a slam.

She would have liked a glass of red wine with her soup, but she thought maybe you weren't supposed to drink before going to a support group. Get a grip, she told herself. It's not AA. Still, if anyone knew she'd been drinking, would they think less of her? She had worried for days about what the other people would think of her. That maybe they'd be like the monsignor, who implied she had been too old for it to be abuse. Or that her going along with it made it consensual and Pete wasn't at fault at all. Or they would be victims of violence and think that was a necessary part of abuse. Those questions almost convinced her not to go. She didn't want to feel like a fool.

A little after seven, she put her bowl in the dishwasher, ran a brush through her hair, stuffed a handful of tissues in her bag, and was off. The church was only ten minutes away, and she parked in a dark corner of the lot with the car turned off for a long five minutes, not wanting to be too late, but not the first one there either. Except for Christmas, this was the first time she had been in a church parking lot in months. At least it wasn't Holy Angels. Suppose it had been, and she had run into one of the priests? She hoped she could just slip in, find a seat near the back, and no one would notice. She would check it out, see if she liked what she heard, and maybe make a quiet exit before the meeting was over. She certainly wasn't ready to say anything. Car doors thunked closed, and there were quick steps as people hurried toward the building. She couldn't see faces, just their dark shapes bundled up in coats against the cold. Then, a few minutes before the meeting was due to begin, she took a deep breath and stepped out of her car.

There weren't rows, as she had hoped, but a wide circle of about 15 folding chairs. So much for sitting in the back. About half of the chairs were taken. The other women seemed to range in age from early twenties to one clearly in her sixties. She was relieved that she didn't know anyone. She'd like to be anonymous for a while, at least until introductions were made. No one was talking, and she noticed several empty chairs between people where they had left their coats as if to insure their distance from others. She had done that herself if she was in a group and didn't know anyone, using a chair as a buffer zone, pretending she needed it for her purse, a jacket, when really she wanted to avoid the physical closeness to the other person. Sitting right next to someone might require a word or two, or even a conversation. And to keep silent could be taken as a dismissal, as deliberate ignoring. Sometimes you just wanted to be on your own island. In this case, how exactly do you introduce yourself to another person when you know she is an abuse victim and so are you? Do you talk about the weather, knowing the weather doesn't matter at all?

This evening she was using all her energy just to be here. To drive through the dark streets, enter the building, walk down what felt like a warren of corridors to get to this room. And now that she was here, her feet on the linoleum floor, her back against a metal folding chair, the real-ness of it pressed in on her. She wrapped her right hand around her left, holding her bones, willing them to ground her.

She imagined they were all as nervous as she was, and it did make her more comfortable that it was a women's group, but even so, they were strangers. The meeting hadn't started. It wasn't too late to leave.

Even though the room was overheated, she kept her coat on, shivering from edginess or apprehension. She wasn't sure which. Looking at her watch, she thought about Will and the kids laughing over egg rolls. She wanted to be with them, wanted an ordinary family outing. She wanted him to smile at her and put his arm around her as they walked into the restaurant, wanted to laugh with him as they tried to manage chopsticks. His taking the kids out was a snub, his way of saying she was on her own and he wanted nothing to do with it. The room smelled like coffee (there was an urn on a table at the back of the room) and the dust of old books. Bookshelves lined one wall, filled with what looked like Bibles and tattered paperbacks. The windows had thick blinds that were pulled closed. She could hear a piano somewhere in the building. Three more women came in, and coats had to be moved. She tried to put her family in a back pocket in her mind and focus on being here. She looked around the circle of chairs, trying not to be obvious or to hold her eyes on any one person too long. It was impossible to tell anything about them from the outside. One woman wore a suit as if she had just come from work. Another, like Olivia, kept her coat on and had her hands in the pockets. The youngest was twirling a strand of her blond hair and looking at the floor. She wondered what the others thought of her, if anything. She wished she could read their thoughts, to see if they mirrored hers.

A woman with short gray hair, holding a clipboard, sat directly across from Olivia. She was wearing jeans and a pale green down vest. As Olivia glanced over at her, she smiled and cleared her throat. "Welcome to Circle Space." She had the kind of voice that made you feel at home, but it didn't still the butterflies in Olivia's stomach.

She introduced herself as Sonia, said she was a social worker and had been leading these groups for several years. "I know each of you is probably uncertain and nervous about being here, but don't worry, no one is going to make you stand up tonight and tell your story." Olivia felt a little tension drain out of her shoulders because it seemed there would be no pressure if she decided not to say anything. She thought she'd talk, but she wouldn't know until she heard some of the others. If she heard hesitation in someone else's voice, she'd feel her own was okay. If, for example, the woman in the suit (who looked so put together) trembled when she spoke, Olivia would think it all right to let her own shakiness show.

Sonia rested her eyes briefly on each woman as she spoke, and Olivia felt her words as a personal invitation. "We're all here for one reason—to support each other in what is probably the hardest thing you've ever experienced. We'll take it slowly over the next several weeks, and you can say as much or as little as you want." And as if to make everyone feel more comfortable, she gave a short version of her own story. "I was eighteen, and he was my economics professor," she began. Eighteen was an adult, so Sonia would understand about Olivia being over twenty-one. Olivia almost teared up with relief. After speaking for a few minutes, Sonia paused to let the words sink in. "So you see, I have been where you are right now." There was a softness to her voice as she spoke, but Olivia could also hear emotion in her words. That even though she had probably told the story dozens of times, she still felt it. She wasn't detached from it. Was this what healing meant? That you could speak about it with confidence and not fall apart?

But it made Olivia wonder about telling her own story. Where would she start? Would she go all the way back to how she had moved to D.C. and hadn't known anyone and had become friends with a priest? Or would she skip that and just get to the heart of it, as Sonia had done? "I was twenty-three and he was a priest in my parish." There were so many ways to tell it, and she wanted to do it the right way, because she wanted the others to feel for her the way she felt for Sonia now.

Olivia didn't want her story to just be a narration of facts; she wanted to relate the tide beneath the facts, because that was where the story lay. And there was the fact that she was speaking up after twenty years. How could she explain what she thought others would question, why she hadn't known it was abuse when it happened? Maybe she should start with "last summer I found out that a man I was in love with a long time ago was accused of sexual misconduct." It wasn't about why she had waited so long. The fact that it had happened so long ago and was just now surfacing was one reason it was tearing her apart. Years of believing one thing had toppled around her, and she didn't know how to pick up the pieces, to reconstruct her life.

Then Sonia showed a video. The first part was a slide show of faces— old, young, female, male, Asian, black, white. There were shots of children blowing bubbles, of nuns in veiled habits, of basketball players. There was an audio track with words like "you are not to blame" and "you were born beautiful." The facial images were interspersed with statistics (1 out of 6 men has been abused, 4 out of 7 women).

Olivia wasn't sure what the purpose of the video was. One of the slides showed an empty swing hanging from a tree in a deserted park and the words "You may feel alone." Well, was this something she didn't know? It felt like the video took the focus off of them, these women who had come to the group, and asked them to consider other stories, or to ease their own. They were looking at the faces of people who were probably actors playing roles for the video, and here were all these real people sitting on the metal folding chairs. She felt herself growing impatient, looking at the stark face of the clock on the wall. This was not what she had expected. She had thought it would be more personal.

Scenes flashed across the screen. It was all so "you are special" trite. Olivia didn't feel special. She felt bruised. She felt alone. When the video ended with soft guitar music and a panoramic view of a field of sunflowers, her legs ached to escape, to step right out the door, and she would have if Sonia hadn't rolled the VCR cart away and flipped on the lights. Leaving would be too obvious, and right now she wanted to melt.

But then the moment passed as Sonia asked each of them to introduce themselves and say just one word about how they felt about coming to the group. She nodded to the woman next to her, who said, "nervous."

Others said, "scared," "hopeful," "lost." The young woman with the long blond hair said, "no comment." Olivia mumbled, "unsure." Then Sonia stood and wrote each word on the chalkboard, and drew an arrow from each one to another word. "Scared" became "courage," "lost" became "belonging," "no comment" led to "having a voice." Olivia's "unsure" arrowed to "confident." Sonia assured them that it would take a while, but that they had already taken the first courageous step. She passed out marbleized composition books, like Olivia had used in grade school, encouraged them to take their words and write about them in the coming week. The rest of the time passed fairly quickly, and when the women left, they held the door open for each other, not talking yet, but acting kind.

Olivia was glad for the silence. She didn't feel like chatting. She didn't know how she felt. Beyond their single words, no one besides Sonia had spoken. They were all still strangers. She had thought she'd leave with at least the sense of a thin thread linking them together.

CHAPTER 68

IT WAS A week later.

The sky had that heavy quilt feeling it gets before snow. The clouds hanging low and thick, the air almost tingly. Olivia thought of skipping the support group meeting, because she didn't want to come out to find a quarter inch of snow had stopped traffic. The D.C. area was famous for not being able to handle even a dusting. But she was curious to see if the second meeting would be better than the first, which had mostly been a disappointment. A slide show. No one saying much.

She wrapped a mohair scarf around her neck, slipped into her L.L. Bean duck boots, and set out. Will had taken the kids out to dinner again, this time for pizza. Would it be like this every week? "It's a meeting for moms," Olivia had told the kids. She hated lying, but she didn't know how to explain where she was really going.

Tonight the same people were gathered in the room at the church. The girl with the blond hair was there, and the woman who had worn the suit was in jeans. Sonia sat with her clipboard and encouraged everyone to help themselves to coffee. The room was still overheated, and Olivia took off her coat but pulled her sweater sleeves down over her hands. She was afraid of feeling exposed.

Last week, Sonia had encouraged everyone to journal about their two words. Olivia hadn't done that, though she had thought about them a lot. She was still "unsure," and she didn't know how she would ever arrive at "confident." She was unsure about being in the group, about the whole process of a support meeting, even about what kind of support she wanted. Would it be enough if everyone just nodded and said, "Oh, I get it. I've been there too"? What would that accomplish?

Sonia said that tonight they were invited to describe why they had joined the group. She looked expectantly around the circle, asked if anyone wanted to start. The girl with the blond hair looked at her shoes, and the woman in the jeans (her name was Phyllis) seemed to be considering it in the way she opened and closed her mouth but then glanced at a spot on the wall. Olivia felt Sonia's eyes settle briefly on her, and something bloomed in her and she started to speak. She didn't look at anyone, not even Sonia, and she began to unravel the story, from her move to D.C., to the counseling, to the growing relationship with Pete (she just called him "the priest"), to her thinking they loved each other, to his decision to stay in the priesthood, and then her discovery last summer that he had been accused of sex abuse with women and young boys. She didn't weigh her words, didn't think about what she'd say, she just let the story pour out, sometimes speaking in slow, measured syllables, sometimes her words rushing like water over stones. The more she spoke, the stronger she felt, and she found herself gaining energy with every sentence. It was all there, how she felt Pete had betrayed her, how her husband was angry, how the church had ignored her, how she was unsure ("that was my word and I'm unsure about everything"), how she didn't know if she should be more angry at herself or at the priest, and she ended with "and I don't know why I've said all this."

But she did know, because when she stopped talking and reached for a tissue to blot the tears she hadn't realized were damp on her cheeks, she felt a lightness she hadn't known before. It was just so good to tell. It was so good to have people listen. She hadn't realized before that this was what she had wanted all along. And not someone close to her like Rebecca, but a room of strangers who weren't going to tell her what to do, who weren't going to question her, who were only going to listen. Maybe that was what a support group was for.

There was silence when she stopped, the kind of silence that feels like it's spinning, and it's alive with what you've said. She sensed her words lifted from her and settling into the room, the room that was too warm but felt safe. She felt empty with relief.

She didn't remember much of the rest of the meeting. Phyllis told her story (an uncle), and another woman (Lou) described what happened with a family "friend," and the young blond woman (Marisa) spoke so softly Olivia could barely hear her. Sonia said some things, but Olivia would never remember what they were. She kept hearing the round echoes of her own words.

When the meeting ended, they straggled out to the parking lot. It had started to snow, and Olivia lifted her face to the sky, let the flakes fall one by one on her hot cheeks and reached her hands out to catch them.

CHAPTER 69

THERE WERE TWO more meetings, two more times when Will took the kids out to dinner. Brent and Lindsay never asked her where she went on Thursday evening. She supposed they were used to her being on this committee or that, or having a catering interview, or doing last-minute grocery shopping for an event. On two of the weeks she did stop at Safeway and left the groceries on the kitchen table (cereal, apples, olive oil). It became a treat for them—dinner out with Dad. They went to an Italian deli, a Mexican place, an old-fashioned diner where they sat in booths and there were juke-boxes at every table. They came home laughing about the songs from the sixties.

At the meetings, more people spoke up. Sonia smiled and congratulated them on their honesty, sending the tissue box around the circle. Nicole (best friend's older brother) got so angry one evening she stalked around the room, crying and curling her hands into fists. "How could he? I was fifteen!" Angie (college date) said she hadn't been able to have sex since it happened and doubted she'd ever marry. She was twenty-five. Barb (a cousin) said she refused to go to family gatherings, and that her parents hadn't believed her. "I came here," she said, dabbing at her eyes with a tissue, "because I feel so alone and betrayed. Why would I make up something like that? What kind of parents don't believe their own daughter?" She had married, had a child, but she rarely saw her wider family. "My parents refer to it as 'that unpleasantness you insist happened,' and they get miffed when I refuse to go to weddings or Bar Mitzvahs. I even missed my uncle's funeral, which was so hard for me, because I knew my cousin would be there. My father actually said I should 'let bygones be bygones.'"

It wasn't just what the women said that touched Olivia. It was the pain in their voices, the way Phyllis always wrapped herself in her coat. Marisa's nails were bitten down to the quick, and Angie had trouble making eye contact. As the weeks went on, though, she noticed little things that showed they were beginning to bond. A laugh shared around the coffee urn. Good-byes and waves exchanged in the parking lot. Fewer spaces of silence for Sonia to fill with questions and prodding. Suddenly, it was eight-thirty. Had it really been an hour?

Olivia heard the others say what she was afraid to say. Like Angie's comment about sex. There were so many nights that Olivia made sure Will was asleep before she slipped into bed. For those long months since summer, Pete had been a constant presence in her mind. And there were also days when her anger at the monsignor trumped the memory of her abuse. Not being believed felt worse than the abuse itself. She started to understand that she wasn't alone, that the other women echoed what she held inside.

Olivia thought she would feel changed. She thought the burden of Pete's abuse would be lifted from her and she would be able to resume the life she had enjoyed before she saw that television broadcast. In truth, she had felt lighter after she spoke that first time, and she grew more comfortable joining in the conversations. But she was still angry and confused, and Pete was still there in her mind, a constant reminder of what had happened. She thought going to the meetings would enable her to let him go, to erase him. To fold him into an envelope marked "things from my past" and seal it up.

But that didn't happen. Pete continued to haunt her. She would wake in the half-light of dawn, swimming up from a dream. In the dream she saw him smiling and pointing to the stars, or lifting a glass of wine in a toast, and then the edges of his face blurred and reformed into a different person, his smile cracking, his hands heavy and calloused. She would bolt upright, heart hammering, sheets tangled around her shoulders. Will slept on.

There were days when it seemed that the meetings, as helpful as they were, scratched at her and opened the wounds that hadn't completely healed. She felt dirty, as if Pete had left smudges on her skin. At one meeting she said this, and the others nodded, and Sonia told them all that it was not their fault. They had nothing to be ashamed of. Olivia tried to believe this, to tell herself that it had happened twenty years ago and she had a wonderful husband and two terrific kids. She could put it behind her. The past clawed at her, though, and she kept being pulled back there. She hadn't intended to get involved romantically with Pete, but was there a point where she should have said no, when she could have stopped what they had started? She remembered telling him, before that first kiss in his office, that they couldn't do that. After that, after she said yes, weren't there so many times when she could have changed her mind? Said no to the motel, no to the trip to Annapolis, no to all the times they met on the dark streets. Said no to the wine in his office, no to buying the Christmas tree, no to going into the deserted school at night. If she had stopped to think, to really think, would she still have said yes? She had accepted his words as true, because they sounded true and because she wanted them to be true. Now she was the woman who planned everything out to the smallest detail, who could spend an hour debating whether or not to use cardamom in a cookie recipe. Where had that Olivia been, when she needed her?

Sonia told her that Pete had orchestrated it all, had played on her naiveté and loneliness. "He used his power to convince you to do what he wanted," she said. "He knew how much you respected the clergy, that you were the 'good' Catholic woman who believed a priest could do no wrong." All those years of Catholic school, Olivia thought. Students standing up at their desks whenever a priest entered the classroom. Her mother setting the table with the good silver if a priest came to dinner, putting the thickest chop on his plate.

Then, one week there was a massive snowstorm, canceling the meeting, and the next week Lindsay was running a fever and Olivia didn't want to leave her (Will had never been good around illness). On the next Thursday, her mother called just as she was about to go out the door, and she didn't know how to cut the conversation short without hurting her feelings. "Your dad's cholesterol is way too high, and he refuses to give up those fatty sausages." Olivia knew she needed to talk. She watched the hands of the clock inch toward and then beyond seven-thirty, and she finally took off her coat and sat at the kitchen table, stirring sugar into a mug of coffee.

After missing three meetings, she didn't see the point of going to the last one. Maybe she had reaped all the benefits there were for her. She had missed so much, and she might feel like a stranger, unable to catch up with the others. Plus, it only widened the wedge between her and Will. Whereas in the beginning she had squared her shoulders and stood up for doing what she thought she needed to do for herself, it was a high price to pay. Watching her family go out without her, while she sat at the kitchen table eating leftovers, as much as she valued the meetings, just made her feel lonely.

When Sonia called, concerned, Olivia listed the reasons she had not attended. The snow. Her daughter. Her mother. She thanked her, and Sonia said there would be another series of meetings in the spring. Olivia said she'd think about it.

CHAPTER 70

SOMETIMES SHE STUDIED Will when he was doing something ordinary like buttering toast or combing his hair or replacing a stripped screw in a drawer pull. She remembered all the times he came to her apartment that first fall, how he was always fixing something. How he lifted the tools he needed out of that red tool box her father had given her. There was something reverent about it, and it reminded her of her father turning a screwdriver over in his hands, checking for dust or dents. Will did that. And he always wiped down the tools before he put them back in the box.

Today he was working on the broken sash in the bedroom window. Spring had arrived, and they wanted to open the windows. He had his tools and materials laid out on an old pillowcase—chisel, hammer, paint scraper, a coil of cording, several bright new nails. She pretended to be folding laundry on the bed, but from the corner of her eye she watched as he studied the sash, as he raised the window and wedged in a board to hold it so it wouldn't crash down. She watched as he used the chisel to take off the molding, as he scraped at the old caulk, as he drew out the old cording. His face was serious as he worked. The furrowed brow, the slightly tightened lips. She saw how sure his hands were as they pulled out the broken cord and threaded the new one down into the window frame, tying a knot at the end and fusing the frayed threads by singeing them with a lighted match.

She picked up one of his T-shirts, the threadbare Penn State one he refused to let her throw away, even though the neck was frayed and the letters shadows of the original bright blue. As she smoothed it out on the bed, as she had smoothed out dozens of shirts, working by touch, she kept her eyes on him, and something turned in her heart. Will was so good. She wanted to be close to that good person again. She watched as a small smile creased his face, as if he was pleased by his work.

If only she could fix what was broken between them as surely and carefully as he fixed the window sash. If only she had the right words, the right tools. A way to make him smile, the way he used to before Pete's shadow fell between them. They were better, the two of them, but they weren't where they had been. Her hands pressed down the crease on a pair of jeans, reached for another T-shirt. Will gathered up his tools, said, "Good as new," and demonstrated how smoothly the window raised and lowered. He left the bedroom, and as always, when he left a room, the space felt empty.

CHAPTER 71

THEY STILL HAD occasional disagreements about the kids (could Brent drive at night? was Lindsay old enough to date?), but the winter of long silences and sharp retorts had passed. One rainy day in April, when Will was finally fixing the wobbly kitchen chair leg that had been bothering her for months, he told her they had to move on. At first she thought he meant he was going to leave her, that he had enough, that he could never forgive her for what she had done. "What I didn't do," she would have corrected him, because she still wasn't sure if he was angry because of her relationship with Pete or because she had never told him. Maybe he saw the look of shock on her face. "Why the frown? I thought you'd be happy."

"That you're leaving? Why would that make me happy?" She had to force air out of her mouth to speak.

Will put down the square of sandpaper. "Who said anything about leaving?"

Olivia sat down on one of the chairs that wasn't broken. "You said— about moving on."

He stepped over to her chair, squatted on the floor. "No. That's not what I meant. Don't you know I'd never leave you?"

She had been afraid of his leaving so many times. All those mornings when he slipped out to work when she was in another room and he didn't seek her out to give her a kiss goodbye. All those nights when she had sat in the pulse of the television light while he slept upstairs. All those times when he came into a room and didn't look at her and the distance between them might as well have been an actual brick and mortar wall. She had imagined life without him. His dresser drawers empty, oil stains on the garage floor where his car had been. The empty place across from her at the dining room table. Would the kids blame her for his leaving? What would they all do on holidays and birthdays?

Now, at his words, she felt her muscles relax, though she was still confused.

"Then what?" She rubbed her finger over a spot of jam on the table.

He reached up and turned her head toward him so she couldn't avoid seeing his face. "I meant it's time for the two of us to get past everything that has come between us since last summer. We can't go on weighing every word, getting caught up in misunderstanding and petty arguments."

"But you still blame me. You still think I was wrong to go to the monsignor, to leave the church, to go to those support group meetings. Wrong about—what I did twenty years ago."

Will sighed, pushed himself up and dragged out a chair. "I won't pretend that I'll ever understand that. Or that I'll not always wish you had told me. But I'm just going to put it out of my mind. I know it's a cliché, but I want to pick up the pieces, get us back to where we were before we saw that damned news broadcast."

Would that be possible? How could she forget all of that? Seeing Pete and feeling betrayed. Being brave enough to go to the monsignor and having him imply she had been a temptress. Telling Will after all those years and seeing the hurt in the way he held his shoulders, turned his head away from her. Could it be as simple as Will said, for either of them?

"I want that too—to get us back. I hate it when we fight. But you still blame me, and even though you say you want to put it all behind us, can you really?" It would always be that one tarnished spot on the silver bowl that you can never remove, no matter how much polish you rub over it. "I don't know if anyone could."

"All I can do is try. What more can I say?"

"Sometimes I feel like it will never go away. I have these dreams, and I think I see him in stores, or two rows ahead in a movie theater." She had never told Will about that. "I want him to go away, out of my head."

"I can't help you with that." He ran his fingers over his brow, as if brushing something off. "I'm sure it will go away with time. You have to let it do that. And in the meantime, here we are. The two of us. The kids. It's almost summer. Time to plan our vacation." He moved the chair back and forth a few inches, to make sure it didn't wobble.

Olivia tried to do what he suggested. She tried to be more relaxed around the kids, bite her lip before giving Lindsay the third degree about her whereabouts, before reviewing traffic rules with Brent every time he drove the car. She found ways to compliment Will. "I love that shirt on you." "It's great that the silverware drawer doesn't stick anymore." Or she'd invite him to go for a walk, make his favorite jalapeño muffins, bring him a beer while he was watching TV. Sometimes she felt like her smile was made of wood, but she persisted. She was afraid the two of them might fall apart again. She was afraid to hope they wouldn't.

Spring turned to summer, and they booked a cabin in Orleans on Cape Cod for the last week of July. She spent hours researching restaurants, booking a whale-watching cruise, making a list of museums. Under duress, she allowed Lindsay to buy a bikini. But no, Brent would not be driving on the highways up to Massachusetts.

Maybe this was what Will meant by moving on. Picking up where they had been before, as if the thing with Pete had never happened. Like finding a dress in your closet that you haven't worn in a long time and raising your arms to pull it down, tugging at the zipper, ignoring if the hemline is too short or too long. Could you actually wear it, pretend it isn't too tight across the shoulders, or too saggy at the waist? Could you forget that you never wear that color anymore, that you don't have any shoes or jewelry that will go with it? You look at the other dresses on the hangers, the new styles you have adopted. Some of them don't fit perfectly, either, but they are a closer match with who you are.

She knew she could sigh and continue to try to be more patient with teenagers. She knew she could feel actual joy at being on the whale-watching boat, at butter dripping down her chin at a lobster restaurant, at walking hand in hand with Will to get ice cream or watch a sunset. But she also knew that there were things she would never forget, that would always be a part of her. Behind her smile, behind her words, behind the hands that French-braided her daughter's hair, there would be a permanent presence, an aching mark deep inside that nothing could scrape away. She would live with it for the rest of her life, even as she pretended it wasn't there.

PART FOUR
2023

CHAPTER 72

OLIVIA TAKES A folding chair down to the beach and places it just behind the water-line. The tide is going out, and as each wave recedes, she watches the bubbles of the tiny crabs as they burrow in the wet sand. The water leaves behind clumps of foam like scraps of folded lace.

Except for a couple farther down the shore walking their dogs, she is alone. This unseasonably warm day might be her last chance to sit out here like this, under a bright sun, wearing sandals. Before too long, winter winds will scour the sand, and only gulls and terns will brave the berm. She wants to soak up every minute she can.

In her jeans pocket she has a scrap of newsprint. Pete's obituary. She has kept it all this time because she wants to be sure. Sure he is actually gone. Sure she didn't misread it.

So much time has passed since those days fifty-two years ago, when she arrived in Washington, D.C. in her secondhand Chevy, with a set of mismatched dishes, an old stereo, and clothes designed for a Minnesota winter. When the world seemed to be opening its arms to her, offering her possibilities. When she and Rebecca haunted secondhand shops for furniture and wine glasses. She was proud of herself then, proud to be taking such a big step, proud of how she could make a meager paycheck get her from one month to the next. So what that she couldn't afford to buy new clothes, had to hunt through grocery store aisles for sale items? So what that she was so tired from teaching at the end of the day? She was independent Olivia living in the Nation's Capital, and she was going to make it work.

And so much time since that first patina of independence wore off and she found herself bewildered by this new life, envious of Rebecca and her carefree ways, working so hard to keep one step ahead of her students. So bewildered that she accepted the invitation of a kind priest to talk it over. A kind priest who was in fact a serial abuser, beguiling her into seeing him as someone he wasn't.

For years, she put that younger self down, chastised her for making what she saw as the wrong choices. For years she bore the smudge of shame, and it is only recently that she has learned how to like herself again.

In the end, it wasn't someone she expected who helped her to do this. It wasn't Will, who never completely understood. It wasn't the support group she tried thirty years ago. She knows now that she was too raw for that group to help, and that as relieved as she was to finally speak, she gathered excuses to stay away from half of the meetings. She didn't know then whether to pardon or excuse herself. And it wasn't even Rebecca, her steadfast and stalwart friend who stood by her from the first moment Olivia told her about Pete.

It was Laura, her yoga teacher, who made the difference.

Olivia had sometimes thought about yoga, and Lindsay had encouraged her to try it. She had thought, though, that maybe she was too old to learn something new, and anyway, why would she want to twist herself up like a pretzel? Lindsay said it wasn't like that, that it was actually very restful and would be good for her bones.

She was heading for the card shop one morning to buy a couple of birthday cards when she saw the sandwich board outside Ananda Yoga. *Special October Offer! Free Class Every Thursday.* It was a Wednesday.

On a whim, she pushed the door open and went in. "I'll just ask about it," she said to herself.

And that was the beginning of what became a year of yoga. After an introductory class, she signed up for a membership, taking several classes a week. All that fall and winter, and into spring and summer. She bought yoga pants, but often wore sweats and one of Will's old flannel shirts. She purchased her own mat (the studio sold them), a striped Mexican blanket, and foam blocks. After a couple of months, she started practicing at home early in the morning. A few stretches to wake up her muscles, standing warrior poses. Soon she could do tree pose without holding on to the wall. Finding her balance.

The studio itself was in a single room off the entrance area. Tall windows looked out over a wood, and the walls were a restful pale blue. The students lined their mats up to face the windows, leaving shoes and purses in the foyer. The instructors were all women, and not the nubile twenty-somethings Olivia had pictured, but middle-aged, and even one gray-haired woman who wore wild-patterned yoga pants. There were no poses resembling pretzels. Instead, she experienced slow movements, focused breathing, short readings, and recorded flute music. She especially liked the deep relaxation, called savasana, at the end of class, when they all lay on their mats, eyes closed, and let all effort dissolve. It was better than a good night's sleep.

One day, Laura, the instructor, introduced a new pose. "This morning, we'll try full frog." It involved starting out on hands and knees, then stretching arms out long on the floor and spreading knees wide, butt up in the air. Olivia was fine for the first few breaths, but then a slow panic began to fill her chest. She felt exposed, wanted to close herself up in a ball. Tears started to spill over, and she bit her lip to try to stop them. She was never comfortable crying in public, and she'd never heard of anyone in tears in a yoga class. What would the others think? Why was this happening?

The room shrank around her, the trees outside blurred in the distance.

Laura's words came to her as if through a glass jar, and she thought she heard her say, "This is a vulnerable pose." Olivia's thighs started to shake, her breath caught in her throat, and she knew she couldn't stay in the pose any longer. Mostly, she wanted to run from the room, but she was stuck in the middle, and it would mean stumbling over other bodies. She glanced around, and no one else seemed to be having any problem with the pose. They all looked peaceful, relaxed. Her breath was ragged in her chest.

It felt like forever until Laura brought them out of it and into the next pose, and Olivia kept her head down, trying to calm her breath, blinking back the tears. She needed a tissue, but her purse was out on the foyer shelf. Somehow, she made it through the rest of the class, but her hands were cold and she barely heard Laura's voice. Lying in savasana, she experienced none of the usual letting go, the deep relaxation. She just wanted to run away. Even her toes felt jangly.

On her way out of the studio, she spoke quietly to Laura, who was folding blankets. "What did you mean when you said that pose was vulnerable?" Her hot cheeks had cooled, and she was able to speak without a wobble in her voice. All through the ten minutes of savasana, the word "vulnerable" had echoed in her mind. She thought of being open to attack, like a town without a seawall. Or unvaccinated children being vulnerable to disease. She wasn't sure what Laura meant, but she did feel like something had attacked her.

Laura paused and set a purple blanket on the pile. "Oh, frog pose? Hip-opening poses can make some people feel uneasy. We store a lot of emotions in our hip area, and when we release the tension there, emotions can be activated." She looked at Olivia for a long moment. "Are you okay? You look kind of pale."

Olivia shifted her bag higher on her shoulder and pretended to look at her watch. "I'm fine. I just—remembered something." Laura opened her mouth like she was about to speak, but Olivia had to get outside. The studio that usually felt so welcoming was closing in on her. She let herself out into the bright sunlight on the sidewalk.

The next week, Olivia missed her usual Monday and Tuesday classes because the plumber came and she had to take her car into the shop. She hesitated about going to her Thursday class because she was afraid that what had happened to her in frog pose would happen again. She talked herself out of her fears, though, saying she was being silly. Grabbing her yoga bag, she headed out for the studio.

Laura was at the desk sipping a latte when she arrived. "You're back!" she said, smiling.

"Of course. You're my favorite teacher."

Laura put down her to-go cup. "I just meant that you seemed upset last week. I thought maybe it was something I said."

Olivia shook her head. "No, it wasn't you." Could she say it? Would Laura think she was nuts? "It was—it was that pose. Frog."

"Ah." Laura nodded. "What happened?"

Olivia hesitated, avoiding an answer while she pulled her mat out of her bag. Finally, she spoke. "It made me feel—" She searched for a word. "Scared. I wanted to run out of the room." There. She had said it.

"Do you know why?"

How could Olivia explain something she didn't understand? The door opened and two women came in, laughing. Laura spoke softly to Olivia before turning to greet them. "Stay for a few minutes after class. And don't worry—no frog pose today." She gave Olivia a small smile.

When the studio emptied out, Laura invited Olivia to sit near the window and handed her a mug of tea. The late morning sun spread in patches on the floor. Olivia, relaxed after the practice, stretched out her legs. Laura was the first to speak. "Remember when I said that some poses can bring up heavy emotions?"

Olivia nodded. The scent of bergamot and spice rose from her mug.

Laura continued. "I don't want to pry. But when someone reacts so strongly, as you did, there's usually something behind it. Sometimes something really difficult to handle." She dipped her teabag in and out of her mug and looked over the steam at Olivia.

Difficult. That would be putting it mildly. As she had thought about it during her drive to the studio, the only conclusion she could reach was that it had been seeing Pete's obituary. She had come across it in a kitchen drawer when she was looking for an index card. But why, after all this time, did thinking about him cause such a troubling reaction? She hadn't seen him for decades. He was dead.

She didn't know if she could talk about him with Laura. She'd kept it all buttoned up inside for so long. But something shifted in her, maybe because she was so relaxed after the class. She thought she could trust Laura, if not with the whole story, but maybe with a hint, an abbreviation.

So, putting her mug on the floor, she took a deep breath. "I was abused. A long time ago." The words dropped into the space of the room, and she felt their echoes, like dust stirred by a breeze. It was the first time in years, since that support group, that she had even mentioned it.

"Thank you." Laura smiled at her.

"For what?"

"For telling me. For trusting me."

"Oh well, it was—a long time ago. I was young." Olivia looked down at her hands, at the wrinkles, at the veins that marked her wrists like roads.

"It doesn't matter. It's been living in you."

Laura spoke quietly. She told Olivia that any trauma can live in the body a long time, even when you think you've forgotten or buried what happened. "Your tissues remember," she said. She told Olivia that that particular pose can bring difficult emotions to the surface. "You're so open, and the open part is toward a space you can't see, behind you. No wonder you were upset."

A whisper of relief began to tremble through Olivia. It might make sense. At the time, she hadn't connected her reaction to Pete, but she had sensed a presence behind her, something unseen, something unsettling. Laura continued, giving Olivia suggestions like not placing herself in the middle of the room, or choosing a spot in the back or next to a wall. She told her that she would be in classes where teachers would include poses like frog, but that she never had to do them. "You don't have to do anything that makes you uncomfortable. Get into child's pose, or just curl up on your side." When Olivia asked her what the other people would think if she was doing something different, Laura shrugged. "That's their problem. They shouldn't be looking at you anyway."

After that first chat with Laura, Olivia began staying after class now and then. Laura told her that there was more to yoga than the poses. She taught her some stress-reducing breathing techniques, and she introduced her to something called the yamas and niyamas.

"The yamas are prescriptions about what not to do, and the niyamas describe observances we should follow." The yamas sounded to Olivia like the directives in the Ten Commandments that the nuns in her Catholic school had drilled into her and her classmates. The yama "asteya" (non-hoarding) sounded like "thou shalt not steal." And "ahimsa" (non-harming) sounded like "thou shalt not kill." Laura explained that ahimsa meant more than simply not harming. "It's not just about not squishing a spider or holding back from saying mean things to others."

When Olivia looked puzzled, Laura continued. "It's about being kind to yourself."

Olivia thought about that. It was easy to see it in a yoga class, when she could refrain from putting herself down for having to hold on to the wall doing a balance pose. Or, on a positive note, making herself a cup of hot chocolate if she was feeling sad or lonely. But what about other things? What about the hard stuff?

She remembered the counselor in the support group who told them every week, "None of this is your fault." Olivia was able to accept those words in a general, abstract sense, but she had not taken them to heart. There was still that inner voice that nagged her, saying, "You shouldn't have gone along with it." She had resigned herself to living with that, like a smudge you can't clean from a window. You don't notice it all the time, but it is always there.

Laura asked her one day if she had perhaps not totally let go of what had happened. "Maybe," she suggested, "you can love yourself not in spite of it, but because of it." That, to Olivia, loomed like a huge challenge, but maybe it was what ahimsa was asking of her.

Olivia began setting her mat up near the back of the room. One day, Laura announced that they would be doing frog pose, but that she was adding something to it. "It's kind of chilly today," she said. Olivia was a bit annoyed at Laura for including it, but she knew she could just fall into child's pose if she had to. She wasn't sure what the chill in the air had to do with anything, until they assumed the position of the pose and Laura came around and draped a blanket over everyone, starting with the back row. As she put the blanket over Olivia, she rested her hand on Olivia's shoulder for a brief second.

Olivia made it through about a minute in the pose before she started trembling. She let her hips sink back toward her heels, curled into herself. She rested her head on her folded arms, took slow, careful breaths. Pulling the blanket closer around her, she felt the soft fabric against her neck, her cheeks. She listened as the frantic beat of her heart slowed into a soothing rhythm.

CHAPTER 73

TODAY, SITTING SO close to the ocean she can feel the salt spray on her face, she thinks about all the others. She knows that she was not the only one. Not just with Pete, but with dozens, hundreds, of priests and bishops. She knows about the cover-up by the Church. She's read about it in the newspaper, saw an episode on 60 Minutes.

She knows there are countless others who maybe sit by their own oceans, on their own porches, in their own rooms. There are thousands of others. They all carry their deep scars. They all have those moments, like she did in the yoga pose, when the smallest thing—a scent, a face in a crowd—brings a rush of dark remembrance. Many are too embarrassed, or scared, or confused, to ever speak about it. She wants to gather them all up, look deeply into their eyes, and say, "You are okay. You have always been okay." She wants them to know, as she has waited over fifty years to understand, that none of it was their fault. She wants them to know that it is more than okay to believe in themselves. It is their birthright.

She will never forget. What happened will never leave her. she reaches her hand into her pocket, feels the thin sheet of newsprint. She knows nothing about Pete as he was after she last saw him. She doesn't want to know. She doesn't care what he did after he was stripped of his priestly powers. She doesn't care where he lived, where he worked. She hopes he never hurt anyone else, but she doubts it. She doesn't hate him, but can she go as far as forgiveness? She accepts that he was sick, but she also knows he used his power as a priest to feed that sickness.

A gull circles overhead, plunges into a wave, rises a second later holding a flapping silver fish.

The breeze carries a chill as the sun lowers in the western sky. Olivia stands and folds her chair. She pulls the scrap of paper from her pocket and steps toward the next approaching wave. As it touches her toes, she drops the paper into the water. She watches and listens as the quiet tide carries it away.

www.ingramcontent.com/pod-product-compliance
Lightning Source LLC
Chambersburg PA
CBHW021217260626
47172CB00002B/476